**TWO WORDS … … … T
VISUA… …
LOW FUEL … … … …**

The flashing red lights came on in that passing second. Their significance was not wasted on him. There was only one way. Eject.

The ground proximity warning light was flashing as he began to count the final seconds. Thirteen … twelve … eleven … the engines flamed out suddenly. In the near total deceleration he felt the greatest sensation of speed he had experienced since take-off. Without checking the airspeed he pulled the top handle out and down, the black cloth blind keeping his head steady against the seat.

Had his face been uncovered he might have realized that something was wrong. The stars were no longer moving—they had left the sky. Only in his mind would the rocket-powered Martin-Baker ejector seat carry him like a blazing meteorite to earth.

ROLLING THUNDER

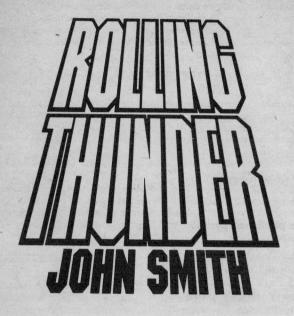

ROLLING THUNDER

JOHN SMITH

ZEBRA BOOKS
KENSINGTON PUBLISHING CORP.

ZEBRA BOOKS

are published by

Kensington Publishing Corp.
475 Park Avenue South
New York, NY 10016

First Zebra Books printing: December 1987

Printed in the United States of America

CHAPTER ONE

One hour earlier they had completed their briefing and sent him out into an electronic dark October night. What they had omitted to mention at the briefing was that their controller would take over three minutes from the end. It was their way of making sure everything went according to plan. And it was not until he felt another hand on the controls that he finally realised there could be no deviation, no escaping the inevitable. He felt as if he had been kicked in the heart. He was living another man's death. The killing game was no longer a game.

Room 19 was typical of most of the rooms in the underground operations block at Royal Naval Air Station Yeovilton: windowless, starkly furnished, painted in drab creams and greys. Its only light came from the two radar screens which swept silent green pictures in endless circles. The building itself had been constructed during the early post-war years and still relied on an antiquated heating system of cast-iron radiators, which in turn were dependent on a supply of heated water from the nearby boiler house. The same boiler house which earlier that Wednesday evening had ceased to function when sheer old age had caused the main boiler to explode.

To the Right Honourable George Hinchcliffe it was utterly depressing. One thing he hated was cold. He felt it now, seeping up from the concrete floor through the thin leather soles of his shoes. He glanced at the expensively uniformed figure to his left. The man seemed oblivious of his surroundings. Remembered words came as an involuntary whisper from Hinchcliffe's lips: "The gates of mercy shall be all shut up, and the fleshed soldier, rough and hard at heart . . ." He faltered and stopped. He could not recall the rest of the lines.

The uniformed figure half-turned towards him. "You said something, Minister?" The voice was cultured. Inevitably ex-public school.

"Said . . ." Hinchcliffe was taken off guard. It was a momentary reaction. He realised almost immediately he had been talking to himself again. It was a weakness he blamed on his years, as he did his aversion to cold. "Nothing . . . no, just thinking aloud. Too many all-night sittings in the House." He doubted if high-ranking officers, no matter how ex-public school, remembered their Shakespeare.

The air vice-marshal smiled thinly in the half-light. Like most professional service men he had little time for politicians, least of all of ministerial rank. Hinchcliffe in particular was everything he despised. The typical working-class socialist, right down to his smoothed-over north country accent which showed through in moments of stress. But worst of all, the man was not even an ex-soldier. How did such a person get to the office of defence minister? Not that Air Vice-Marshal Alister Southgate-Sayers ever publicly betrayed his feelings; he was too discreet for that. As were his NATO counterparts. The operation in hand would prove just how discreet they were. Southgate-Sayers consulted his watch. "Two minutes thirty seconds to run, Minister!"

Hinchcliffe rubbed his eyes. He felt tired. "Where's our man now?"

Southgate-Sayers lifted his right hand and indicated the small moving echo on the radar screen directly in front of him. "That's Bluestar One."

Hinchcliffe peered closer and nodded. He was aware that the pilot's callsign was Bluestar One but found it difficult to slip into the serviceman's easy use of military jargon. In his world fancy names and numbers did not fit people—not until this ministry of defence job, at least. Then again, he had a deep-rooted fear of saying the wrong thing. Most self-made men, he supposed, carried the same cross. "And the Russian chap?" he said. "What's his position?"

Southgate-Sayers maintained his thin-lipped smile. "Redstar . . . lower right quadrant . . . four

7

o'clock . . . there!" He pointed to the almost white blip converging on Bluestar One.

"Our controller here is still in charge, I take it?"

"Not exactly, Minister. We lost full radio contact approximately one minute ago. That is, we can receive his transmissions—albeit weakly—but he cannot pick up ours." The air vice-marshal paused, searching for layman's words to explain the situation. "At the same time we lost two-way radio contact, Bluestar One lost computer control of his aircraft. It also appears that the emergency system reverting the aircraft to manual control also failed."

Hinchcliffe had done his homework. "Which means," he interrupted, "that your controller assumes direct control and brings the plane back?"

"Fly-by-wire, you mean . . . yes. Under normal circumstances that should be the case. However . . ."

"The Russian, you mean?"

"The Redstar aircraft . . . yes."

Hinchcliffe could feel a cold uncomfortable dampness in his armpits. He blinked his eyes. It was crazy for him to feel so trapped, an unwilling witness to an impossible disaster. His mind raced back over the long sequence of events. Hundreds of millions of pounds spent on research and development to produce the ultimate strike aircraft. An airborne killer twenty years ahead of its time. An aircraft the planemakers had promised would be unstoppable. The added insurance of a triple fail-safe system had only enhanced what in the early days had been a very convincing argument. Then, seven days ago, on the eve of entering squadron service with all of the NATO air forces, one had crashed in mysterious circumstances, and now in a grim action replay was about to crash again.

He swore under his breath, his eyes now locked onto the two radar echoes closing rapidly upon each other. If Southgate-Sayers was correct, only one echo would emerge from their apparent collision. And that echo would be the Russian.

The pilot was amazed at how quiet it had become. He sat staring out into the dark, moonless night beyond the cockpit. There was no sensation of speed. No way of confirming the LCD readout on the visual display unit which told him he was travelling at over twice the speed of sound. He felt detached. It was almost as if the world had ended, leaving him exiled in space for ever. He checked the stopwatch.

Fifty seconds. He remained calm. Eyes still and unblinking. One thing his test pilot training had taught him—panic kills. Even so, he knew fear. No pilot worth his salt would admit otherwise, and the secret was to learn to live with it. And that was what he was doing now. He ran quickly back over his earlier analysis, convinced he had overlooked something. He hadn't. His aircraft was fixed in a shallow descent, its speed relentlessly increasing. Fuel was being consumed at an alarming rate, and would shortly run out. In time, however? He doubted it.

Forty seconds. The pilot reselected the emergency frequency on his UHF radio and tried to transmit. Nothing . . . it was still dead. Dead. As the original pilot of this plane was dead. His flesh crept—it was as if he was actually sensing a dead man's feelings. He shook his head, letting willpower take over, forcing him to recall the briefing. His eyes moved up towards the heavens, and the transcript of the dead man's words came back to him, one by one: "Now that really is crazy . . . the goddamn sons of bitches are moving!" He stopped talking and looked down at his gloved left hand, the thumb of which according to his instructions was still depressing the radio transmit button. He released it.

Twenty seconds. There was a way. The one the dead man would have fought all along. Eject. He reached for the overhead seat handle and stopped. At this speed it was non-surviveable. The human body was incapable of withstanding a direct airblast of over 1,500 miles per hour. So the only choice, it seemed, was in the manner of the dying. Which way would be the quickest? To crash or to burn up in the air? Which way would offer the least pain? At that moment even his training could not prevent a sudden dilation of surface blood vessels as the colour drained from his face.

The flashing red lights came on in that passing second. He reached forward, cancelling the central alert system. The flashing red lights ceased, leaving only two words pulsating on the left visual display unit. Low fuel . . . low fuel . . . low fuel.

Their significance was not wasted on him. A close thing, but in time. No fuel meant no engines, and no engines would hopefully bleed off enough speed for him to eject safely before he ran out of sky. The ground proximity warning light was flashing as he began to count the final seconds. Thirteen . . . twelve . . . eleven . . . the engines flamed out suddenly. In the near total deceleration he felt the greatest sensation of speed he had experienced since take-off. The seconds passed . . . seven . . . six . . . five . . . four . . . Without checking the airspeed he pulled the top handle out and down, the black cloth blind keeping his head steady against the seat.

Had his face been uncovered he might have realised that something was wrong. The stars were no longer moving—they had left the sky. He, however, unlike the dead pilot, would be spared the final scene. Only in his mind would the rocket-powered Martin-Baker ejector seat carry him like a blazing meteorite to earth.

Room 18 was larger than Room 19. It also had a thirty-foot deep pit at its centre. Suspended over that pit was the nose and cockpit section of a fighter aircraft. The steel gantry was swinging out towards the cockpit as Hinchcliffe followed Southgate-Sayers through into the room.

"The Blackhawk simulator," Southgate-Sayers announced.

Hinchcliffe gave him a tired look. He had seen the mock-up for himself at Warton a year earlier,

11

had in fact sat inside the machine and grunted intelligently as an electronics expert demonstrated the "simplicity" of the computerised gadgetry. In fact he had been appalled, wondering if human beings really belonged in what was fast becoming an electronic world. He and Southgate-Sayers stood in silence by the guard rail as a junior officer helped the pilot from the cockpit. To Hinchcliffe, the emerging figure had all the appearance of an astronaut; from his white anti-g suit to the over-large bonedome, which trailed green oxygen tubes and multi-coloured radio communication leads. The pilot approached them slowly, removing his helmet as he came.

Southgate-Sayers inclined his tall frame towards Hinchcliffe.

"Minister, may I introduce Squadron Leader Maudsley?"

Maudsley, face damp with perspiration, removed his chamois leather gloves and held out a hand. "Good evening, sir."

Hinchcliffe smiled grimly. "I would have thought the word 'macabre' summed up the evening more accurately, Squadron Leader." Maudsley, clearly not knowing how to take the man or the statement, remained silent. "So, what does she fly like?"

Maudsley turned his face towards the simulator, Like? he thought. It's like nothing on God's earth, that's what it's like. It's like getting into a pretend aeroplane to play the pretend part of a man who seven days ago was killed for real. It's like hearing the distant thunder as the engines start. It's like feeling a toy come to life around you. It's like concentrating so hard at twice the speed of sound that you forget it's a bloody game. It's like scaring yourself shitless when you suddenly realise you are about to die. It's like witnessing a small fair-haired boy kneeling in prayer at the foot of his bed pleading with God to make him into a pilot. It's like damning the boy for succeeding, and the God for letting him . . .

Maudsley wiped his lips nervously with the back of his hand and turned back to face the minister. His smile was in place before their eyes met; he had come too far to be frightened by an aeroplane. He'd been through staff college. He was a squadron leader. It was only a matter of time before the permanent desk job, and then the satisfying ascent through the ranks. "Brilliantly, sir," he said, pleased at how controlled his voice sounded. "She flies quite brilliantly. The next best thing to space travel, I imagine."

Hinchcliffe muttered: "Good . . . good," and turned his thoughts to the plane itself. The Blackhawk had promised so much—but that had been before the crash seven days earlier, before Major Eugene Kitrell had been killed, before the press release.

Maudsley, sensing he had lost the minister's interest, turned eagerly to the air vice-marshal instead. Still thinking of his promising future career, he said: "I think I've found the answer to one of the puzzles, sir."

The senior officer frowned. Non-standard procedure. All information on Blackhawk classified, to be discussed primarily with the intelligence officer at de-briefing. And never in front of civilians—not even if those civilians were government ministers. "Good show, Henry; pass that on to the IO will you?"

Maudsley snapped smartly to attention, and with a brief nod and "sir" to the minister, tactfully dismissed himself.

Hinchcliffe was still staring at the simulator, picturing the Blackhawk it represented, and the mess his department was now in. That press release! His face twisted into a bitter smile. There shouldn't have been one in the first place—and there wouldn't have been if that bloody, small-town newspaper reporter hadn't thought he had a scoop and contacted Fleet Street with a few highly dramatised suppositions. Still, what the hell, they could always stick to their story; that the plane had been a captured MiG-25 being flown on evaluation work. Except that now they had another problem. Now the military chiefs had dreamt up a potential headline even more damaging: "Soviets Down Blackhawk". The unstoppable aircraft sunk without trace. Another bloody Titanic. True or not, just let Fleet Street get their sticky fingers on that one in the present political climate!

Hinchcliffe turned to Southgate-Sayers. "You did say, Air Vice-Marshal . . . earlier in the radar room . . . that Major Kitrell ejected in the final seconds?"

"Three-point-five seconds prior to impact. Yes, Minister."

"Is it possible that that kind of action could have affected the attitude of the aircraft?"

"In what way?"

"You mentioned that the aircraft turned upside down as the pilot ejected. Could that have been caused by the ejection procedure itself?"

Southgate-Sayers considered the question briefly. "Not normally, no. All systems are independent. The roll manoeuvre which inverted the Blackhawk should have been nothing more than the direct result of pilot command."

"But, you're not sure?"

"Not until the experts have sifted through the wreckage, no. However, I feel confident that their findings will be in total accord with what you have witnessed here tonight."

"Speaking of wreckage, have we found the 'black box' yet?"

"The flight recorder . . . no. But once we do you will have all the proof you need."

"Back to blaming the Soviets, you mean?"

"In other times we might have put it down to pilot error; but here and now the implications of the transcript seem pretty conclusive. The Tupolev's radio transmissions must somehow have unlocked the Blackhawk's computer and then assumed total control of the aircraft. All they had to do then was maintain the descent path. The resulting crash was of course meant to look like an accident."

Hinchcliffe said: "But you're still officially stating the cause as pilot error?"

"For the record, yes. At this stage I don't see

that we have any alternative."

"One thing puzzles me," Hinchcliffe remarked as they left the room. "How could the Soviets have known we would have a Blackhawk aircraft in that exact place at that exact time . . . especially as we operate on a random procedure?"

"A question to which I have no immediate answer. All I know for certain is that the Tupolev was out of Murmansk on a routine high level reconnaissance mission. According to the radar plot for the night of October the second he was returning home as Bluestar One exited the arctic circle on track for Kinloss."

Hinchcliffe scratched his chin thoughtfully. "Nothing more than a chance encounter then?"

Southgate-Sayers offered a condescending smile. "With anyone else, Minister, I would be inclined to agree. With the Soviets, however, chance encounters are invariably planned twenty years in advance."

George Hinchcliffe was standing near the bar in the Yeovilton ward room. He was drinking a bloody mary. All around him were naval officers; some in uniform, some in civilian clothes. Southgate-Sayers had excused himself on the pretext of wanting to check the readiness of the minister's aircraft for its departure to Northolt. His real reason was curiosity over what Maudsley had said about an answer to one of the puzzles. A few words with the intelligence officer would ascertain what action needed to be taken, if any.

At Hinchcliffe's left elbow a vice-admiral was talking animatedly about fleet requirements in the Mediterranean. The minister was only half-listening; he had recognised the young air force officer who had just entered the room. And he, like Southgate-Sayers, was curious. He made his excuses to the admiral and approached the younger man. "Squadron Leader Maudsley, isn't it?"

"Yes, sir. Good evening again."

"Just thought I'd thank you personally for playing the part of Major Kitrell. Nasty business . . . you knew him well, I take it?"

"Briefly, sir. He'd only been with us for a short while."

"So what sort of man was he?"

Maudsley studied the man before him. Grey hair, thin face. An austere, basically gentle individual. But a member of the cabinet—and that was what was important. Ever ready to seize an opportunity which might further his career prospects, Maudsley chose his words carefully. "As a pilot, sir, Major Kitrell was absolutely first class. Good company too. The squadron won't be quite the same without him."

"Yes . . . yes. They can be quite endearing, can't they?"

"Sir?"

"The Yanks. A lot of charm."

Maudsley smiled at the dated reference. "Yes, sir. As you so aptly put it. A lot of charm."

The minister adopted a serious pose. He too had his career to think of. "You know, Squadron

Leader, you mustn't imagine that because we are locked away in what some may term ivory towers, we don't worry about our young men. These accidents only highlight the dangerous job you're all doing." His face softened with a vote-winning smile. "And we do appreciate it, you know. We might not say so often enough, but we do."

"Very kind of you, sir."

Hinchcliffe hesitated, still not ready to make his move. "Anyway, to change the subject, and if it's not too personal a question, how old are you? Seem a bit young for a squadron leader."

"Twenty-nine, sir," Maudsley said with some pride.

"Eyes set on higher things, I take it?"

"I'd like to think I have the ability . . . yes, sir."

"And I'm sure you'll make it, Squadron Leader." He looked at his watch. "Now I suppose I'd better go and find my transport back to London." He looked around for somewhere to put his glass.

Maudsley said: "Allow me, sir."

Hinchcliffe handed him the glass. Now or never, he thought. "Oh . . . one other thing. As I won't be getting the transcript of tonight's little episode until next week . . . you mentioned earlier you had found the answer to one of the puzzles?"

Maudsley, eager to please, never even considered the classified status of the Blackhawk. And if he had, after all, Hinchcliffe *was* the defence minister. *And* they were getting along rather well. "Perhaps it's nothing, sir, but there was a passage on Major Kitrell's final transmission, when he said something along the lines: 'That

18

really is crazy . . . the goddamn sons of bitches are moving.'"

"Yes . . . I seem to remember that. So what was it?"

"Well, interestingly enough, the Blackhawk simulator has full external projections; night sky for instance. Gives you the impression you really are out there." Hinchcliffe hid his impatience. Maudsley continued: "It was when I had to repeat Major Kitrell's words that I happened to look up, and I saw the stars. And that must have been what he was talking about."

Hinchcliffe, not having been a pilot, missed the point. "There's some significance in that, I assume?"

"Indeed there is, sir. You see, the stars are far too distant to seem to move. They always appear still."

"Even at the speeds this new machine flies?"

"If you remember that the earth's surface rotates at roughly a thousand miles per hour, and then observe the stars in the night sky, still, motionless, you'll understand that another thousand miles or so per hour isn't going to make the slightest bit of difference."

Hinchcliffe was working it out for himself. "And you have a theory on this? This moving star business."

"Well, I'm not altogether certain, sir. It needs to be checked out, of course, but I believe that Major Kitrell clearly never ordered the—"

Air Vice-Marshal Southgate-Sayers's appearance at that moment stopped the conversation dead. He gave Maudsley a chilling look before turning to Hinchcliffe. "Your aircraft is ready, Minister."

"So soon," Hinchcliffe replied, controlling his annoyance. He rubbed his hands together briskly. "I was just thanking the squadron leader for playing the part of Major Kitrell tonight." He turned to Maudsley and exchanged goodbyes.

Walking out to the waiting jet, Hinchcliffe said: "Well, thank you once again for arranging all of this. Only wish the circumstances could have been a little more auspicious."

"So do I, Minister. Notwithstanding which, I do feel we should take steps to prevent a recurrence of tonight's drama . . . don't you?"

Hinchcliffe knew what the man was referring to. "An oblique reference to your *Space Strike* report, Air Vice-Marshal?"

"If you wish, yes. You will be reviewing its findings on the strength of this evening, I take it?"

Hinchcliffe smiled in the darkness. "Most definitely. Can't have the Soviets stealing a march on us, can we?"

Thirty-five minutes later George Hinchcliffe was drinking yet another bloody mary, this time on board a twin-engined air force jet high over southern England. He took the latest newspaper cutting from the sheaf of papers on the table in front of him and read the latest:

RAF PROMOTES SCOTTISH CRASH
CONFUSION.

The death on October 2 of a United States air
force officer in a flying accident near a top
secret Scottish military base remains a
mystery.

The RAF has not changed its story from
the original press release that Major Eugene
Kitrell, USAF, on an exchange posting to
RAF Strike Command, was killed whilst
flying a "specially modified test aircraft".
The service has allowed press speculation to
continue and most reports, quoting various
unnamed sources, say that Kitrell was in fact
killed while flying a MiG-25 Foxbat. The
RAF, in conjunction with other NATO air
forces, operates around twenty Soviet types
on test and evaluation work.

However, although the area in which the
aircraft crashed is not usually used for this
type of flying, it is within thirty miles of the
top secret Scottish base, Kinloss. Speculation
is therefore now rife that the aircraft involved
was in fact NATO's new top secret interceptor
Blackhawk One, which is currently believed
to be on final air force acceptance trials, and
that the MiG-25 story was leaked to maintain
Blackhawk's cover.

Major Kitrell, a highly qualified American
test pilot, was far more likely to have
sampled MiG aircraft some time ago, at the
United States air force base Nellis, Nevada;
it is also more than plausible that a pilot of

Kitrell's experience would test NATO's most advanced strike aircraft.

Hinchcliffe finished the dregs of his bloody mary, swore twice, and made a note in his diary to curtail the press's interest in the Blackhawk. They were getting too bloody close for comfort. The second entry in his diary was more cryptic. It read: "Private meeting with Squadron Leader Maudsley—STARS"

He stood apart from the gathering of air force officers round the grave, at first glance an unremarkable figure. Medium height, slight build; the collar of his dark civilian raincoat turned up against the cold driving rain. He had missed the church service deliberately. He was not a religious man. The only reason he had come to this place was because of a long-forgotten promise. One he had failed to honour. And now, as so often, he was too late. For a moment his blue eyes examined the rows of neat white crosses as if counting off those who had been ex-patriated forever. The naval chaplain's voice reached him briefly and then was lost again in the wind and rain. He watched as the Stars and Stripes were removed and the coffin lowered slowly into the freshly dug grave. His eyes appeared to blink back tears before focusing on the footprints in the soft damp earth beside the grave. They reminded him of something. Something once at the boundaries of his vision. A place now fixed in his mind as distant blue hills. Almost unreachable. Almost the limit of known things. Almost, but not quite.

It had been shortly after dawn when they had gone down to the muddy, slow stream under the feverthorn trees, and there, clearly impressed in the soft red clay—footprints. The Masai with the name Ole Renterre had turned slowly towards the two young white boys. *"Simba,"* he whispered. The brothers nodded, casting nervous glances over their shoulders, half-expecting to see a lion about to pounce. When the initial fear had subsided they turned back to the Masai. He had smiled in that benevolent way of his before adding, "So now we have a part of him. Something with which to catch his spirit. Something with which to draw him in."

The man smiled sadly at the memory. Gene would have remembered that. Or would he? It was a long time ago. Sometimes in the loneliness of night that long time ago took on an air of unreality, as if it belonged only to some dream. The mornings told him otherwise. He hated mornings. They were cold, harsh, loveless places. Places with footprints. Places much like this bleak military cemetery. He wondered idly where Gene had left his footprints.

The group of umbrella-sheltered air force officers were all men, with one exception—Flight Lieutenant Erica Macken. She stood in their

23

midst, head bowed, eyes red with the tears she had failed to control. And still she could not accept it. Would not. Gene couldn't be dead; not this way. Pilot error. He was too good a fast jet pilot to have made so elementary a mistake. She knew it. They all knew it. Yet they had accepted his death with indifference, and were only here now to pay lip service to their so very British code of decency. It was a game they were very good at: disliking a man when he was alive, and deciding he was a thoroughly good chap once he was dead. Yes, it was typically British. They were always at their reserved best at strangers' funerals.

There was a lull in the wind and rain. Even the voices around her seemed to have stopped. She closed her eyes. There had been a day. Just once. The first day. She had been standing in an empty office. The top half of the door had been glass. And she turned and he was standing there. The moment could have been no more than a second, but to her it had lasted a thousand years. A thousand years of standing, watching, waiting. Of being drawn slowly in through the startling blue eyes. Into his very soul. There had followed a week of small talk—of getting to know each other. To her it seemed almost unbelievable that he should accept her so readily—as an equal. The first woman fast jet pilot in the Royal Air Force, and quietly tolerated by the other pilots, she had still been passed the unwritten and unspoken message that she did not belong. That she was, and always would be, an outsider. Gene Kitrell was different. He listened and advised, sharing his vast experience of jet aircraft with her. He had the happy knack of resolving the most difficult aeronautical problems into nothing more than a piece of brilliantly explanatory artwork on the back of a cigarette packet. To him, if it could not be resolved in such practical ways it carried all the signs of a biblical miracle: something to be accepted, gratefully, but never questioned. In a lot of ways Gene Kitrell reminded her of her father. In a lot of ways but one. She wanted to go to bed with him. Explore his body. Make love to this blond-haired, blue-eyed man. The thought did not shock her, although if she thought back on her strict upbringing she had to wonder where the change had occurred.

She was twenty-seven, beautiful in a sensuous way, with red hair, a flawless creamy complexion, and green eyes which she had been told on more than one occasion could be very wicked. She had never had plans to marry. Flying had always come first. Then Kitrell entered her life. The change was dramatic, taking less than a month. One month, followed by five more. Six months of being happier than she had ever been. She thought now through their weekends together, grasping them tightly in her strong white hands, afraid that if she didn't they would be lost to her forever. Only when all the days had been carefully gathered and stored did she pause. That was when the cold autumn rain in the cemetery caught her face. She shuddered, raising her clenched fists to her closed eyes. She pressed tightly until the pain made her feel sick. That was when a po-faced flight lieutenant tugged at her arm. "It's time to go," he said. She let herself be led away then, the clenched fists falling to her sides. An unconscious gesture of defeat.

It was as she turned down the pathway that she looked up and saw the man standing apart from the crowd. Her step faltered. She quickly wiped the tears from her eyes and looked again. She couldn't believe it. His face! The fair hair pressed wetly to his head. The startling blue eyes of the man they had just buried. Gene Kitrell! She was vaguely conscious of a great silence as her vision narrowed and darkness engulfed her.

Howling wind and lashing rain brought her back. Arms were supporting her, easing her gently forward. A voice said: "The car . . . not far now . . . come along." It took a little time for her to realise she had fainted. And even longer to recall the reason. Then she was pulling against the arms, twisting her head to where she had seen him. Except that now there was no one there. No one. Nothing. Nothing but the rows of neat white crosses and the wind-scattered confetti of spent flowers. She stared wildly in all directions, whipering "Gene! Gene!" as if calling his name would bring him back.

The supporting arms steered her forward. "Come along, Lieutenant," the man on her left said. "We're almost there."

"Did you see him?" she cried. "Did you see him?"

"Who?" the man questioned.

"Gene . . . he was standing," she turned her head. "He was standing over there."

26

"He's dead, Lieutenant," the man said sadly. "Do you understand? Major Kitrell's dead."

At four o'clock, British summer time, that October afternoon—when a still confused Erica Macken was arriving back at the Royal Naval Air Station Yeovilton, in Somerset, England—it was 6 p.m. Eastern European time in Murmansk, Russia.

The pilots' rest room at the Soviet air base was filled with an air of tension, the only sound the rapid series of dull thuds as the blade of the flick knife stabbed into the table top. Two young lieutenants were watching Captain Sergio Dzerzhinsky with an almost hypnotised fascination.

Dzerzhinsky, who was about the size of Peter the Great, and weighed nearly three hundred pounds, was beaming all over his flabby face. He often used this Chekist knife exercise to win wagers, the stakes taking the form of bottles of vodka. He had long since forgotten that the exercise's purpose was to develop speed and dexterity. The oldest serving, and most passed over captain in the Soviet air force, he was considered by most an eccentric, if not affable, rogue. A rambling bear of a man. Short on discipline and good manners. An old soldier, who for no apparent reason had always been tolerated. There were those of course who thought he should have been transferred to a labour camp in the Urals long ago. Many had tried it. All had failed. Dzerzhinsky didn't give a damn either way. At fifty-four years of age he was still an able pilot. Also he had the luck of the devil. His last trip had shown that. True, there may have been a moment's mental aberration over the North Atlantic, and he still could not explain how his orders had ended up being flushed down the toilet. And maybe he *had* accidently strayed into the northern fringes of United Kingdom airspace. But his infra-red pictures of NATO's top secret interceptor—Blackhawk One—were brilliant. Quite brilliant. His opportunist Cossack image, it seemed, had survived for another day.

The first young lieutenant, whose tunic carried the name tag KASPAROV. A., glanced at his watch. Thirty seconds to go. He looked back at the table; at Dzerzhinsky's left hand its palm flat, the fingers spread. He watched the knife blade arcing down between each pair of fingers in turn. Faster . . . faster . . . Anatoly Kasparov checked his watch again. Five seconds left. *"Pyaht . . . chyeetiryeh . . . tree . . . dvah . . . ahdyeen . . . STOY!"*

Dzerzhinsky stopped; flicked the knife upwards in a double somersault, caught and retracted the blade in one smooth practised movement. The two young officers applauded enthusiastically. Even though they had lost their wager, the possibility of failure, the drawing of blood, had seemed real up to the very last moment. If they had known, however, that Sergio Dzerzhinsky had first learned this party piece at cadet school over thirty years earlier they might have chosen to risk their meagre allowance elsewhere. Thirty years was a long time to hone a particular skill. And Dzerzhinsky never failed. But never.

The big man got up from the table and ambled over to the corner of the room.

"You are coming with us, Sergio?" Kasparov said.

Dzerzhinsky poured tea from the samovar before answering. "Me . . . with you?" He shook his head. "I am too old, Lieutenant. No good for what you are hunting."

"You, *old?*" Kasparov said in mock disbelief.

"Yes me . . . old. Now be off. And remember what your father told you. No colonels or generals in my crew!" This Russian serviceman's slang for contracting gonorrhoea or syphilis brought sly laughter from the two young men as Dzerzhinsky followed them through the doorway. He watched them march smartly down the dimly lit corridor. They had almost reached the exit when he bellowed, "And don't forget the vodka you owe me." They raised their hands in mock salute and were gone.

Dzerzhinsky returned to the empty room, finishing the strong sweet tea as he went. Above the sink, by the samovar, was a small cracked mirror. He looked into it now. Saw the unruly shock of snow-white hair which crowned a tired and uncared-for face. "When did you grow old, Sergio? When did the young girls stop smiling at you?" He stared down at the empty glass in his hands before hurling it into the sink where it shattered. Dzerzhinsky turned to the uncurtained window and a night sky heavy with stars. The sky was all that remained. A timeless mistress who gave much and sought little in return.

It was long moments later that he turned from the window and laughed. To hell with it. He would go and visit Rokossovsky in the briefing office. Rokossovsky would be there. He always was. He had an ugly wife. But also Rokossovsky always had a bottle. They would talk about the old days.

Dzerzhinsky was halfway down the poorly lit corridor when he saw a man approaching him. Slouch hat, round steel-rimmed spectacles, and a black leather overcoat. The man stopped. He waited until Dzerzhinsky drew level, then said: "Comrade Captain Dzerzhinsky?" The voice had authority, the grey-blue eyes something reminiscent of cruelty or madness. Or both.

"Perhaps . . . and who are you?"

The man stiffened slightly at the insolent tone in the other's voice, then withdrew his left hand from his pocket and flicked open a slim leather wallet. Dzerzhinsky had a fleeting glance of an official badge before it was snatched away. "Karolyov. Alexei Karolyov, state security." He looked quickly over his shoulder. "I wish to have some words."

"Words?"

Karolyov took Dzerzhinsky's elbow and steered him back down the corridor. "Yes, Comrade Captain . . . words. And in private."

The following morning Professor William Blakeley arrived at the ministry of defence at exactly six. It was Friday, October 10. There was no one in the large reception room apart from the private secretary, a sour-looking young man with a turned-down mouth, whose name appeared from his desk tag to be Morriss. He eyed the blue ID label on Blakeley's lapel with little enthusiasm.

"Sit down and wait," he said in a voice which matched his expression. "And when you get in there," he nodded towards the oak-panelled door, "keep it brief and to the point. He doesn't like superfluous explanations. Just keep it short and simple—got it?"

Blakeley jerked his head dumbly. He felt sick. He was a bad traveller, especially in the back seats of cars, and the long drive down the M1 to London had been sheer torture. He had scarcely slept at all.

Three minutes later a bell on the secretary's desk rang softly and a red light flashed. Morriss leapt to his feet and disappeared round the oak-panelled door. After a pause he reappeared and motioned the professor to enter.

Blakeley nervously straightened his tie and went forward. The first thing he noticed in the well-lit, fairly small office, was the tooled leather desk. On it stood a brass lamp with a green shade. Beside the desk stood the defence minister, George Hinchcliffe, whose rumpled suit, unkempt hair, and unshaven chin indicated he had been working all night.

He waved Blakeley to a chair, at the same time taking in the thin, almost emaciated form, the over-large balding head, and the heavy horn-rimmed spectacles which had the habit of sliding down the slender blade of nose. "Good of you to come at such short notice, Professor," he said.

Blakeley gave a wan smile. He was not aware he had had any say in the matter. The telephone call to his house in St. Annes, Lancashire, the previous evening, had told him he had a 6 a.m. meeting with the defence minister in London. The black Jaguar saloon, with a driver and a security man, had arrived for him at one in the morning.

Hinchcliffe came straight to the point. "It's concerning the Blackhawk One aircraft, or to be more specific your Vocal Interface Command System." He paused. "What are the odds against the system being penetrated by a third party?"

"I . . . don't quite follow, Minister," Blakeley stammered.

Hinchcliffe sighed audibly and moved around behind his desk. He settled into the high-backed leather chair. "All right, Professor, we'll take it from the beginning. Step by step . . . and you can correct me if I go wrong. Fair enough?"

Blakeley nodded. "Minister."

"Firstly, we are phasing out the Tornado aircraft and the two-man crew concept in favour of the single-pilot, computerised Blackhawk. The reasons are many and various, and not least is the argument that a two-man crew element—that is pilot and observer or electronics officer—is a sometimes hazardous proposition." He smiled, trying to put this stiff little scientist at his ease. "Two men having to react like one at a hundred and fifty feet above the ground whilst traveling at close to the speed of sound—I must say that seems bloody alarming to me. I'm sure the same thought was in your mind when you designed the VIC system!"

It hadn't been, but Blakeley nodded politely. To him it had been simply a matter of cost/time effectiveness. A programme to remove human error from the cockpit. His studies had shown that any two-man crew needed many months of working together before they could reliably anticipate each other's thoughts. And even then it didn't always work. The accident figures proved that.

"So," Hinchcliffe continued. "We design a one-man interceptor which will fly at seven times the speed of sound—at mach 7—and install computers to do the mechanical work of flying it. Computers which will react to the pilot's voice. Right so far?"

"Yes." Blakeley cleared his throat. "Except that the computer also has its own synthesised voice. It can reply to the pilot's questions. Among other things."

"Isn't that more or less what I said?" Hinchcliffe was getting edgy. A sign of tiredness. "Now, where was I . . . ah yes, computers. The sticky world of micro-electronics, of which I know less than nothing. Except that in the late 1970s the French experts at Crouzet started work on a voice command system for France's ACX experimental fighter. Also that voice activation was being successfully carried out on a Mirage III at around that time." Hinchcliffe sat back. "Perhaps you'd like to take up the story from there?"

Blakeley smiled weakly, searching his mind for simple explanations to complex problems, at the same time remembering the secretary's instructions to keep things brief and to the point. "You asked me originally about third-party penetration," he said. "That might have worried the French, but hardly us. This new system employs four computers altogether." He hesitated. "Hence the aircraft has a triple fail-safe element. Basically the first computer, which we can call Mode One, is the normal everyday system. Once the pilot is strapped into the aircraft he keys in the daily code word to unlock the computer. Thereafter it will react only to his voice, to his voice and none other—"

Hinchcliffe interrupted. "There's no way to copy it then . . . the voice, that is?"

"No. Voices are like fingerprints. No two are entirely identical."

Hinchcliffe picked up a pen and scribbled a note on his desk pad. "Good, go on."

"Should the first computer fail for any reason it keys a second computer, Mode Two, which reverts the aircraft to manual control. That means the pilot now flies it as a normal aircraft, and takes care of the first fail-safe situation.

"Now we go a stage further and assume that the manual control servos malfunction. When this happens an automatic trigger device activates the third computer, Mode Three. And this is where things become interesting, because under Mode

Three control is handed over to a ground operator. Hence the term fly-by-wire. Something along the lines of flying a model aircraft—the man on the ground is in effect the pilot. This takes care of the second fail-safe situation.

"Finally we assume that for technical reasons this computer also fails. Another trigger device activates the fourth and last computer mode. This one is also operated by the ground controller. So he, like the pilot, has two bites at the cherry. If we get to this situation we have failed-safe three times.

"Should anything go wrong with this last computer, we have of course lost the aircraft. But certainly not through third-party penetration." Blakeley dried up quite suddenly. He folded his arms and waited awkwardly for some sort of reaction.

"And that's it?" Hinchcliffe sounded almost disappointed.

"In a nutshell, yes."

The minister sat, pensively drumming his fingers on the desk. How much could he say, that was the question. True, Blakeley would have signed the Official Secrets Act. True, he had designed the VIC system. True, he was the chief scientist with British Aerospace who were building the Blackhawks. It was also true, however, that officially no Blackhawk had crashed. Any such admission, even to Blakeley, was dangerous. Production figures were: sixteen already built including three prototypes, and an order book full of promise. If all went well sales to foreign air forces alone would keep British Aerospace going into the beginning of the next century.

"So," Hinchcliffe said finally, "according to you this computerised aeroplane is a fairly idiot-proof piece of hardware?"

Blakeley blanched at such crude terminology. "I think it does have a high safety factor, yes."

"And the possibility of a third party penetrating any of its four computers?"

"Virtually nil."

"Virtually?" Hinchcliffe sat foward sharply. "Wouldn't you say totally?"

Blakeley clasped his hands tightly in his lap. "I can't be sure. You see, computer technology is always vulnerable. It advances at such a rate that obsolescence is almost certainly built in. What was impenetrable yesterday need not still be so today."

Hinchcliffe rubbed his aching eyes. He was worried. It was possible they had jumped the gun on this one. Taken a snap decision, and the wrong one. Political expediency, someone had termed it. Political expediency! And yesterday at the American cemetery at Cambridge they had buried the remains of a Major Kitrell. "Pilot error", the record said. But if this Blakeley was right, then perhaps "unlawful killing by person or persons unknown" would be the fairer verdict.

Hinchcliffe made up his mind. He looked up and said to Blakeley, "Okay, how long for your people to run tests with the air force? They think they've found a problem."

"It depends, Minister. Days . . . weeks . . . until we know the exact circumstances it's difficult to gauge, you understand."

Hinchcliffe said fiercely, "No, Professor Blakeley, I definitely do not understand. What is more important, however, is that we ensure this computer system of yours is totally secure. The entire Blackhawk project and many thousands of jobs depend upon it. Now, do *you* understand?"

Blakeley cleared his throat again. "Yes sir, I think I do."

Hinchcliffe picked up a fountain pen and began to write something rapidly on an official form. When he had finished he folded the paper and handed it to Blakeley. "Give this to my secretary as you go out. He will arrange transport to the naval base at Yeovilton."

Blakeley stood up. "When will that be, Minister?"

"As fast as they can deliver you to Northolt, I imagine."

Blakeley felt like saying he had not slept all night. Had brought no overnight bag and no money. They had promised, after all, just a short meeting in London, following which he would be returned to his home. Most worrying of all; who would feed his cat, Caversham? Caversham was old and practically blind, she needed a lot of care. But Hinchcliffe's cold unfriendly stare commanded him to silence. Perhaps—although he doubted it—the secretary could advise him. The sickness was still lying heavily on his stomach as he left the room.

It was bitterly cold when George Hinchcliffe stepped out of the Daimler in Downing Street two hours later. He had stopped off briefly at his flat in Eaton Square; showered, cut himself shaving, and changed into a freshly laundered white shirt and dark grey suit. The red tie, he thought, set it off rather well. His wife had still been asleep so there had been no opportunity for breakfast. He had fixed himself another of his bloody maries; more vodka than tomato juice. He would have preferred a stiff whisky, but whisky left traces on the breath. It was on the drive from Eaton Square to Downing Street that he decided he was getting too old to be playing these silly bloody games. Yet retirement and a country cottage were as remote now as they had ever been. His wife, Elizabeth, still had designs on Number Ten.

His talk with Blakeley had told him predictably little. Certainly it had not allayed his fears that the Soviets were up to something. Not that he intended saying that to the prime minister. The PM had other, more pressing problems, the most important of which was the pending general election. The opinion polls were looking anything but convincing.

No, at this point in time the crash had come about through nothing more than a computer malfunction, the direct result of pilot error. The fact that the air force chiefs were crying "Soviet

Wolf" must be put down to nothing more than a mild outburst of childish hysterics. The PM would like that.

And it would teach Air Vice-Marshal South-gate-bloody-Sayers not to act in such a dictatorial manner.

CHAPTER TWO

A smile touched Erica Macken's lips as she began to undress. The Jekyll and Hyde transformation had begun. The silk-lined uniform skirt rustled quietly to her feet. She stepped out of it, kicking off the black high-heeled shoes as she did so. The remainder of her clothing followed. Then she showered and towelled down her body with vigorous enthusiasm. It was a part of the preparation she loved, for no other reason than for the excitement which was to follow. She glanced down briefly at her naked body; the firm breasts, the small waist, the long shapely legs. It pleased her.

The smile was still there as she pulled the string vest down over her head. Next came the loosely fitting long johns; the thick off-white seaman's stockings; the sloppy pale-blue sweater; the cotton flying suit. Finally, and with some exertion, she struggled into the drag green immersion suit—known to pilots as a "goon suit"—its watertight rubberised wrist and neck openings clinging uncomfortably to her skin.

Ten minutes from the beginning of the transformation she emerged from the women's aircrew locker room. She was once more a bulky, sexless figure carrying a hard hat stuffed with radio leads, oxygen face mask, and pale green chamois leather gloves. Any trace of feminine charm had disappeared, except perhaps for the faint lingering fragrance of expensive French perfume.

Making her way down the narrow corridor the happiness which had touched her earlier suddenly vanished. She was remembering Gene. The seven days' sick leave had been a mistake. She had brooded far too much. Had found it impossible to sleep at night. The grief of those long lonely hours had somehow wrought in her mind a new clarity; a definition more finely etched than life itself. Nothing she could do would drive the remembered images from her. And the images always led her to the final scene in the American military cemetery near Cambridge. That was when the sharpness of focus faltered and the living face of Gene Kitrell was framed impossibly against a rough sky. The same image had haunted her for most of the seven days.

Today, October 13, the Monday following the funeral, she was back on duty, and the conditioning process had begun. She was able to believe that the face had never existed. Could plausibly explain it away as the imagination playing tricks. Could even reconcile herself to the unwanted

42

truth that Gene was gone forever.

The briefing room was filled with expectant chatter. Twelve fast jet pilots who had been selected for conversion training to the new Blackhawk One interceptor. Two navy lieutenants were the only exception in what was a predominantly air force operation.

With the death of Major Kitrell, the RAF, guided by NATO, had drafted in another American to take over as squadron commander. His name was Jason Hood. His reputation had preceded him. Former boss of the Red Flag war game team in Nellis, Nevada, he was known as the "iron man".

Lieutenant-Colonel Jason Hood. Marital status: widower. Children: two, one boy and one girl— both deceased. Age: forty-nine. Education: gradudated Putnam City High School, Oklahoma, with straight As. Had rejected place at Yale in favour of pilot training with the United States air force. Military record: Vietnam veteran. More MiG kills than any other pilot. The Silver Star, Distinguished Flying Cross with oak leaf cluster, thirty air medals—one for each enemy aircraft destroyed, seven more air medals for seventy-seven missions, and five Purple Hearts. Beyond that the man was a fitness fanatic. Slept only four hours a day. Always ran ten miles before sunrise. Dislikes: alcohol, smoking and navy pilots. Likes: fast jets, the Star Spangled Banner, and the air force. Especially the air force.

The American media had of course lionised him. Had created a living legend. A true patriot. An All-American hero. A superstar. In reality Hood was feeling his years and fighting a daily battle with his physical and mental condition. That he was clinging to an impossible peak in both was the result of a phenomenal will power. The reason for his arduous training programme was a secret known only to the man himself. He was preparing himself for another war. And it was sure to come. Not necessarily a Vietnam; a smaller war would be quite adequate, just as long as it was a shooting war. A place to use the only skills he possessed. The aggressive combat skills of the warrior.

Someone called the room to attention. Amid the rattling and scraping of chairs Hood swept into the room and up the three steps to the stage. He turned and faced the gathering. "Okay, at ease . . . take your seats." He waited until the brief noise had died and then added a few more seconds. Those seconds were to ensure his presence was felt. It was. The magnificent Hood, hair greying slightly at the temples. Lean, tanned, rugged face. Cool grey eyes. His uniform was beyond immaculate. It reflected the man. The man to whom perfection was zero on a scale of one hundred.

"First off," he said, his accent deep mid-western, "I guess I should introduce myself. Lieutenant-Colonel Jason Hood; detached from the 429th Squadron of the 474th Tactical Fighter

44

Wing, United States Air Force. Now I guess the majority of you are trying to figure out what an American fighter jockey is doing here, taking over the role of squadron commander . . . am I right?" A long silence greeted the question. Hood continued. "Sure I'm right . . . so I'll fill you in as far as I can. The most significant issue on this course is not fast jet flying; you are all capable of that or you wouldn't be here. No, the issue finally is combat readiness. Recent exercises have indicated that our pal Ivan and his buddies have the drop on us, that the next war puts us on the losing team!" Hood paused, letting his final statement register. "Okay, so let's analyse this little problem. Starting with Korea we had a superiority rating in air combat of twelve to one. Moving up to Vietnam that rating had closed to five to one, and by the end of Vietnam the Commies were running at evens." The grey eyes narrowed. "Now don't suffer from the delusion that these are a bunch of figures picked out of the air. They are not.

"So bearing these figures in mind, what's the answer?" Hood glanced down the rows of watchful faces. "Any of you guys think you know?"

A pilot sitting near the front said: "Improved hardware?"

Hood shrugged dismissively. "Improved sure, but it's still up to the guy in charge of that hardware. Which brings us to Hood's Theory." He paused again, then held up the first finger of his right hand. "Number one. We in the West live under the umbrella of democracy. A democracy administered by politicians." A second finger joined the first. "Two. Those same politicians slash defence spending from time to time. Forget the reasons, they're not important. Move on to number three. Cost cutting in the defence department reduces your time in the air. Which brings us to number four. The only way I know of being superior in the sky is to live in the damned place."

A fifth digit joined the other four. "Finally and I guess most importantly, Ivan does not suffer from defence cuts in the way we do. The opposite in fact. We do a great deal of our training in simulators . . . Ivan does the majority of his work in the real sky. The results speak for themselves. As I mentioned earlier, Vietnam, was the clincher."

A voice from the back of the room said: "Bearing in mind Hood's Theory, sir, does that mean we will be getting unlimited flying time?"

Hood had studied the records and photographs of all pilots on the Blackhawk training programme during the past thirty-six hours. He said: "Flight-Lieutenant L'Estrange, isn't it?"

L'Estrange looked mildly impressed. "Yes sir."

"Unfortunately, Flight-Lieutenant, I—like you—drive airplanes for a living; had I been a member of the Senate or your House of Parliament, I could perhaps have answered you. As things stand, however, I will do my damnedest to increase the flying programme, but it's still up to you—all of you—to make sure that every minute counts." He walked across the stage to the three steps. He paused at the top one. "Before I leave you, a parting thought. In less than six weeks we have the NATO exercise in Norway—code name

46

ROLLING THUNDER. Past records have been abysmal. I, for my part, intend to change all that. You, for your part, will be required to work harder than you've ever done before. The dropout rate on my courses has to be seen to be believed. You have doubtless heard rumours about me. Stories about the 'iron man' and his impossible standards. Stories that every day in his outfit is of thirty hours duration. That may have been true once, but not any more . . . the going rate is now forty."

Half an hour later Jason Hood was waiting out on the flight line. He had been intrigued to discover that he had a woman on his training roster. Now he wanted to find out if this Flight-Lieutenant Macken was all her records cracked her up to be. He doubted it. Still, forty-five minutes in the air would tell him all he needed to know.

Hood had been well-known back at Nellis for his "ass through the wringer" missions. Get through the first run and there was hope. The failure rate however indicated that Hood's standards were too high for most mere mortals. His only passion was flight. People with aspirations to share his sky were treated with mistrust. As an instructor he sought only perfection. In his students he never found it.

Erica Macken approached the aircraft uncertainly. Until this moment she had pushed the thought of Hood himself from her mind, the most

47

important matter being her selection to the new Blackhawk squadron. Lieutenant-Colonel Hood had meant nothing then. Now he meant everything. She knew she had only the one chance to succeed.

Hood waited until she was standing in front of him, until some form of greeting was inevitable. Then he said, "That there has been no formal briefing on this flight may strike you as odd. It is not. You are not a student in the true sense of the word, but an experienced fast jet jockey who is simply taking me up for a ride around the sky. That ride is to convince me you have a natural aptitude." She tried to keep her eyes on his as he spoke. His hard stare made that impossible. "Either you have some God-given talent Lieutenant, or you will be another average Joe who flies by the numbers. And in that unhappy event, Lieutenant, we will not meet again after today's ride. You get my meaning?"

She stiffened. "Perfectly. Sir."

Hood's voice lifted against the background noise of taxiing jet aircraft. "One other pointer. That you are a woman makes not the slightest difference to me. What will matter, however, is your dedication. I ask and expect nothing more than one hundred and ten percent...at all times." Turning on his heel towards the aircraft he called back over his shoulder. "Now if you'll follow me I'll introduce you to a friend of mine."

Eight minutes later Erica was settling into the front cockpit of the Blackhawk T.1 trainer, Colonel Hood's "friend," a Blackhawk One modified for dual control. A young mechanic clambered up the steps, leant over her, and began tugging at straps and buckles. Legs, waist, shoulders. He removed the top safety pin from the ejector seat and held it up for her to see. She completed the ritual by reaching between her thighs and removing the second pin. The mechanic took it and stowed them both. The seat was now armed. Its rocket-powered motor required only the activation of one of the two handles to blast it out of the aircraft at over eighty feet per second. Above Erica's head the canopy motored shut with a dull thud.

Hood's voice came over the intercom from the rear cockpit: "How do you read me, Lieutenant?"

"Fives . . . how me?"

"Good enough . . . one last tip, one you've heard a thousand times before. It concerns fast jets. You don't fly them in real time, because real time is too late. You must anticipate everything. With this bird that goes threefold."

By the time the pre-start checks were complete it was raining; the sky a dull metallic grey. Erica watched as the throttles by her left hand jinked forward and back. Hood was doing the work from the rear cockpit. The start-up was a rushing thunder, diminished to bearable levels by her hard hat which contained glycerine-filled inner ear pieces. She scanned the cathode ray tubes (CRTs) which flashed words and pictures and numbers, then smiled as she thought of her

49

father. He would scarcely have considered this piece of advanced technology an aeroplane. To him aircraft had instruments with dials, the smell of gasoline, oil, dope, hydraulic fluid. They also had recips., radial for preference, and a propeller which became a great silver disc. Standing behind his sort of aeroplanes you felt the slipstream buffeting and tugging at your clothes, lifting your hair, filling your nostrils with a unique aroma, plucking tears from your eyes . . . to him, aeroplanes had been ladies. Old, young, beautiful, plain, ugly. Some kind, some cruel, some faithful, some harlots. But to all of them he had spoken gently. He had convinced his daughter those long years ago that aeroplanes were living things, that they needed as much love and understanding as real people. And his words must indeed have worked some kind of magic, for not one of his "ladies" had ever let him down.

The memories faded and she went back to scanning the CRTs. Towards her left knee she saw the placade VICS INOPERATIVE. Hood had mentioned during their walk-around inspection that the computer system was out of action. Apparently the scientists were doing some fine tuning work on it. Not that the vocal command system would have applied today, anyway. Today was a purely manual operation. Getting to know the machine. Attempting to satisfy the exacting standards of Jason Hood.

The Blackhawk started to roll forward. The nose dipped as Hood checked his brakes. "You have control," he said. "Check your brakes."

Erica took control and depressed her feet gently on the brake pedals. The nose saluted once more, then Hood's voice was back issuing a stream of curt, clipped commands. The rain was sheeting down by the time they reached the runway. Erica felt nervous. But not because of a new aircraft or the wretched weather conditions. Pilots were a very special breed of people: the only breed on God's earth who spent their entire working lives separated from it. No, she could cope with that. Flying was a part of her make-up; her stock in trade. What was getting to her was the man in the back seat. Examiners, instructors, check pilots, all flyers suffered at their hands. Attempting to fly the perfect check ride with eyes boring into the back of your skull: knowing you're having an off day when you find your altitude out by a hundred feet, your heading by ten degrees, your airspeed by fifteen knots; and as you're juggling to put the figures right you miss a radio call and a navigational fix, and as you're trying to gloss over them you fly into the biggest and blackest storm cloud in the northern hemisphere. Now you're icing up and you've forgotten to switch on the anti-icing gear ... and all the time the check pilot is quietly taking notes. You can almost hear his pen scratching across his knee pad. You also know that pilots are not allowed to have off days. And at the end of the flight you realise that you have spent more time worrying about your "passenger" than the job in hand. Next time, you resolve, it will be different. It never is.

And all that's with a routine check pilot. Not

Colonel Hood.

Hood's voice growled through the intercom. "Follow me through on the controls during take-off."

Erica acknowledged and waited. Hood, holding the aircraft on the brakes, advanced the two throttles slowly forward. The rushing thunder grew steadily in volume. A slight vibration ran through the cockpit. Then the afterburners were coming in, and the brakes were off. The acceleration was a brutal kick in the back as the runway ahead started shortening at a heart-stopping rate. A necklace of raindrops shivered around the edge of the windshield, trapped in some invisible pressure pattern. Almost as suddenly as the take-off roll had commenced they were airborne, screaming up towards the black rain clouds.

"You have control," Hood said.

And suddenly it was going to be all right. Erica cleared her mind of everything but the task in hand. She continued the climb up through the frontal weather. Twenty seconds later the cloud turned to lighter grey. They were going to switch worlds any minute. The light grey turned whitish, then white ... then that final brightness as they exploded into blue sky and dazzling sun. She felt like mentioning it: the beauty. But she knew Lieutenant-Colonel Hood would not appreciate that kind of remark. As if anticipating her thoughts his voice was back. In compliance with his commands she cancelled the afterburners and levelled off at 24,000 feet.

"I have it," Hood's voice drawled from the back

seat. She relinquished control and waited. "Now I'm going to show you what I can do, then I expect you to better it . . . okay?"

"Okay." She said it, but she didn't believe she would.

Jason Hood was in his heaven. He ran through the book. Slow rolls, hesitation rolls, Immelmans, chandelles, then on to cloverleaf turns, figure eights, loops. All was done with elegance and precision, a precision which marked him out as more than a natural pilot. He possessed a rare brilliance. It was a brilliance most people saw only once in a lifetime, and only then if they were lucky. Erica Macken had seen it twice.

Her father had emigrated to Canada from Northern Ireland in the late 1950s. Shortly after their arrival at a place called Sept Illes her mother had died, of pneumonia. In such circumstances her father, a bush pilot, had done the only thing possible. He had raised his daughter in the cockpit of his aeroplane. Wherever he went, she went. At the age of three he had taught her to stand on the co-pilot's seat of the old Beaver floatplane and fly straight and level. To her it had seemed the most natural thing in the world. As natural as walking, or breathing, or sleeping. With no government agents in the sparsely settled areas where her father operated, she had unofficially soloed the old floatplane at the age of eleven. Up until then her scholastic education too had been taken care of by her father. The classrooms had ranged from noisy cockpits, to lake shores in summer, and snowed-in log cabins during the

53

long winters. The curriculum had been broad based. Arithmetic, English, a brief history and geography of the world—or at least the places her father had been, which seemed to be everywhere with the exception of Russia and South America—and a smattering of science subjects. Apart from all this, and her lessons in flying she had been taught to fish and make dead-fall traps, and had been schooled in arctic survival.

Then, shortly before her twelfth birthday, her father decided she now needed formal education and sent her to a Catholic school in Quebec. After the freedom of the wilds she fought against the move, but to no avail. She knew her father. Knew that once he had made up his mind about something he was immovable. He did make compromises however, always arriving in the plane to collect her on Friday evening and returning her to school on the Sunday afternoon. And the long summer vacations had been the best time anyway, the time when she could build up her already considerable flying skills.

By the time she was seventeen, and old enough to hold a pilot's license, she had amassed over seven thousand flying hours. Not that those hours could officially count for anything; but they had given her a feeling for aircraft which had since confused and amazed flying instructors in Canada and England alike.

She had been nineteen when her father died. It was inevitably the most traumatic moment in her life. He had always been there, patient, kind and understanding. A man who always found time for her, even when it seemed no time existed. Before school in Quebec he had tucked her in bed every night of her life, and sat reading stories. Sometimes he would nod off. It was when the book slipped from his lap to the floor that he usually awoke. Then he would carefully pick up the book, mark the page, and place it quietly on the bedside table. She would of course pretend to be asleep, while all the time squinting through half-closed eyelids. Then his beard would be tickling her nose as he bent down to kiss her forehead. He would blow out the candle next, and from somewhere in the darkness whisper "Sweet dreams". Then, distantly, she would pick up the next sounds; logs being thrown on the fire downstairs; the clatter of dishes; doors opening and closing.

Years later when she was home from school and the bedtime stories had long ceased she would still lie awake listening to the old familiar noises. It was if they would always be a part of her life. His dying had left an emptiness; an unbelievable void. She sat in the house for two weeks after his death, grieving. It was as if God was calling in a marker. Too much happiness, it seemed, had a price.

The local doctor, a Scotsman and a good friend of her father's, visited her frequently in those two weeks. He was of the opinion, he told her, that her father had worked himself into an early grave. "Twenty years in this God-forsaken wilderness are enough for any man. If I were you, lassie, I'd find a kinder place to give your life to."

She had taken the old doctor's advice, sold the house and the Beaver floatplane, packed what few personal belongings she had, and moved south to Montreal. Upon her arrival she had signed on with Won-Del Aviation at Cartierville airport for a commercial pilot's course. She passed with the highest marks ever graded by the Department of Transport. Even so she found it impossible to get a job. Companies didn't take on women pilots, not when there were men around. She kicked her heels a month longer, walking from airline office to airline office, from charter company to charter company, from flight school to flight school. In the end she decided to move to England. Perhaps things would be better there . . .

They weren't. Even so she did all the necessary courses to obtain her British licences. Then, amazingly, the Royal Air Force suddenly announced that they were accepting women pilots. The anti-female bias was still there of course, but in her case, with her abilities, there was little it could do. When a student outflies her instructors something is wrong! Or conversely, something is right. With Erica Macken they decided on the latter, and after two years of training posted her to a Tornado squadron. That she was not accepted there at first had been understandable, to her at least—she was after all a woman. Fast jets were for aggressive steely-eyed young men. And the young men made their feelings known. But even when her skills began to outweigh theirs nothing changed. Until Gene Kitrell came along. And then, for the first time, it had all seemed worthwhile. He loved her for herself. Respected her natural aptitude in the sky. To him she had been an equal . . .

Hood's aerobatic sequence ended with all the grace of a ballet. He handed over the controls: "Okay, Lieutenant, show me what you can do."

For long moments he sat watching the back of her bonedomed head. It was as though she had frozen up. Nothing moved. Nothing happened. The aircraft whispered on in straight and level flight. Perhaps I've unnerved her, he thought. Perhaps she realises she hasn't got what it takes. Damn it, I just knew those records were wrong. No one is that good. No one . . . not even the fucking birds.

Hood was about to call out, to say something cruelly appropriate. The words never left his mouth. They couldn't. Suddenly, quite suddenly his entire world exploded around him. He didn't know what had happened. One moment they were cruising sub-sonic at twenty-four thousand feet, the next . . .

The sky and lower cloud deck blurred and tumbled like a fast moving kaleidoscope as Erica transformed the Blackhawk into a living thing. It was now a part of her, and she a part of it. The sleek black interceptor roared its thunder at the heavens as she flashed through a breathtaking sequence of manoeuvres. There was no transition from one to the other, just a constant flowing movement. A fluid motion catching and bending shadows with a definitive kind of magic.

The magic ended as quickly and dramatically

as it had begun. An eight point hesitation roll around a perfect loop. Hood sat wide-eyed. Seeing but not believing. Not even when the aircraft hit its own slipstream at the bottom of the loop. The altitude read out was exactly 24,000 feet; the height at which they had started. Had Jason Hood been sharper he would have also observed that the sequence ended at precisely the same latitude and longitude readout as it had commenced. A point above the English Channel exactly seventeen nautical miles southwest of the navy base at Portland.

Erica switched to intercom. "Anything else, sir?"

Hood recognised the tone in the voice. The cool, calm, easy-going banter he had heard so many times over 'Nam. And the guys who had that sort of quiet confidence were the ones who had been around forever. The real pros. He wondered where the hell the woman in the front seat had been taught. The air force, sure. But there had to have been some other battlefield; some other sky. His tone when he eventually spoke was as it had been earlier. Jason Hood was a past master at hiding his feelings: "Anything else, you say, Lieutenant? Sure . . . if you think you can manage it, get me home."

Erica allowed herself a quiet smile as she wheeled the Blackhawk across the sky and picked up a heading for the base at Yeovilton. In between radar headings from the fighter controller, she let her mind return briefly to her childhood in

Canada. To the man who had taught her everything he knew about the sky. To a pilot who was the equal of Jason Hood. Her father.

At Supreme Headquarters Allied Powers in Europe (SHAPE), a chateau near Mons, Belgium, Air Vice-Marshal Alister Southgate-Sayers was standing at a second-floor window. It was raining. One of those squally, blustery days which strip the autumn leaves from the trees. He was watching them now, blowing across the long lawn which stretched away from the building. Off to the right a black Mercedes sent up clouds of spray as it sped away down the narrow access road.

The man himself was tall and broad-shouldered; six feet four and two hundred pounds. His black hair flecked with grey was regulation short, parted on the left, and neatly combed. He was wearing a charcoal-grey suit, white shirt, and an air force tie. His left hand was in his pocket absently jingling coins; his right hung loosely at his side. The letter had slipped from it unnoticed, and now lay face down on the carpet.

His eyes left the lawn and glanced skyward at the low scudding clouds. Above those clouds would be sunshine. There was a brief moment bordering on regret for his lost youth. To be free again; up there at the controls of an aeroplane . . . The moment passed. He despised sentiment in all its forms. That was why through all his postings his wife had always remained at the family home in Buckinghamshire. Of course marriage had been, and always would be, essential. It offered stability to a career officer's prospects. Even so, he—they—could perhaps have socialised more. Was that the reason he had been passed over at the last round of promotions? He shrugged, set his mouth in a firm angry line, and turned back towards the conference table. His foot caught the letter, and he registered surprise as he stooped to pick it up. He hadn't even noticed that it had left his hand. The surprise changed to concern when he remembered other occasions. They were all quite recent, of that he was sure; but clearly he was losing the feeling in his right hand. He made a low priority mental note to consult the family doctor when he was next home; then he joined the two men at the conference table. They, no doubt, sensing something was wrong, remained silent as he seated himself at the head of the table and laid the letter down before him.

Southgate-Sayers said: "Bad news, I'm afraid."

Rear-Admiral Charles Greenaway, a small grey-bearded man with watery eyes, glanced at the letter now on the table. "The Blackhawk project?"

Southgate-Sayers frowned and nodded. "They've given it the green light." There was a brittle silence as the words registered.

Greenaway said: "As from when?"

Southgate-Sayers took a deep breath and smiled ironically. "It's already started. This morning at 0700 hours, Monday, 13 October." He glanced at his watch. It was now one o'clock. Noon in England. "By now the Blackhawk squadron is officially five hours old."

"Why did the letter take so long getting here?" Greenaway asked.

"Held up in Brussels. That's the problem with NATO; too many damned committees."

"What about the VIC system?" It was Major-General George Foulkes, seated to the air vice-marshal's right, who spoke. A lean cadaverous man in his late fifties, in his younger days he had been known throughout the army as "Joker" Foulkes; a man with a ready wit and an easy smile. These days he had neither.

Southgate-Sayers picked up the letter. "According to the Right Honourable George Hinchcliffe the British Aerospace people have located the problem. They're doing some modifications on the computer at this very moment. In the interim the aircraft is being flown manually."

Foulkes snorted. "But the damned thing is vulnerable. Your report showed that, Alister . . . it proved the Soviets had knocked it down."

"Not quite, George. It was never one hundred per cent certain. Ninety-five, but never a hundred. And the five per cent doubt is enough for Hinchcliffe."

Foulkes's face darkened. "We haven't retrieved the black box then?"

"Still searching . . . but no."

"So that is in effect the missing five per cent?"

"More or less."

61

"And the proposals on Space Strike? They're still considering bringing it back on line, I assume?"

Southgate-Sayers slid the letter across to the general. "Not according to this. Too much tax-payers' money tied up in the Blackhawk project. Too many advance orders . . . too many jobs at stake."

"The trouble with socialists," Foulkes snapped. "Too bloody sentimental." He snatched up the letter and started to read.

Southgate-Sayers said nothing, waiting for him to digest the contents of the letter and pass it across to his navy counterpart, while his thoughts drifted back to the "Space Strike" plans.

The Reagan administration had of course started it in the early 1980s. The Americans had termed it "Star Wars". It was at the end of Reagan's second term of office that he appeared to have a change of heart and decide that pursuit of detente and arms reduction talks would benefit mankind. In reality he needed to reduce the American budget deficit which was terrifying even Republican voters. By slashing defence spending, especially in the alarmingly costly Star Wars programme, he was able to boost his administration's waning popularity.

The British Conservative government, riding the last of their dwindling oil revenues, had funded their own programme instead: Space Strike, a system of rocket-borne probes in space trajectories that would be equipped with long wavelength infra-red sensors able to detect hostile missiles at ranges of up to 3,500 miles, and computer and communications technology capable of handling data for as many as 20,000 targets.

To destroy the hostile missiles a ground-based laser site would fire a beam at an orbital mirror fitted to the space probe. The probe would sight each enemy missile through its infra-red sensor which in turn would realign the mirror onto the target. The laser beams, bounced off the mirror, would hit the missile with devastating accuracy. It was a foolproof system. Unlike the project it superseded, Blackhawk, it was the ultimate deterrent.

The Space Strike programme had been well advanced when, in the most recent general election, the Conservative government had been defeated. The continuing high unemployment figures had been their downfall. The Labour Party had cruised to victory on a "Jobs For All" manifesto, had immediately cancelled the low labour-intensive Space Strike, and had revived the more marketable Blackhawk project instead.

Admiral Greenaway, who had put on a pair of half-moon spectacles to read the letter, eventually laid it down before him. He had always been a cautious man, a reasonable man. He saw both points of view in an argument and prided himself on choosing the winning side more times than not. Had he cared to analyse this state of affairs further he would have realised that the reason for his success was quite simple. His prevarications let others make mistakes. The issue was usually as good as settled by the time he added his vote. He removed his spectacles now and stroked the bridge of his nose gently with one finger. "A difficult problem," he said, addressing the air vice-marshal.

"Difficult?" Southgate-Sayers said stridently.

"In view of the government's policy. I think . . ."

"You think?" Southgate-Sayers exploded. "That is one thing no one could ever accuse you of. Government policy, you say. Let me remind you about Labour government policies, Charles, before you end up voting for the bastards at the next election." Greenaway had turned pale. He didn't like angry scenes. Southgate-Sayers went on: "Barnes Wallis, the man who invented the bouncing bomb in the last war, he'll do for starters. It was at the end of that war when he went to the government, a Labour government I might add, with a radical new concept in war planes. He had designed a swing-wing aircraft called the Swallow. The government told him he was wasting their time and why not take the idea—and himself—off to the USA? And that's what he did. Now we go forward nearly twenty years to the early sixties, a Conservative government, and the TSR2 project. Nothing like it had been built before. It was going to revolutionise the entire aviation world. Then there was an election and the socialists came to power. The next thing is, the TSR2 is scrapped. But not only that; the government, acting like a gang of Gestapo thugs, sent in a wrecking crew to Boscombe Down and physically smashed all the jigs and tools."

Southgate-Sayers paused long enough to lean forward across the table. "And the reason? Political chicanery. The socialists had made a deal with the Yanks to buy hundreds of their latest fighter bombers; the F-111 ... the new swing-wing aircraft. Now, if you think back that far, you will remember that they had sent Wallis to the States with that very concept because they felt he was wasting their time. Now we have the same socialists buying back something they didn't want in the first place and at the same time writing off millions of pounds which had gone into the research and development of the TSR2.

"There is of course a nice little sting in the tail. The Yanks started having problems with the F-111. The problems went on and on, and in the end the British government cancelled the order. The only problem with that was that they had infringed a clause in their contract. And that meant that the British taxpayer had to pay out something like 800 million pounds. And we ended up with no aircraft; just years of wasted development and a catalogue of disasters instigated by different Labour governments. And now I suppose you're going to tell me that they're doing the right thing with this Blackhawk project?"

Greenaway was paler than ever. He felt sure that Alister was telling less than the whole story. But he lacked the necessary facts and figures. He said, "I submit to your superior knowledge,

Alister. It was just that I see a great deal of difficulty with this problem . . . I mean, how does one reverse the thinking of a government?"

Foulkes, who had been brooding quietly, said, "One thing's for certain, we can't back off now. Space Strike could be only two years away from being fully operational. Why the hell we couldn't have done without Blackhawk and held on with the Tornadoes, God alone knows. What do you say, Alister?"

Southgate-Sayers, whose anger had been entirely for effect, smiled. "I think you're wrong in your assumption, George. I'm sure God knows as little about this as we do." His face became serious. "But I think you're right. We can't back off now. Basically as I see it we are being foisted off with an aircraft which I consider already obsolete. Of course we can patch up the computer, change the damn thing if necessary; but at the end of the day it isn't going to help, because by then the Soviets will be out there—in space—with their own version of Space Strike. And then you can have all the aircraft in the world and you'll still lose."

The room darkened as storm clouds gathered over the chateau, adding to the general air of foreboding which had settled on the three men.

"Ideas?" Southgate-Sayers said shortly.

Foulkes, after some consideration, said eagerly, "What if another Blackhawk went down . . . in public, as it were?"

Southgate-Sayers frowned. "I don't like losing

pilots, George."

"Who the hell said anything about pilots? I'm talking about planes . . . they do have ejector seats don't they?"

"That's no guarantee after the last incident."

Foulkes said grimly: "Guarantees, Alister? Since when did any of us deal in those?"

"Point taken. But the circumstances would have to be similar to last time. Soviet intervention. Which means we need a Tupolev. We can't very well phone up the Kremlin, can we!"

"I know that. But I also know that the Soviets do fairly regular reconnaissance flights out of Murmansk. Couldn't we position a Blackhawk into the appropriate area . . . much the same sort of thing as last time?"

"Not that easy. I can't order flights night after night without good reason. Besides which, we can hardly rely on the Soviets doing the same thing again."

"Of course not," Foulkes replied. "But couldn't we . . . give them a helping hand, as it were?"

There was a long silence.

"Even assuming that," Southgate-Sayers murmured I still can't have planes going out night after night."

"But you could try it once . . . or twice?"

"It's possible."

Outside the windows rain had begun to fall. Greenaway, who had been listening in quiet disbelief at this sudden turn in the conversation, said: "I thought you indicated earlier they could patch up the computer, or replace it if necessary. So what happens if another does crash? Surely they'll just modify the system; I mean, it's no guarantee they'll scrap the aircraft."

Foulkes gave the admiral a hard stare. "As I said earlier, Charles, we don't deal in guarantees. However, if this was picked up by the press, who then found out it wasn't the first time . . . that the government had been doing a cover-up job . . . you get my meaning? Emotive stuff, Charles. *And* with a general election in the offing."

Greenaway nodded weakly. He didn't like what he was hearing. It sounded distinctly subversive. The distant rolling of thunder was like a warning to him. For perhaps the only time in his life Rear-Admiral Charles Greenaway had no reason to prevaricate. He knew, positively and definitely, that he was on the wrong side.

It was raining in Yeovilton, too, as Erica Macken contemplated going to the locker room to change. She had been sitting for the past hour drinking coffee and half listening to other members of the squadron comparing notes on Jason Hood. Henry Maudsley was fulsome in his praise—unsurprisingly since Hood had appointed him a flight commander on the new squadron. Another pilot, Michael L'Estrange, was now baiting him.

"Thought you didn't like Americans, Henry?"

Maudsley caught Erica's eye before he answered. He had stirred up a lot of ill feeling against Gene Kitrell, the reason being nothing more than simple jealousy. Erica Macken had rejected his advances on more than one occasion, and to see her take up with Kitrell so readily had been hard to accept. "This one's different, old boy," he said to L'Estrange.

"Different from what? . . . I mean the jolly old playing fields of Eton are still the same distance from the colonies."

Maudsley smiled offensively. "Not really the point. This one has definite leadership qualities . . . if you get my meaning?"

L'Estrange instantly saw the direction the conversation was leading. Comparisons being odious, especially between the dead and the living, he quickly changed the subject. "I hear he doesn't like navy pilots!"

"Colonel Hood, you mean?"

"I do. I gather he's not altogether sane on the subject."

Maudsley tapped the side of his nose knowingly. "Ah yes. Interesting story that—"

A corporal from operations came into the room. Maudsley turned to him but he went straight over to Erica Macken. He told her in a quiet voice that someone was waiting to see her in the briefing room. She left her chair and followed the NCO into the corridor.

"Do you have a name?"

"I'm not sure, ma'am, but I think it was Mr. Kitrell."

A wave of dizziness swept over her as she

69

walked down the neon-lit corridor to the briefing room. Kitrell? Gene's uncle, it had to be. His parents were dead: that much she knew. An uncle then? Or perhaps a cousin?

She opened the door and went into the room where earlier that day Jason Hood had said his piece. Her visitor was looking out of the window, his back to her. He turned as she entered. It was the man from Cambridge, the one she had seen at the funeral service. The who who looked so much like Gene. She stood, wide-eyed, her words of greeting trapped hopelessly in her throat.

The man moved across the room towards her. "Miss Macken?" he said with a little smile. His voice was accentless—in that respect he differed from Gene. She continued to stare at him. The same longish blond hair, the startling blue eyes, the same lean, athletic body. What she hadn't noticed at the military cemetery was his sun-tan. His face was a golden bronze. She wondered where he'd recently been to acquire it. Around his eyes sun spokes radiated in small white lines.

"Yes." She heard her own voice as if from a long way off. "I'm Erica Macken."

"I didn't realise . . ." His voice faltered as his eyes took in her flying suit with its air force wings. "You're a pilot."

"Yes . . . and you are . . . ?"

"Me? . . . oh, I'm sorry. I'm Gene's brother. Paul. Paul Kitrell." He held out a strong sunburnt hand. She felt it close warmly around hers. Felt the same tingling sensation she had experienced

70

with Gene. Their hands remained together as they sat down on the hard-backed chairs which faced the deserted platform, the backdrop of which was a huge map of Europe. "I heard that you were engaged to Gene . . . I came to collect his personal belongings." He gave that little, half-apologetic smile again. Gene's smile. "I thought I should come and see you before I leave."

"Leave?" the word echoed down the rows of empty chairs.

"Yes. I live in East Africa, you see, but I've been in London for the past week or so. Someone at the ministry of defence said they would arrange to have Gene's things forwarded. But I wanted to see the place he had spent his last months." He added, almost as an afterthought, "We weren't very close, I'm afraid. Not in later years, that is."

"Where are you going when you leave?"

"Back to Nairobi."

"You live there?"

"Some of the time. We were raised there, Gene and I."

"In East Africa!" she said in amazement. "But he . . . you're American."

As if becoming suddenly aware of their contact he withdrew his hand from hers. She saw something like embarrassment in his face. "It's a long story. Gene didn't tell you, I guess!"

"No, not exactly. He didn't talk much about his family." He hadn't, she now realised, talked about it at all. "But please go on. You said it's a long story."

He was quiet for a moment, his eyes caught up in some distant past. "Too long to be worth telling," he said suddenly. "But briefly, our parents—they were American—died out in Nairobi when we were both in our teens. I was the older, eighteen at the time. Gene was just thirteen. An aunt, my mother's sister, came out from St. Louis, Missouri. She took him back with her. I stayed put and got a job."

"I didn't know," she said quietly. Suddenly there was a lot she didn't know. A lot she had to find out about. The first of which was Paul Kitrell. She couldn't let him walk into her life and back out again in the same breath. It was like having a part of Gene returned to her. And any part, no matter how small, had to be kept; treasured for as long as was humanly possible.

She was aware of his voice again. "Have you heard the result of the enquiry?"

"Enquiry?"

"Gene's accident."

"Yes . . . they normally take months to sort those things out, but in this case—"

"That's interesting," he said. "Anyway, I was in London. I managed to find out too, if by unorthodox means. So stop me if I've got it wrong. Gene, it seems, was flying a specially modified Russian jet—a MiG-25. Apparently he was too low . . . at night. They're saying he just flew into high ground. Pilot error, simple as that."

Erica's eyes flashed with anger. "I know. And it's impossible. Not Gene. He was too good for that. He was too good . . ." The anger turned suddenly to tears.

He put a comforting arm around her shoulders. "I'm sorry, I shouldn't have brought it up."

"I'm glad you did." She controlled herself. "You don't believe it, do you—their conclusion, I mean?"

"If it's any consolation, no. We may have been apart for a lot of years, but I remember him as a boy. Everything he did he did well. Then when he went into the air force, back in the States, he started to write to me. We never met again, but we wrote. The only change I noticed was for the better; always getting better." He turned his face towards the window and the sound of rain on glass. "I suppose I'll always find it hard to believe he's dead . . . I'll still find blue airmail envelopes in the mailbox and think they're from him." He withdrew his arm from her shoulders and smiled at her wryly. "We always exchanged Christmas cards, you know. The same two cards, year after year. It started out as a joke, and they were getting a bit dog-eared, but we said we would send the same two cards back and forth across the world until they—or we—finally became too old and fell apart."

She watched him closely now in the failing afternoon light, thinking all the time how very much like Gene he was. His voice when he spoke again had dropped so that she had to strain to catch the words. "It's sad, really. Once we were going to live forever . . . and then our parents died

73

and the spell was broken. And we were no longer children." He paused. "I would have liked to have seen him again, though. Just once."

Without thinking she reached out and took his hand. "I understand," she said. "You'd have liked him, I know. He was a wonderful man."

They remained together quietly as the rain-sodden skies brought on a premature evening light. Autumn it seemed was already over; winter had its foot firmly in the door.

She said tiredly, "I suppose I'd better go and change."

He sighed. "I suppose so. Do you mind if I wait for you?"

"No, of course not. Give me ten minutes."

"One other thing," he said as she moved towards the door.

"Yes?"

"Was Gene involved with this new aircraft? The Blackhawk?"

"Yes . . . why?"

"Perhaps it's nothing, but there was a newspaper report at the time of the accident which suggested that Gene had died testing NATO's latest aircraft."

"Yes, I read that." Suddenly she was wary. These were high security matters. And what did she really know about this man? She temporised. "You know what newspaper men are like! I doubt any reporter would know a MiG-25 from a Boeing 747."

Kitrell shrugged. "That particular one would."

"What d'you mean?"

"The crash in Scotland was observed by a semi-retired reporter who telephoned the details to Fleet Street. The *Daily Telegraph*, to be exact."

"And?"

"He was formerly with that same paper . . . as their air correspondent. He was also once an air force pilot."

She hesitated, still unsure. "How . . . how did you find all that out?"

"I'm in the same business. Journalism."

She believed. And felt herself blush in the semi-darkness. "I'm sorry . . ."

"Sorry? For what?"

"My dig at newspapers and journalists." And for her suspicions.

He laughed. "Don't be. Most of the time it's true."

"So what are you going to do?"

"About the crash? What would you suggest? The air force are sticking to this pilot error nonsense. And to their story that Gene was flying a MiG. And as it was night when it happened, and as our expert on the spot was probably on his merry way home from the pub . . . I don't really know what I *can* do."

She nodded thoughtfully. "I'll go and get changed then."

He followed her out into the corridor. She was halfway towards the locker room when he called her name. She stopped and turned. "Yes?"

"Could I take you to dinner? Tonight?"

Just a little part of Gene. Something to keep. Something to treasure. "Yes," she said carefully, "that would be lovely. Don't go away, I'll be right back."

Paul returned to the briefing room and turned the lights on. He sat down and took a notebook and pen from his inside pocket. The Masai, Ole Renterre, had been a good teacher. A lion's footprints not only told where he had been but also where he was going. With Gene it was the same. Paul had already found out that "pilot error" verdicts in flying accidents were used somewhat too readily; usually after exhaustive investigation had failed to pinpoint any other apparent reason. And now this Erica Macken had mentioned that military enquiries usually took months. So why in Gene's case had it only taken days?

It was nine o'clock. 2100 hours Eastern European time.

The border was quiet. Too quiet? Alexei Karolyov moved silently through the skeletal shapes of silver birch trees, the deep carpet of snow muffling any sound he might have made. He stopped at the top of the rise, body straining, head cocked, listening for the guards. Only the silence came back, ringing insistently in his ears.

There was no moon or starlight, the sky was overcast. A fresh breeze had sprung up out of the east bringing with it the threat of more snow. Karolyov reached forward and parted the branches of a young birch. In the distance he saw the twinkling lights of the town of Kirkenes. Finnmark—northern Norway. Not far now. His eyes swept to the left and picked up the vague outline of the Russian watch tower. He had seen it before, in daylight, and had marked the area in his mind as an unlikely crossing point. The watch tower, he recalled, was a tall grey concrete structure, the top of which had reminded him of an airport control tower. Three hundred and sixty degrees of vision. He knew that the soldiers on duty in that tower would be scanning the area through high-powered infra-red night-scopes. For that reason alone he would have to move further north to make his run.

Karolyov swore under his breath. He was cold. His hands and feet, then his legs and arms—all had passed the stage of belonging to him. He knew his body core temperature was dropping to the point where he could not survive. He squatted on his haunches, then jerked upright, then down, then up again. He counted silently to thirty-five before giving up on the idea. There was no welcome resurgence of warmth from an increased circulation. The only result had been a tightening in his thigh muscles, and a laboured breathing of arctic air which cut painfully into his lungs.

Before moving off to his right his eyes took one last covetous glance at the straight kilometre in front of him. At the end of that kilometre was the Russian Gate. He could just about make out the white ribbon of road that ran from the watch tower to the gate. Once over that insignificant obstacle he would have been in Norway. Except that a rifle bullet would have picked him off long before the final step.

He shrugged. No, he had to move north. Get to the denser tree cover, where firs mingled with the dwarf-like silver birch. A few more kilometres maybe, but then, once in Norway, his problems would be over. His mind went back to Captain Dzerzhinsky at the Russian air force base in Murmansk. The information he had extracted from that ill-mannered Cossack bastard would be well received at the end of his journey. If Blackhawk were blown then certain people would be very glad. He trod carefully, keeping to the growing cover of trees, heading for the spot he had fixed in his mind as the turning point for the border.

He did not see the two soldiers in white winter uniform moving into his eleven o'clock position. Did not know that they had picked up his movements in the trees seconds earlier. They were now moving round to outflank him. Both men had unslung their Kalashnikov rifles from their shoulders. Both men carried identical orders concerning unauthorised border crossing. Shoot to kill. . . .

Suddenly Karolyov froze in his tracks. In what had seemed an impossible darkness his night vision had detected motion. It was a reverse overlay. Whiteness drifting across the darker outline of trees. A reindeer perhaps? No . . . He was up-wind of the movement. A reindeer would

78

have picked up his scent, would have waited—transfixed—until the danger had passed; or else would have bolted. Certainly it would not have chosen to maintain a converging path with the man scent. Which left the one possibility he had wished to avoid. Soldiers. A border patrol.

His stomach tightened at the gambit which now seemed his only recourse. It was a trick he had never used, one he had been taught a long time ago. He had laughed at it then, remarking on its dangers. Anyone foolish enough to get themselves into such a no-win situation, he had reasoned, deserved everything they got. But that had been then. And then he had been young, and sharp, and wise, and indestructible. Whereas now . . . he shuddered at the "now" element of his life. The wily old fox had been caught in the chicken house and the farmer was about to blow his balls off.

"Please" he whispered, "if there are to be bullets . . . let it be the first one." Then, bracing his body, he took a deep breath and shouted at the top of his lungs. "Sergeant . . . this is a bloody disgrace. I've been tracking you for twenty bloody minutes. Now get your arse over here . . . at the double." He had taken the flashlight from his pocket. It now sent a long bright beam in the direction of the movement, white against white. "Move, Comrade Sergeant . . . move!" His voice was confident, giving the lie to his fearful awareness that words were a poor defence against bullets.

The two soldiers had frozen in shock. A voice shouting? A Russian voice? The anger denoted authority, as did the flashlight which seemed to have them trapped in its narrow beam. Karolyov's aim had been lucky. What had also been lucky was the fact that one of the soldiers was indeed a sergeant. He spoke now, somewhat nervously, raising his rifle towards the blinding white light. "Identify yourself!" he shouted.

"What do you fucking mean, identify myself? What do you think this is . . . a training programme at Komsomolskaya barracks?" Karolyov's voice ricocheted through the trees like a rifle shot. Before the last echo had died he screamed again: "Well, do you?"

The last words need never have been uttered. The sergeant knew of Komsomolskaya barracks; as clearly did the voice. And if the voice knew, that was good enough for him. He nudged the soldier by his side, and slowly both men moved forward.

Karolyov caught the movement and adjusted the beam of the flashlight, keeping it purposely low. Trying to destroy their night vision might turn surprise into suspicion. When they were practically upon him, he shouted, "All right, Captain Valenkov . . . you can bring your men in now." The sergeant and the private stopped and looked back over their shoulders. They saw nothing. Karolyov snapped, "Do not worry, comrades, they will be here very shortly. Now, which one of you is Sergeant . . . damn, where is that order!" He fumbled in his pocket.

"Sergeant Vrubel," the sergeant volunteered.

He was an old soldier. A little simple in some men's eyes, but that was all a part of the act. He had been around too long to lose his stripes at this late stage of his career. Anything he could do to placate this officious bastard—that was the order of the day.

Karolyov said: "Yes . . . Vrubel. Right, get this man of yours over to the checkpoint at the double. Tell them Major Gorochenko and Captain Valenkov—KGB border guard—and six of their men need a hot meal . . . now."

The soldier, helped by a thump in the back from Vrubel, hurried off through the snow. His bladder had noticeably weakened during the last few minutes. Now, as he stumbled towards the distant checkpoint he kept muttering, "Fucking KGB . . . fucking Sergeant fucking Vrubel . . ." All the time his mind was telling him that his fourteen days' leave, due to start the following morning, was sure to be cancelled. He wouldn't get to screw Natalia. Thoughts of her welcoming body had tortured him constantly for the last seven days . . . and nights. He had even . . . he tripped and fell face down in the snow. "Shit!" he muttered, heaving himself up again onto his feet. And then he was off again, lifting his boots high as he tried to run . . .

Sergeant Vrubel accepted a cigarette from the KGB major. The officer had calmed down now. Vrubel felt happier. He was playing the role of the straight man, agreeing with everything, offering glowing praise on the major's stealth—but then

81

the major was a member of the elite KGB, while he himself was but a simple sergeant in the infantry.

Karolyov listened patiently to the sergeant's flattery. When the man had exhausted his limited powers of invention Karolyov said: "In fact, Vrubel, I liked when I said I had been tracking you for twenty mintues." The sergeant was momentarily confused; then Karolyov went on, "It was only eighteen."

The sergeant smiled obligingly at the joke. Things were going well.

Karolyov, after a moment of fumbling through his pockets, said: "A light, Vrubel . . . I can't find my damned matches."

The sergeant quickly tugged off a glove and produced a light from his breast pocket. He offered it to the major.

"Light yours first . . . the wind!" Karolyov waited his moment, watched the sergeant struggling with cupped hands to keep the flame alive. Vrubel's eyes were on the flickering light. And that, thought Alexei Karolyov, is enough. You have destroyed your night vision.

Directing his voice beyond the sergeant's left shoulder, he said, "Well done, Captain Valenkov," at the same time stepping forward as if to greet his brother officer. Sergeant Vrubel turned also. There was a moment of struggling to refocus his eyes; then a half-moment of realising something was wrong. There was no one there! He was moving back towards the major, words filling his mind, when Karolyov's blade slashed his throat open. The words never left Vrubel's lips, the only sound being a gurgling of blood as he slid silently to the ground. His dying thought was of a place called Komsomolskaya barracks.

For Alexei Karolyov the action had been necessary. Unfortunate but necessary. Now he was off at the run. Making straight for the border. Once through the trees there was a road. That road belonged to Norway.

CHAPTER THREE

Over seventeen hundred miles away Paul Kitrell and Erica Macken had just arrived at a small restaurant in Taunton. The table was candlelit. She was wearing a simple off-the-shoulder black dress and looking stunningly beautiful.

"An amazing transformation," he said.

"You said that earlier."

"I know. I still can't get over it. That uniform hardly did you justice."

"Which is probably the point."

"And I can quite see why. If you went to work in that outfit the entire air force would grind to a halt."

She laughed. "Oh, I don't know. They're a pretty serious lot. All they really care about is flying."

"You're joking, of course?"

"Perhaps. Anyway, enough about me. I want to hear about you," adding as an afterthought, "and Africa."

"Africa," he said gravely, thinking of what

it had once been, what it had become, and what it would always be. He considered her request a moment longer, then said: "First of all, there's something I meant to ask you this afternoon. Why a *naval* base?"

"For an air force squadron, you mean?"

"That's right."

"It's an idea picked up from the navy. They have itinerant squadrons; that is, aircraft normally based on carriers. When the carriers are in dry dock the squadrons have no official base, so they're temporarily transplanted to other stations around the country. The air force simply took it a stage further and decided that all their front line squadrons should be nomadic."

"And the reasoning?"

"Reasoning? Your guess is as good as mine. To stop the Soviets knocking out key strategic bases should a war start? Also, if a war did break out we'd be on the move anyway—better be used to living out of a suitcase now rather than later." She paused. "I don't really know if I should be telling you all this . . ."

He smiled. "I'm sure the Russians know the game plan. In fact if the truth were known we probably stole the idea from them in the first place."

She returned his smile. "More than likely. Anyway, you're not getting off that easily."

"Getting off?"

"You were going to tell me about yourself and Africa."

"Ah yes, me and Africa. There's not very much,

I'm afraid. Me. Forty-two years of age. Journalist, among other things. Home the place I rest my head ... much the same as your nomadic air force."

"And Africa?"

"A place I keep my yesterdays." He couldn't tell her now, there was really no point. And no reason. "It's a very long story. I know I've said that before. But ..." He tailed off.

She didn't press him. The waiter came then and they ordered. Afterwards she tried to regain their former intimacy. Anyway, I've learned something else about you."

"What?"

"Your age. You're forty-two."

"Ah," his face grew mock serious. "That puts me at a disadvantage—I don't know yours. But then the English would consider that an ungentlemanly question, wouldn't they?"

"They would, but as I'm a product of Irish parents raised in Canada I think a little differently. I'm twenty-seven."

"And forthright."

"Life's too short to be any other way, isn't it?"

"Too short indeed." He laughed. "I felt depressed for months after my fortieth birthday, thinking all the time had gone."

Her voice softened. "But it hadn't?"

"Yes and no." His eyes caught hers through the flickering candlelight. "Things were different. Twenty-odd years of working the foreign desks of different newspapers was suddenly a poor consolation."

87

"And now?"

"Now I have to make the appropriate payment."

"Payment?" She didn't understand.

He frowned, as if reluctant to be taken so seriously. "I don't believe life's free, that it should be taken for granted. I think we must pay for its pleasures. The price is left to us, of course; as is whom we believe we're paying it to. Mother, father . . . or perhaps a dusty white-robed God smiling benevolently from his heaven."

"And your payment?"

"I'm writing a book," he said.

"That's wonderful. What sort of book?"

He folded his arms tightly across his body. His eyes were drawn by the candle-flame, lost in the halo of yellow light. "Not an ordinary book. A big book. A history. My dream is that it will turn out as I imagine it. Real people . . . the smells of woodsmoke and animals, dust and excitement. Never just words. A journey through time . . . a living experience." He stopped talking, his eyes slowly refocusing on the present.

She felt herself being drawn, as though he had cast a spell over her. She told him as much.

He laughed, trying to lighten their earnestness. "Perhaps I'm a magician, a throwback from the court of King Arthur. Merlin's apprentice!"

She joined his laughter, before saying, "And if you write your book, who will the payment be to?"

"I've said it already: a man, a woman, and God, whoever or whatever he may be. The man, my father. The woman, my mother. I owe the three of them that, and more . . ."

It was later, over the coffee; he was sitting back smoking a small cigar; she watching him and feeling a little heady from the wine.

"So tell me why you never married?" she asked.

"How did you know that?"

"I guessed. It takes one to know one."

"No good reason," he said thoughtfully. "Perhaps I've never found the right woman. Or perhaps all the right women have been spoken for."

"That sounds like an excuse."

"It is. I'm a traveller. I could never give myself to any one place for very long. What sort of woman would stand for that sort of life?"

She smiled over the rim of her coffee cup. "You'll settle. I guess it'll take some time. But when you've paid your debts you'll settle . . ."

Still later. They left the restaurant and he drove her in his hired car to the house she shared with two other WRAF officers. They sat quietly in the glow of the car's instrument panel lights. The dinner, for her at least, had been a great success. Now she was trying to find a way to make the evening last a little longer. As it transpired there was no need. He did it for her.

"About Gene," he said.

"Yes?"

"If that reporter was right, and it was a Blackhawk . . . why the cover-up?"

"That's not too difficult." She welcomed the change of subject, the chance to be practical. "It's a new aircraft, to be used throughout NATO. And besides that, the military always keeps accidents on the classified list, as you probably know from your years with the press."

"Same way the Soviets do. Yes, I gathered that. Even so, I can't accept the 'pilot error' verdict. And neither can you."

"No," she said quietly. Even as he had been speaking her mind had gone back to her flight with Colonel Hood. The Blackhawk with the placard in the cockpit—VICS INOPERATIVE. Of course Gene had been in a Blackhawk on the night of October 2. He'd told her that was what he was going up to Scotland for. What if the vocal interface system had malfunctioned then and somehow caused his death? That would account for its present inoperative state. She stopped. Would the authorities be blaming Gene in an attempt to cover up a serious technical fault? She wished she could tell Paul about it: confide in him. But the Official Secrets Act loomed before her.

"You've gone very quiet," he said.

"I'm sorry. I was thinking . . ." Then, more brightly. "Is there nothing you can do?"

"About Gene's crash?"

"Yes."

"I intend to try. First of all I'm going to Scotland to find that reporter guy, the one who witnessed it."

"When?"

"Depends. I'll have to go to London tomorrow. Once I've established who he is and where he lives I'll catch a flight to Scotland."

"How will you find out his address?"

"A few enquiries around Fleet Street."

"And that's it?"

"If you know who to speak to, yes."

She turned her head slightly and peered up at the night sky. It had stopped raining and the clouds had blown away. The stars looked down with a disinterested hard energy. "I wish I could go with you," she said.

"What's stopping you?"

She laughed. "I'm a working girl."

"So when does all this dangerous hurtling around the sky take a day off?"

"Friday as a rule."

"I should be back in London by Friday week, so why don't I phone you and let you know how I got on?"

She tilted her head to one side. "I've got a better idea. Why don't I come up to town on Friday night and you tell me over dinner . . . my treat this time."

He had never known anyone like her. In a way she unnerved him. He was discovering that women pilots, trained in making instant decisions somewhere beyond the speed of sound, suffered an overspill into their private lives. "That would be nice . . . except I buy the dinner."

She didn't argue. They arranged a meeting place, and he shook her hand. "Until Friday next, then," he said.

She watched the car tail lights turn the corner at the bottom of the deserted street, then walked lightly up the footpath to the house. He was an

unusual man she decided. Old fashioned, and . . .
most unusual.

Alexei Karolyov reached the small mining town
of Kirkenes at ten thirty local time. Across
the border, back on the Russian side, it was an
hour later. He had been thinking about that on his
lonely five kilometre walk to the town. Thinking
about the extra hour of sleep he would get. Walter
Kristiansen had been expecting him.

"It was good?" the young Norwegian air traffic
controller said.

Karolyov, shaking with cold, replied, "Good and
bad. Ran into a patrol."

"How many?"

"Two."

They were speaking Norwegian. Kristiansen
handed him a glass of hot weak tea with lemon. He
didn't know what it was about the Russian that
frightened him most. The appearance—cropped
steel-grey hair, round silver-rimmed spectacles
framing cold grey-blue eyes; the fit muscular
body which appeared to have the hardness of
tempered steel. Or the voice: quiet, controlled, not
so much cruel as indifferent. Kristiansen wondered if the man had ever possessed any of the
kinder human feelings, or if this was all there
was.

"What happened?" he said at length.

Karolyov shrugged. "Not much . . . I had to kill
one."

"And the other?"

Karolyov sipped the hot tea. "Amazing," he said, lapsing into Russian, "how simple things are always the best." He held up the glass lovingly to the light.

Kristiansen said sharply: "Norwegian, for Christ's sake . . . speak in Norwegian. We may be safe here, but it's a good habit. You should know that."

The Russian said nothing, but put down the glass and removed his spectacles. He carefully rubbed his eyes and face, kneading out the frost. The movement when it happened was lightning fast, taking Kristiansen completely off guard. He jumped in surprise as Karolyov's left hand clamped the back of his neck like a vice. He didn't know where the knife blade had come from, but he felt it now pressing lightly against his exposed throat. "One thing *you* should know, Norway," Karolyov said coldly. "You never use that tone of voice with me . . . you understand?"

"Yes . . . yes . . . I understand." Kristiansen kept very still.

Karolyov removed the knife, folded the blade, and put it back into his breast pocket. "Now, what was it you were asking me?"

Kristiansen was shaking. He tried to think back but his mind was confused. It took him a few more seconds before he remembered. "The other soldier," he said. "The one at the border. What happened to him?"

"He returned to the guard post."

"So this place is of no more use."

"For what?"

"This crossing point, we cannot use it again. He will tell his story. You should have killed him also."

Kristiansen had made another mistake. You did not tell Alexei Karolyov what was right or what was wrong. The Russian stared at the blond-haired Norwegian. The man was too weak. Karolyov had somehow missed that when he had been here last, or he would never have relied on him again. But then, weakness could be harnessed. The man could still be of use to him.

Karolyov said: "Give it time, it will be quiet once more."

"I doubt that. Kirkenes has a population of no more than five thousand and that includes the outlying districts. We know your KGB people are here . . . how long before they uncover this operation?"

Karolyov moved over to the wood-burning stove to find more warmth. He had replaced his spectacles and held the glass of tea in his right hand. "Not that Polish so-called rock group again?" he said tiredly.

Kristiansen perched himself on the edge of the kitchen table, pushing his long yellow hair from his eyes, gaining confidence. "The Hotel Rica," he said. "They are there again this week. They play pop songs by night, and in the early mornings are out in the fjord to take soundings."

Karolyov replied impatiently, "Okay, so they have a cover as musicians, and perhaps they are mapping strategic areas for Mother Russia; but beyond that I think they will be no problem.

Anyway, all you do is stay on the right side of the border . . . you should try my job sometime."

The Norwegian smiled uneasily and reached across the table for the briefcase. "It's all in here," he said, handing it to Karolyov.

"And the routing?" Karolyov enquired, dropping the briefcase onto the chair by the stove.

"Air to Bodo, then train to Oslo. You change trains at Trondheim. At Oslo you take the flight to London."

"Why the train? That's over a day's journey, isn't it?"

"About twenty-one hours total. My instructions were exact. Perhaps the British think you will be followed. This way you have plenty of time before you finally depart for London."

Karolyov finished his tea and put the empty glass on the mantel shelf above the stove. "Anything new from Starling?"

"No, just my report to go in." He took a plastic pouch of Petteroe's tobacco from his shirt pocket and began to roll a cigarette. When he had finished he held out the pouch to Karolyov. "You want one of these?"

Karolyov shook his head. "My fitness is all I have left, Norway; start smoking those bloody things and I'm a dead man . . ."

It was half an hour later when Kristiansen began to pull on his cold weather gear.

Karolyov, who had been dozing in the chair by the stove, looked up and said: "You're on duty tonight?"

The Norwegian stifled a yawn and nodded. "I swapped with another controller to make sure I was in the tower when you depart. If anything seems to be not right I will telephone."

"Your wife is not here then?"

Kristiansen said, "No, she is staying with her sister in Hammerfest." He went toward the door. "Take the Datsun in the garage. When you get to the airport leave the keys under the seat—I will arrange to bring it back."

Karolyov lifted a hand in acknowledgement and watched him go. Listened as the car engine started up and the muffled sound finally faded down the high snow-banked roads. Then he sank back in the chair and closed his eyes. He would go through the contents of the briefcase later, he decided. Now, he was too tired. Even so he found his mind retracing the past two weeks. The coded message from London covering the crash of the computerised Blackhawk. The request that he should proceed to Murmansk and find out what the Red air force were using to be able to knock down the West's most sophisticated aircraft. His controller in London, code-name Starling, had been quite explicit on what was required.

For Alexei Karolyov, a Soviet double agent who was really a triple, it had been an easy enough task. His masters in Moscow had been more than helpful in supplying him with all the papers he needed. But then he'd been on his own. It was the way he liked to work, on his own: and it stopped the British from ever getting suspicious. After he had obtained the information from Captain Dzer-zhinsky in Murmansk he had stolen an army truck and made his way to the Russian-Norwegian border. And meanwhile Starling had notified their men in Kirkenes.

Once in London, of course, Karolyov was to try and find out the true circumstances of the Blackhawk crash. Certainly a Russian Tupolev had taken a series of infra-red photographs of the aircraft flying into high ground at night (and the Russian pilot had supplied copies of those photographs), but that was all. There'd been no attack. Still, if the British wanted to believe that the opposition had some secret weapon capable of knocking down their latest interceptor, there was no harm in encouraging them.

As for Alexei Karolyov, he would remain in Britain for as long as he felt he could be useful there. At the first sign of trouble he would return to Moscow.

Karolyov left Kristiansen's house at first light and drove slowly up the hill past the Rica Hotel. Away to the right at the top of a small mountain above the fjord, the tall chimney at the ore mine sent a steady cloud of white vapour into the early morning sky. Karolyov however was not inter-ested in the sights; he was concentrating on his driving. The road before him was a solid layer of ice. He eased the accelerator down and picked up another twenty kilometres per hour before check-ing the brakes. The spiked winter tyres held well.

He resumed his normal speed.

He was less than one kilometre past the Rica when he noticed the vague outline in his rearview mirror. He recognised the car as a Saab. Two hundred metres further on, instinct took over and he made a sharp left and went up an access road to one of the mine sites. From his last visit to Kirkenes, and the hours spent pouring over local maps, he knew that this road was a dead end. It led to a large wire-mesh double gate that was always closed. At the side of the gate was a small office containing a uniformed security guard. Without a pass you didn't enter. But Karolyov didn't want to. He was simply checking out a possible tail.

The access road to the mine site was a narrow snaking affair with dangerously high snow banks on either side. Karolyov kept the speed on, rushing into corner after corner. He checked the rearview mirror and caught a brief glimpse of the Saab, then he was drifting through the next corner and the mirror was filled with nothing but snow. He reached the gates two minutes later—it was the only place wide enough to do a three-point turn. Then he was roaring back the way he had come. He met the Saab on the first bend from the mine gates, squeezing at high speed through what seemed an impossible gap; taking in the two dark figures in the front seat.

Once on the airport road Karolyov slammed the accelerator to the floor. It would never be enough. The Datsun had seen better days; and besides, the Saab was the faster car. It was somewhere past a fork in the road and the next gas station that he picked up the now familiar shape in his mirror. Whoever they were, he thought, it was a poor job of surveillance. They had to be Norwegian; his own people would have been more subtle. Even so it spelt danger. He tried to think ahead. Somewhere before him, at the top of a long steady climb, the road swept to the left. After that it descended a steep hill toward a sharp right hander which led to a bridge over the fjord. From the top of the hill to the bottom there was a sheer unguarded drop to the icy waters below.

Minutes later he was nearing the top of the incline and the sweeping left-hand curve. He dropped down to second gear and switched on his side lights at the same time. The Saab driver, seeing the red tail lights of the Datsun suddenly flare, believed that he was braking and did likewise. It only took him a split second to realise that the Datsun was in fact pulling away, but by then the other car had disappeared around the top of the mountain road.

The Saab driver cursed and gave chase. The early morning sun had slipped behind the mountain as the Saab drifted dangerously around the bend, the driver using all of his skills to combat the icy conditions. It was as he straightened up to negotiate the steep descent that he saw headlights coming up the middle of the road towards him— out of the shadow of the mountain. His first realisation was that the oncoming car wasn't going to move over. He was braking hard when the second realisation hit him. The oncoming car was the Datsun.

It was all too late. The Saab went out of control. Karolyov had a fleeting glimpse of hands being raised as it plunged over the side of the road. He did a hand-brake turn and brought the Datsun to rest facing down the hill. His face was covered with sweat as he stretched across the passenger's seat and looked down. Far below the Saab exploded into the frozen shoreline of the fjord. A brief cloud of smoke and spray was all that remained.

He waited, and checked his rearview mirror before releasing the hand-brake and setting off down the hill. For the first time since his arrival in Norway he felt uncomfortable. One interception might be coincidence. You could never guarantee to cross a border without running into soldiers. But this was twice. Twice in a matter of hours. And the only person who had known his movements had been Walter Kristiansen. He increased his pressure on the accelerator and continued on down towards the airport.

The rain which had persisted for most of the week had finally gone. The early morning blue sky over London seemed to promise a fine day. The two men strolling through Green Park appeared not to notice it. They were deeply engrossed in conversation. And even if the early morning weather report had indicated unusually warm weather for the time of year neither man, it seemed, was taking chances. Both wore top coats and gloves. The older one also wore a bowler hat.

The minister for defence jerked his head round in surprise. "Satellites, you say?"

Squadron Leader Maudsley, thoroughly enjoying his unexpected audience with the high and mighty, said: "Yes, sir, although I'm inclined to think it was just one. Even if anything was there at all."

"So, to recap, the air vice-marshal believes that Major Kitrell saw a satellite which would appear as bright as a star, and as that star would have been seen as a moving object amidst the night sky of stationary stars . . ." Hinchcliffe smiled. "Yes, yes. Quite plausible, Squadron Leader, quite plausible."

"Which leads us to his next possibility," Maudsley said.

"Which is?"

Maudsley side-stepped as two ageing joggers, oozing sweat and misery, pounded their way down the footpath. "It's very hypothetical, of course, but assuming it was a satellite in the first instance and that it was Russian in the second, we could have a possible reason as to why the Blackhawk crashed."

"We could?"

"From my limited knowledge of computers I have to admit it seems quite plausible, sir."

Hinchcliffe, ever short on patience, snapped, "Well, go on, man, go on."

"Computers have been able to talk for some time and with the latest generation of microchips

101

have also started to listen. Speech recognition systems can be programmed by repetition to understand a set number of words. The air vice-marshal thinks it very possible that the computer in that satellite eavesdropped on the Blackhawk flight and then, by reproducing Major Kitrell's voice-print pattern, interrogated the Blackhawk computer. We now have two computers talking to each other. The one in space, in the Russian satellite, is, however, the master's voice. It could therefore command the Blackhawk to crash and also punch in a code to make the order impossible to rescind."

Hinchcliffe slowed to a halt. "But you don't agree with this."

"To be honest, sir, no. As I told you, Minister, I think it's all much simpler. I'm not a technical bod, of course, but I *was* in the simulator. The stars were moving because the Blackhawk was rolling on its logitudinal axis. And if Major Kitrell hadn't ordered that roll, then of course he'd be surprised."

Hinchcliffe started walking again. Maudsley immediately fell in step alongside.

"Nice morning," the minister said at length.

"Yes, sir, very nice."

"Mind you, I doubt if the rain will stay away for long . . . the time of year's against it."

"Indeed, sir."

"Have you ever visited the Houses of Parliament, Squadron Leader?"

"Afraid not, sir."

Hinchcliffe gave a little smile. "Have to do

something about that then, won't we? I'll get my secretary to arrange something . . . perhaps we could have a spot of lunch together."

"Terribly kind of you, sir."

"Think nothing of it. Thursday's my favourite day. They have curry on the menu; you do like curry, I take it?"

Maudsley, who detested hot spicy foods, said, "One of my favourite dishes, sir."

Both men emerged into Piccadilly. It was nearly ten o'clock. The place was full of traffic and hurrying pedestrians.

"Which way are you going?" Hinchcliffe asked.

Maudsley indicated to his right. "The Green Park underground, sir."

"In that case I'll say goodbye now, my car's somewhere at the back of the Air Force Club . . . A very enjoyable chat—oh, and my secretary will be in touch over that luncheon date."

"Very kind of you, sir."

Maudsley was turning to go when Hinchcliffe said, "One last thing, Squadron Leader. Not that it's important, but you did mention your theory to the air vice-marshal, I take it?"

"Yes, sir. I suggested that if the Blackhawk had rolled spontaneously, without Major Kitrell's instruction, that could simply point to mechanical failure. No need for enemy intervention at all . . . I have to say that the air vice-marshal wasn't impressed."

"Quite. In that case I don't think we need press the matter—just for the time being, of course. Give me time to discuss your theory with the experts . . . I mean, we don't want to ruffle any feathers. Better to be armed with all the facts, eh?"

Maudsley said willingly, "Absolutely, sir. I just felt it right to bring it to your attention."

The two men smiled, shook hands and parted, and were soon lost in the hubbub of a bustling Piccadilly.

It was one hour later in Bergen, Norway. Alexei Karolyov peered out of the airliner's window at the low grey terminal building. Above the ploughed-out main entrance the sign BERGEN-FLESLAND-LUFTHAVN was painted in large white letters. Elsewhere the wind was tugging relentlessly at the frozen snow banks, sending swirling clouds of ice crystals towards the control tower, adding more misery to the bleak monochrome scene. Even so Karolyov would have liked to disembark and stretch his legs, if only for a few minutes. His recent memory of events in Kirkenes decided him against it.

Following the Saab incident he had driven flat out to the airport. He needed a few minutes to speak with Walther Kristiansen before his flight left. Kilometre after kilometre he tried to remember the Norwegian's exact words of the previous night. Tried to find the smallest hint of his treachery. He was on a flat road now, foot hard on the floorboards. To his left the three man-made mountains, almost perfect cones with flat tops, covered with snow, the residue from over a hundred years of mining. He turned right into the airport access road thinking about the phoney Polish rock group. There was nothing else out of line in the entire operation.

He parked the Datsun in the AVIS ONLY parking slots which were nearest to the terminal building and leapt out of the car. Three men emerged from the baggage hall end of the terminal at the same time. Karolyov checked then ducked out of sight as they got into a black Mercedes. One of the men was the Norwegian, Kristiansen. The Mercedes sped away down the airport road, Kristiansen sandwiched between his two escorts on the rear seat. He might have been a willing passenger but Karolyov didn't think so. He gathered up his bags and went across to the terminal, loitering in the empty baggage hall until the flight was called five minutes later. A quick dash through the check-in procedure and he was running across the snow-swept tarmac to the waiting Wideroe airliner.

The flight to Bodo, like the long train journey to Oslo, was uneventful and he finally arrived in the Norwegian capital the following evening at seven o'clock. His first action was to book into a small hotel near the railway station. The second was to cancel his British Airways ticket to London the following morning. The third was to book with SAS on their early morning Heathrow flight via Bergen on Friday. The fourth was to run through the details of his new identity. The forged Norwegian passport Kristiansen had provided gave his name as Arild Hansen. Age: fifty-two.

Place of birth: Oslo. Profession: insurance broker. The reason for his visit to England, a business trip to Lloyds of London to obtain favourable rates for two oil tankers recently acquired by Viking Seaways, a new shipping line with registered offices at Karl Johansgate 1, Oslo. Apart from the new identity there were endless sheets of details on super-tankers, crude oil movements worldwide, a table of the latest spot-market prices, and general shipping information anyone in the business would automatically know. It was heavy reading and kept Karolyov up half of Wednesday night.

On the following day, the Thursday, he played the tourist for a few hours and went into the city centre. From there he took the Number 2 tram to the main entrance of the Vigeland Park/ Frogner Park, meeting Gustav Vigeland's world-famous art right at the gates. Having dutifully appreciated the seven wrought-iron gates he wandered on into the park, across the bridge with bronze sculptures, past the enormous bronze fountain and up to the monolith, an impressive fifty-four foot high obelisk with 121 human figures carved out of a single block of stone. After that he left the park at the south end and crossed over Halvdan Svartes gate to the Vigeland Museum. An hour or two there and he caught a tram back to the city centre. Following a meal at a small restaurant he returned to his hotel near the railway station. It was early evening as he went through the double doors of the building. He had not been followed.

Now, sitting in the Boeing 757 at Bergen airport, he looked out at the snow and the movements of ground-crew as they prepared other aircraft for departure. Passengers emerged from the terminal then, making their way towards his aircraft. He had checked the plane out at Oslo, making sure he was the last to board. Nothing unusual. Which left here, Bergen, and of course the London end. Either way there was little he—or any watcher—could do until he had cleared customs at Heathrow. And after that he could hope to melt into the crowds.

He reached down for his briefcase and took out Kristiansen's report. The one going to Starling in London. Moscow would want to know what was in it. He had read it for the first time the previous evening and now silently cursed himself for not having checked it earlier. It was coded, obviously. The only problem was it was not in regular format. It was something he did not understand. On the surface it was a story, an episode in Russian history. But its two pages had to mean something more than the title suggested. He started reading it again. "The Story of Boris Gleb. A monastery bordering on to Norway."

It was Sunday evening and as the sun went down the wind began to blow. Dark clouds formed behind Ben Uarie and the whole west face was caught in a ghostly grey light. What little heat the day had offered was now gone, the air turning to the bitter cold of premature winter in the Scottish highlands.

Paul Kitrell helped Finlay pitch the small tent. "I thought you said we would be there before nightfall!"

Finlay looked up. An old man with a craggy weatherbeaten face and long white hair. "Aye, laddie, that I did. And maybe if I'd'a been younger we would. As it is, the weather," his eyes flickered towards the sky and the ominous brooding clouds, "has made the decision for us."

They worked on in silence, pitching their tent on the difficult mountain slope, using pitons as tent pegs. Kitrell glancing from time to time down the dead ground between themselves and the base of the mountain. It would have been warmer down there. They could have found a place out of the wind. He had mentioned that to the old man, who had simply pointed at the sky. "Rain, laddie," he had said in a low growl. "Poor drainage down below. I don't sleep too well in a foot of water."

It was dark by the time they got around to eating. Cold beans from a tin and warm tea from a thermos hadn't sounded much to Kitrell before they set out: now it tasted like the best meal he had had for days. The old man turned in early, leaving Kitrell to smoke his customary after-dinner small cigar by the flap of the tent. Eventually it became too cold for anything but sleeping and he hauled himself into the narrow confines of the tent and wriggled into the down-filled sleeping bag. Finlay's snoring made sleep difficult but he didn't complain. The old man was after all leading him to the proof; or at least a part of the proof. Once he had that he would know what to do.

He eventually began to doze, his mind reliving the events of the past few days. The few short hours spent with Erica Macken; a beautiful, intelligent, remarkable woman. It would be easy to fall in love with her. But she had belonged to Gene, and in a lot of ways she still did. The healing would take time. Anyway, she was too young for him. It would never work. They belonged in different worlds.

The next four days had been spent in London tracing the Scottish reporter who turned out to be an old Hong Kong buddy of his, Jamie Finlay. It was never difficult finding the answers to such questions, simply a matter of endless legwork, eternal optimism and the odd name and telephone number to start the ball rolling. In this instance it had been an old friend, a Guernsey man, Winter Le Cheminant—a staffer with Associated Press— who had uncovered all the right particulars.

The Sunday morning—that morning—had seen the flight from London up to Inverness via Edinburgh. Then the long drive up the east coast to Brora and the meeting with Finlay himself. James Finlay, former RAF pilot, former air correspondent with the *Daily Telegraph*, current eccentric who had turned to bird watching. And it was due to that very pastime that he had been secreted in a hide for two days and witnessed the aircraft crashing. What was even better, he had stumbled upon a piece of wreckage.

Jamie's first instinct had been to go to the crash site and search for the pilot, but the explosion had decided him against it. If the pilot had still been in the plane he would be dead. If he had baled out he could be anywhere in a number of square miles. On a dark night finding him would be an impossible task. So Jamie had set off for the nearest house to telephone the authorities, dragging the piece of wreckage with him. For three miles at least—then it became too cumbersome, so he hid it for safekeeping and continued his night journey through the mountainous terrain.

It was a good three miles more before an exhausted and bedraggled Jamie Finlay was beating on a cottage door. By that time the authorities were aware of the accident and had search parties and SAR helicopters deployed. Finlay's fix on the crash location was received by the Inverness police with something less than enthusiasm: the RAF, it seemed, had already informed them that one of their aircraft was down, but as it had crashed in a military defined area they would be handling it. It was not a civil matter. The civil police could however oblige by blocking off any roads into the area and would be notified in due course when to reopen the roads.

Jamie's final action before collapsing into a long and well-earned sleep was to telephone his old newspaper. He didn't mention the piece of wreckage: that was an air force matter and could wait. It was safe enough. He'd tell them about it in the morning. And that is what he would have done, before even having his breakfast, had not the owner of the cottage where he'd spent the night chosen that moment to switch on the radio. The early morning news conflicted dramatically with the information he had phoned through to Fleet Street the previous night. He had seen the crashing aircraft quite clearly, had observed the delta wing form, the canard foreplanes at the front of the fuselage. He knew aircraft as well as birds. And this aircraft was very similar to an artist's impression of the new Blackhawk One he had seen on the pages of *Flight International* a few weeks earlier. He had called the *Telegraph* again and was informed that the ministry had issued a press release stating categorically that the crashed aircraft was a MiG-25 being flown on secret tests.

Jamie knew differently. It was like claiming a ballistic missile was a barn owl. He said as much. Fleet Street said they would look into it. Jamie being Jamie, a somewhat cynical eccentric, he had the feeling he was being fobbed off. But then he still had the piece of wreckage—his ace in the hole. He held his peace, and spent the next week researching the Blackhawk. Not that there was much on the surface, but a little gentle digging produced enough information to convince Finlay the aircraft had indeed been a Blackhawk: his final proof was that the air force had sealed off Kinloss as a top secret base at the same time they had started flying the first prototype of the new aircraft from Warton in Lancashire.

It was nine days after the crash that he again contacted Fleet Street with enough information to convince them. He was twenty-four hours too late. The defence ministry had slapped a "D" Notice on the entire business. And that meant no one could print Jamie's story. True or not . . .

The following morning Kitrell awoke to the sound of a squally wind buffering the tent and the eerie dawn light filtering through the canvas walls. It was unbelievably cold. He shivered and turned towards Jamie. The old man had gone. All that remained was his rolled-up sleeping bag.

Paul ducked outside, calling Jamie's name. Nothing came back, just the rush of the wind on the steep hillside. He scrambled back into the tent and lit a small cigar; the nicotine quelled the pangs of hunger which had already started in his stomach.

Smoking was a part of the job. Many newspapermen smoked, especially the ones packed off to cover some faraway war. Mealtimes on battlefields usually came and went unattended. The reporter, as the soldier, smoked. It eased tension as well as hunger pains. It might be unhealthy, but that went with the lifestyle.

It was some time later when Kitrell moved out of the tent and stubbed out his cigar on a wet boulder. He was turning to crawl back in when Jamie appeared over the top of a ridge, dragging a large piece of black metal.

"What the hell happened?" Kitrell shouted, more in relief than anger.

The old man stopped, wheezing noisily. "You were sound asleep, laddie. Didn't want to disturb you. Besides—isn't this what you were wanting to see?"

The black piece of tail fin was almost as big as Kitrell. Jamie laid it down gently in the heather.

"So how do you know it's not from a MiG-25 as the newspaper reports said? Just looks like a piece of metal to me . . . could be from any aeroplane."

"It could be, but it's not. Pick it up."

Kitrell picked it up. It was surprisingly light. He said as much.

"And there's your answer, laddie," Jamie retorted. "Carbon fibre, or something similar. I remember reading an article about its use in aviation some time ago. MiG-25s are metal . . . aluminum, mainly. The MiG-25 is an old kite. This sort of technology was in its infancy at the time."

"I accept that, but couldn't it have been from some other aircraft. Something more modern?"

"It could, but I doubt it. We've been through this before. I saw the machine going down. I know it was dark, but the stars were bright enough for me to make out the delta shape and the canard foreplanes."

"Maybe," Kitrell said.

"No maybes about it laddie! That aircraft was a Blackhawk. I'd stake my life on it."

Kitrell stared down at the piece of wreckage of the plane which had carried his brother to his death. He bent down and turned it over. The sides were identical—except for an access panel in one. Approximately fifteen inches by ten, it was retained in its recess by a number of countersunk screws.

"What's in there?"

Finlay sniffed and wiped his nose with the back of his hand. There was a look of childlike innocence on his face when he said: "Something, I'm hoping, that will convince you ... always assuming that you can believe your luck."

"I'm listening."

"Ever hear of a thing called a flight recorder?"

"The black box, you mean?"

"Aye, except it's not black. Usually red or orange, if memory serves me right."

"And it's in there?"

Finlay produced a multi-purpose pocket knife and selected a stubby screwdriver blade. He handed it to Kitrell. "Only one way to find out, laddie ... open it."

Early that Monday morning, in London, George Hinchcliffe replaced the telephone in its cradle and moved over to the drinks cabinet. He removed a bottle of Smirnoff de Czar and broke the seal. Never too early for a celebration, he said to himself. With a shaking hand he poured a straight vodka into a small sherry glass and tossed it back. He shuddered slightly as the drink caught in the back of his throat. The coming appointment with top executives from British Aerospace decided him against a second shot and he put the bottle of 82.6% proof Smirnoff back in the cabinet.

He returned to his desk and pressed the buzzer. Phase one was complete. His premature report to Air Vice-Marshal Southgate-Sayers at SHAPE had been justified after all, thank God. He had never been a gambler, but it had taken Blakeley until today to confirm that the VIC system was fully serviceable and that the Russian Tupolev aircraft could not have caused the accident by tapping into the Blackhawk's computer. The problem, if there was a problem, lay elsewhere in the aircraft. On that Blakeley was quite adamant.

Hinchcliffe's secretary came into the room wearing his customary sneer. "You rang, Minister?"

"Indeed, indeed," Hinchcliffe said with unaccustomed brightness. "Signal to Air Vice-Marshal Southgate-Sayers, SHAPE: Blackhawk VIC system fully operational as of this time."

"Minister."

"One more thing, Morriss. Make a lunch appointment for me at the House some time soon with that Squadron Leader Maudsley. He may have difficulty getting off, so push it all you can."

Morriss acknowledged and left the room. Hinchcliffe sat doodling on a pad before him. It seemed logical—to him, at least—to assume that if the Tupolev could not penetrate the Blackhawk system then a satellite would do no better. So Maudsley was right, and Southgate-Sayers wrong. And now he must have words with British Aerospace. If the computer wasn't at fault they would have to get their damned fingers out and find the real cause.

CHAPTER FOUR

"They've lifted Kristiansen!"

These were the first words to greet Karolyov when he walked into the tiny office above the Chinese restaurant in Gerrard Place. It was seven minutes past noon. The Russian had arrived from the transitsafe-house via the underground. He had changed trains four times, before walking the last mile. The office was a new location, he hadn't been here before. The plate on the side door at street level announced: "Jarret, Meyers & Wong—Accountants."

The red-carpeted hallway was shabby and sour with the smell of stale Chinese food. At the end of the hallway was an old-fashioned cage lift, beyond which was a cream-coloured door leading to the stairs. Karolyov used them in preference. He had a dread of not being in control of his own destiny. Of being locked in a metal box which relied on electricity, cables, pulleys, and maintenance men —too much fallibility in a few cubic feet.

Now, past Jarret, Meyers and Wong's formidable receptionist, he was looking at the same man with the code-name Starling. Medium height, heavy build, fleshy pallid face, sad pale-blue eyes and thinning grey hair. He was wearing a dark worsted suit, check shirt, and mustard-coloured tie. His name, which Karolyov did not know, was David Courtney. His role, assistant director-general, MI5.

Karolyov placed the briefcase on the desk and dropped into the chair. "In Kirkenes?" he said.

"Yes."

"Tuesday morning?"

"Possibly."

Karolyov shrugged. "I was probably there then. Black Mercedes saloon. Registration BL 72737. There were three men in all. One driving. But I saw the other two clearly. Young, twenty-five to thirty, Caucasian. Both tall. Both with light hair."

Courtney said, "Is that all?"

"Yes. Except for a Polish band. They were playing at the Rica Hotel in Kirkenes. Norway was worried over them."

"Norway?"

"My name for Kristiansen. He summed up his people; dull and slow . . . you take my meaning?"

Courtney frowned. "Yes, well, we won't go into that. You have the information I asked for?"

Karolyov opened the leather briefcase and removed the Murmansk report. "As much as I could get. The eighth commandment. I like to be careful."

Courtney took the envelope and opened it. He

118

was fully aware that the eighth commandment—out of the ten commandments which govern the world's most ruthless profession—simply states: "Do what you like with traitors." Neither side had a responsibility towards the spy who operated against his own government. The Soviets didn't mind their former contacts rotting in a Western jail; while in the same way the British didn't worry when a Russian who had been a double for them was shot by a KGB firing squad.

"And Kristiansen's report. You've got that, I take it?"

Karolyov took it from the briefcase and handed it across the desk. For a moment he had considered keeping it. Saying that the Norwegian had never passed it over. Moscow might have been able to decipher it. But then he considered the possibility that Kristiansen's pick-up might have been British. They were always testing him. And always he had to stay one step ahead.

Courtney picked up a packet of Rothmans, took one from the packet and lit it with a gold lighter. "Anything else?"

"Nothing of importance. It will be in my report."

Courtney flicked his cigarette absently at the ashtray. "Good. If you see Miss Nicholson as you go out she will arrange transport and accommodation."

Karolyov stood up and moved towards the door. "One thing puzzles me," he said, turning back to Courtney. "Why would my people bother to lift Kristiansen?"

119

"A message to us, I'd say. They were on to you, and then they lost you. They somehow found out he was your contact in Kirkenes, so they took him out instead."

"And got there before me? Impossible."

"No, we think they were already there."

"But there are no legals in Kirkenes. In fact the only ones would be in Oslo."

"I'm not talking about diplomats; I was referring to the musicians."

Karolyov said, "Of course. The Polish rock band!"

Courtney was not smiling when he replied: "And you let them. The Norwegians aren't the only dull and slow ones, I'd say. And now you're blown. Well, you won't be going anywhere. We'll find you an odd little job or two, I expect."

Karolyov did nothing to conceal the scowl on his face as he left the room.

Courtney muttered "Bloody Russians" and picked up Kristiansen's report. It read very curiously:

"The Story of Boris Gleb. A monastery bordering on to Norway.

"At the end of what is commonly known as the Dark Ages, several monasteries were erected in the north of Russia, of which the one at Solowetski in the White Sea is the most famous. Of the others, the monastery in Petchenga was the closest to our region. At this time there were no fixed borders between Norway, Denmark and Russia, but vast stretches—far larger in extent than today's Great Britain—known as 'The Common Districts'."

Courtney pressed his fingers to his eyes, then read on.

"A few miles north of Moscow, in the Tver district, a young boy named Trifon developed into a gang leader. By his side he always kept a young girl called Elina—generally known to be of high breeding—whom he loved above all else. It was during this period that the young girl felt sorry for the treatment being received by one of the gang's captives. She asked Trifon to be more lenient towards him. Trifon wrongly assumed Elina had fallen in love with the prisoner and decided to behead him. It was at the execution ceremony that Elina rushed forward and received the blow which was meant for the young man. Her head was split wide open. Trifon fell to his knees in an agony and despair which would remain with him for the rest of his life.

"It was a night nearly one year later that Trifon had the dream. It was a dream in which he met his beloved Elina. She told him he had to make amends and lead a better life. His task was to journey to the far north; to a people living in total darkness as to the existence of God and his earthly plans.

"So it was that the rebel became a Christian. His wanderings took him to the sinister districts of Petchenga where he built a small chapel. This later became a monastery with more than one hundred monks. Trifon's way of behaviour towards his fellow humans became generally known to be that of a saint, and people came great distances to talk and pray with the holy man. Even the Tsar came to hear of him and sent a letter to the monastery saying they could take anything they wanted from the land, the sea, and rivers as far as Neiden."

Courtney paused to light another cigarette. He read on now because he was actually caught up in the story.

"It was after this that the holy monk came to the area which is now known as Sor-Varanger. He lived in a cave near the edge of the sea. It was the place he kept his ikons (pictures) and made his daily prayers—this to the great amazement of the Lapps (heathens as they were). Trifon tried to dispel their beliefs in trolls and pagan idols, and there are a lot of stories (in this area) telling of the bitter conflict with the Lappian shamans or noaids.

"It was some years before the battle was won and it was then that the holy monk built the monastery of Boris and Gleb. The date was 24 June 1565. The names by which the monastery is called were originally the names of two Russian princes. They were both brutally slain by their elder brother whose name was Svjatopolk. This happened in the immediate years following the death of Vladimir the Holy (1015), and all information about this may be obtained from the Nestor Chronicle found in the Grotte monastery of Kiev. Briefly it tells of the great sorrow throughout Russia when Vladimir died and his evil son took over. And so it was that the two murdered princes became martyrs. Their names are never forgotten and closely link several monasteries all over Soviet Russia today.

"What is written above is taken from no book or open source. It is not even generally known, and although I cannot claim it is FIRST-HAND, I am sure it will help your research.

"My wife Kari sends her thankyous for the new edition of the *Concise Oxford Dictionary*, she says it will help her English greatly.

"Reference your request for poetry by the Norwegian EGIL, I think you may have meant Egil Skallagrimson. If so all I have found is the odd verse in a book called *Stave Churches in Norway*. I'll send you a copy with anything else I might find.

Best wishes
Walther."

Courtney dropped the papers on the desk. His cigarette, resting in the glass ashtray by his elbow, had gone out so he lit yet another and went across the room to the bookshelf. He removed two books. The first was the *Oxford Dictionary*— 1979 edition; the second a coffee-table book entitled *Stave Churches in Norway*. He then returned to the desk to decode Kristiansen's report.

The first part was easy. The words in capitals denoted the title of the report. FIRST-HAND being the first reference meant taking the first letter of each word, F and H. Their numerical sequence in the alphabet was 6 and 8. The hyphen always indicated a zero. Therefore the number was 608. Courtney turned to page 608 in the dictionary.

The second separate word in capitals was EGIL and represented numerical values of 5, 7, 9, and 12. Added together they came to 33. And the thirty-third word on page 608 was "Laser".

"At bloody last," Courtney said with some relief. "Perhaps I'll get Christmas off after all." He stubbed out his cigarette and went to work on the more elaborate second part of the message.

It was a long and laborious task. He took every capital letter in sequence and wrote down the alpha-numeric value. Then he took every odd number in the sequence and paired them together. The first number denoted the page in *Stave Churches in Norway;* the second the line. Taking every even number in that line of words, he resolved once again the first letters of the words to alpha-numerics, then paired them off in sequence. Once again the page was the first number, while the second was the line. And the word from the start of each line so arrived at produced the message in plain English. It was simple, idiot work. But without the right books the finest computers in the world could not perform it.

Erica Macken stood on the Yeovilton flight line. It was night. A damp cold filled the air. Between the black shapes of war-ready fighters she appeared as one more lifeless figure. Even her eyes were motionless; locked on to the end of the runway.

The distant sound of jet engines rose suddenly to an ear-piercing scream as a shadow began to move. Slowly at first, then faster, until its acceleration seemed to be limitless. The scream grew in volume. In her heart and mind Erica was with the pilot. She didn't even know his name, but she was with him, pushing those same throttles to the limit of their travel. As the afterburners lit up the explosion shook the flight line. Two long torches of violet fire scorched the night air; pulsating thunder tingled through her feet as the shock waves vibrated the pre-stressed concrete.

Then the pilot was pulling back; rotating the fire-thrusting mass towards the sky. The escape was complete. He was free. Her eyes followed the Blackhawk towards the heavens. The flames, as the thunder, diminished with time until all that remained was a dwindling pinpoint of orange flame and the ghostly whisper of jet efflux rustling down through the night air. She watched a moment longer, until the flames had turned to white, merging and drifting amongst the stars . . .

"If the guns don't kill them . . . then I guess the noise will!"

Erica started at the unexpected voice. She turned and saw the unsmiling face of Colonel Hood. "It's a thought," she replied.

"I sure hope the poor goddamned villagers about here see it that way too." Hood shifted his gaze towards the night sky and the moon low on the eastern horizon. There was a brief silence before Hood said: "You were raised in Canada, isn't that right?"

"Yes."

"I thought so. You've got a lot of accent still . . . That where you learnt to fly?"

"Yes."

"Bush operations?"

"Something along those lines."

"Yeah. I've kicked around that neck of the woods once in a while . . . lot of good flyers up there."

"I like to think so."

"Of course bush flying isn't quite the same as our line of work, is it, Lieutenant?"

"No, sir."

"My point is—and I'm sure you've already guessed that this conversation is leading somewhere—is that bush pilots tend to be loners. They don't mix much. Now on a squadron we are a team. We have to be. We work together or not at all . . . you get the drift?"

"Quite clearly, sir."

"Good." He turned to go. "Oh, two other things, Lieutenant. First off, we pull out in the morning and move up to Kinloss in Scotland. Three-day exercise. Most of the guys know by now. 0600 briefing." There was a moment's pause before he added, "The second thing concerns people who wear their heart on their sleeve. Forget Major Kitrell, he don't live here any more ... you do. Make the most of it. 'Night, Lieutenant." He turned sharply on his heel and was gone.

Erica turned her eyes back toward the stars, remembering something her father had once told her. Flying is like doctoring, it's a gift of life. Forget that for too long and you die yourself.

She walked slowly down the line of silent aircraft. One thing had to be said for the single-minded Colonel Hood—his obsessiveness certainly showed you where you were going wrong. Even to join the RAF she'd had to disregard her father's words. And if Colonel Hood had his way her soul would die of it too.

It was late the following day, Tuesday, when Lieutenant-Colonel Jason Hood was handed the signal from SHAPE, Mons, Belgium. His anger reached new heights when he read it. That he should be given the almost impossible task of whipping a new, untrained squadron into a first-rate outfit had been quite acceptable, providing that he was left to get on with the job. But now some jumped-up bloody air vice-marshal—the very same as yesterday had ordered the three-day exercise in Kinloss—was requesting that he put up a Blackhawk on a night penetration mission.

And, as if that wasn't enough, he was being told how to do it. He read the order again before screwing it up in a ball and hurling it across the room. Just how the hell did they think he could maintain a highly intensive day training programme together with random night operations! He'd already had to ground two aircraft due to technical reasons, and even with the technicians working all night there was no guarantee they'd be serviceable by tomorrow morning. Putting up another flight only added to his difficulties—as well as removing a pilot from the following day's programme. He snatched up the phone and dialed the officers' mess.

Ten minutes later Squadron Leader Maudsley was sitting in a hard-backed chair facing Hood. "Okay, Squadron Leader, that's the deal. But we will not be using the VIC system even though the order asks for it. The reason, in case you're looking for one, is that I think you all need some time getting into that kind of night flying. The old-fashioned way will do for this trip."

Maudsley, more aware of the dangers involved than even the colonel, agreed with him. "Yes, sir."

"One other thing. We win this operation; remember that. If they want to play games with us, then we damn well play our own games back. You get my meaning?"

"Sir."

"Good, because if you screw up you're out. Squadron Leader or not, it's as simple as that." Hood got up from his chair. He had omitted to mention to Maudsley that he had been chosen for this operation by the same air vice-marshal who was screwing up the training programme. This way Maudsley would be under the impression that he was working solely for Hood. And from now on, so he was.

Moving towards the door, Hood said: "So, having established that we're taking part in tonight's little game, I will now let you in on the plan. Follow my instructions to the letter and the northern defence system will wonder what the hell has hit them. Okay, let's go."

Maudsley, ever the gentleman, said, "May I enquire where to, sir?"

"The meteorological office, as you cloth-mouthed limeys would have it known. The reason? To find out if Thor is playing for them or us!"

If Maudsley had missed the colonel's reference to the god of thunder he was soon to discover its significance.

Captain Sergio Dzerzhinsky was asleep—cat-napping away the flying hours until his co-pilot informed him of one of four things. Number one would be an in-flight emergency. Number two, radar plotting of unfriendlies or interception by the same. Number three, feeding time. Number four, the end of the patrol and descent into Murmansk.

In short, the co-pilot's main responsibility was to ensure a smooth and uneventful ride for his master. For fifteen hours at a stretch the operation was total boredom: weary trips to the toilets, back-ache caused by sitting in one position for too long, the crew's jokes as old as the faded paint-work and scuffed surroundings. Fifteen hours locked away inside a complex prison cell, with the constant drumming of the four engines and the high frequency whine of the pressurisation system. It was less than once in six months—like a couple of weeks ago—that the patrol actually saw or heard anything worth reporting.

The co-pilot Lieutenant Kasparov, nudged Dzerzhinsky's shoulder. The captain opened his eyes, blinked, grunted and took the food tray. He sighed when he saw the dark bread curling at the corners. "How can fighting men be expected to live on this sort of diet, Lieutenant? What do they promise you in cadet school these days?"

"I was assured it would be caviar and pink champagne. At worst they said stuffed Ukranian dumplings and a bottle or two of Dark Eyes . . . if I'd known the truth I would have probably applied to the Bolshoi."

Dzerzhinsky laughed. "You are right, my young comrade. Prancing around in tights showing off your manhood does seem to be a more rewarding pursuit. Warm flat in Moscow, the occasional decadent party, trips to the West . . . lots of girls." Dzerzhinsky paused reflectively. But that's not really what I miss, you know—the girls. No, it's the children. A son. Bit of advice for you, Lieutenant Kasparov. Find yourself a good wife with big child-bearing hips. Give her lots of children and when you get to my age make sure

130

you are as far away from aircraft as is humanly possible." He took a silver hip flask from his flying suit pocket and splashed vodka into his glass of tea. "This is fine for a while, but the sky's a jealous bitch. She'll try and keep you forever . . . Vodka?" He held out the flask to the lieutenant.

"Thank you no, Captain."

"No, you are quite right, Lieutenant. Young men's dreams should be realised in more noble ways." Dzerzhinsky finished his tea, grimaced, and gave the food tray back to the co-pilot. His eyes made a cursory sweep of the instruments. "Mid-Atlantic?"

Kasparov, passing the tray on to the flight engineer, said, "Yes. We turn back in ten minutes."

"And the weather?"

"According to transmissions from commercial traffic, the low off Iceland is deepening. Iceland Radio is warning of severe CAT above 10,000 metres."

Dzerzhinsky made a few grumbling noises before pulling the weather folder from the pouch at the side of his seat. CAT—clear air turbulence—made for an uncomfortable ride. Old aviators always looked for the smooth air. No point in putting unnecessary stress on aircraft and crew when a few hundred miles' deviation would keep them in the clear. "We'll use Stornaway on the return leg then. Might even pick up a good tailwind."

Kasparov, who had already decided on that routing, said nothing. Their master/apprentice relationship was a good one, so good in fact that he could not imagine himself in that treasured left seat. Not that he did not want a command of his own; it was just that flying with Captain Dzerzhinsky was special. The old man had become more like a father than his real one. "Stornaway it is, Captain," he said, setting in the coordinates on the inertial navigation system.

Dzerzhinsky smiled and closed his eyes, and went back to dreaming of Svetlana—the girl he should have married twenty-five years earlier. And if that had come to pass perhaps there would have been a son. One not unlike Anatoly Kasparov. As sleep filled his eyes Dzerzhinsky decided that after this flight he would recommend his co-pilot for a command. What finer gift could a father give a son? And long overdue.

His head dropped then; the steady rhythm of his breathing inaudible as the huge Tupolev droned on into the night.

Squadron Leader Maudsley was beginning to understand. The hurried briefing had been taken in but hardly comprehended. Now, as he headed south into the night sky he saw that Hood's plan could work. His scheme to foil the electronic northern air defence system was simplicity itself, especially as the met. room had reported that Thor was indeed playing on their team. An active cold front was lying in a line from the Faroes, through Stornaway—on the northwest tip of

Scotland—to the north of Ireland. The intense thunderstorm activity in that frontal system would conceal the Blackhawk at a critical moment. That concealment would prove fatal for the radar defence operators.

Flying subsonic at sixty thousand feet Maudsley maintained the southerly heading until he was over the Isle of Wight. Then, on radio instructions from London military he swung right and took up a westerly heading. Beyond Shannon—over the Atlantic—he had a rendezvous with an air force tanker.

The link-up was made half an hour later; a delicately poised few minutes wavering beneath the mother ship, taking on fuel from the parabolic curve of pipeline. Then Maudsley was out on his own, running north at mach 4.

He swept in a high level curve over Iceland, causing mild panic among their radar operators. They tracked the unexpected fast-moving target a few seconds more, then radioed to the UK military network that a possible hostile was on direct track for Stornaway. At 60,000 feet Maudsley's mach 4 presence was being plotted for the moment with confident accuracy.

Sergio Dzerzhinsky was wide awake. The weather had seen to that. The cold front had moved east with unpredicted speed. It was one of those situations that all pilots may have to face. Meteorological prognosis charts are always deduced from current isobar spacings and the geostrophic wind scale, and are therefore somewhat theoretical. Frequently—in the more unsettled temperate latitudes at least—theoretical conclusions are made worthless by the actual movements of the converging and diverging air masses. This was one of those times.

Dzerzhinsky flicked off the auto-pilot, went to maximum power, and hauled the Tupolev into a long steady climb.

"Position, Kasparov?"

"Twenty miles to run to Stornaway."

Dzerzhinsky scowled at the DME—distance measuring equipment—counter. The red bar remained firmly locked across the instrument, indicating its unserviceability: it had been that way for the last three trips. He had complained, of course. The technical officer at Murmansk had not taken kindly to Dzerzhinsky's tone—shortage of spares was hardly his fault. "Besides, Captain," he had added, "you still have the inertial navigation system." And if that fails, Dzerzhinsky had thought, what do I rely on then? But he hadn't bothered to ask the question. The seat of his pants was what he used mostly, anyway.

Turbulence rocked the Tupolev's wings violently. It was turning into a rough night. For Dzerzhinsky and his crew it would become a lot rougher.

Maudsley was on the run-in to Stornaway when

he released the decoy missile which would extend the original path of his aircraft. Within the missile a signal generator would give the radar defence operators an exact "paint" of the Blackhawk. Maudsley reduced power and deployed dive brakes, commencing his descent towards the ocean at over 20,000 feet per minute. The decoy continued sedately on its way.

Sweating with concentration, he timed his pull-out and levelled off at a hundred feet. There was a moment of fear—of reaching the coastline, and high ground, before his instruments had registered the fact; of doing what Kitrell had apparently done. His legs twitched nervously. Seven miles to go . . . six . . . five . . . rain exploded noisily against the canopy, drowning out all other sounds. He hung on. Four miles . . . three . . . now he was close enough to move the throttles forward to maximum, sending the Blackhawk up the faces of the cliffs ahead in a steady three-g climb. His legs stopped twitching as the interceptor screamed up through the eye of the storm. He was climbing now at eight miles a minute—vertically.

No radar could pick him up yet as he would be concealed by the weather clutter on the operators' screens. Besides which, the decoy missile would still be the object of attention, being chased now by a pair of defending Tornadoes. Once he had topped the weather it would be different; but, since Colonel Hood had ascertained that the radar height information in that quadrant was out of action, then all the radar operators would see would be a slow-moving target—in terms of forward movement at least. They would have no means of knowing that the slow forward-moving target was in fact climbing at a heart-stopping rate.

Once at 60,000 feet Maudsley would level off and streak inland at five times the speed of sound. The radar operators then would not believe what they were seeing. Would not believe that slow, almost stationary traffic could suddenly accelerate to over 3,000 miles per hour ... unless it was a flying saucer! The heavy weather clutter on the screen could be partly responsible, of course. Also the set could be playing up—they did from time to time ... The operators' disbelief would waste significant seconds. It would be after those seconds that they might check for confirmation. By then it would be too late. By then Maudsley would be far to the south, at the nerve centre of the United Kingdom. Once there he would release two small transmitter missiles, each screaming "invasion" signals at the UK's military defence 'scopes.

And Air Vice-Marshal Southgate-Sayers would be reminded that, fine as his radar defences were, they could still be beaten. One man, given intelligence and luck, could defeat a thousand computers. And he could put that, Colonel Hood had said, in his extra night operations pipe and smoke it.

If Maudsley hadn't been so busy with the horrendous weather conditions he was now encountering he might have found time to worry about his career. After this he would hardly be the air vice-marshal's Golden Boy. And this transfer to Kinloss had already cost him his lunch with the defence minister ... He was thundering through 38,000 feet, clipping the tall battlements of cumulonimbus, when a blinding flash of white light smashed into his eyes. There was an adrenalin-enhanced milli-second of confusion: was it a lightning flash? No—it was lasting too long. Was he flying level, then, straight into a lighthouse? His confusion ended abruptly with an ear-shattering explosion. Then the Blackhawk was spinning uncontrollably down the tall night sky.

Maudsley, who had blacked-out as the aircraft flicked out of control, now fought in vain to effect a spin recovery. He was unaware of everything else. Unaware of his collision with the Tupolev. Unaware that his left wing had been completely destroyed. He stayed with his aircraft a moment longer, struggling in the fearful confusion of flashing red lights and audio *whoops*; then, reaching down for the seat pan handle, he ejected.

He didn't know where he was, or what had happened. It was cold, and his face was wet. It felt like rain! There was no feeling in his arms and legs. But he was sitting in a seat. Ejector seat, that was it. He remembered now. He had ejected. For the first time in his life he had ejected. Amazingly it didn't feel as bad as he had imagined. In fact it was almost a pleasant sensation. How high was he? Obviously above 10,000 feet—he remembered that once through 10,000 the seat automatically separated from the pilot by a barometric device, deploying the parachute as it did so. What if the barometric device had failed? Go for "mansep"—manual separation. There was a small handle on the left side of the seat. He tried to move his left hand towards it. There was no feeling. Perhaps he had injured himself in the ejection! No . . . it was simply the cold. He was numb, that was all. Anyway the seat would separate at ten thousand feet. They always did. Why was it so dark? Why couldn't he see?

The heavy metal seat plummeted out of the low cloud base seconds later. One mile away from the angry Atlantic coastline near Stornaway. Maudsley, still believing he was above the barometric separation height, was nothing more than a torso strapped to a Martin Baker ejector seat. The seat had been damaged in the collision. Apart from that, the result of his arms being thrown out by centrifugal force, and the leg restraining straps failing to pull back his legs, was that he had been dismembered as he left the stricken aircraft.

His brain was still clinging to the belief that he was above ten thousand feet when his eyes finally parted, and through the blood which he had mistaken for rain he saw the dark moving waves below. Funny how the clouds looked like water, he thought. Like waves. It was his dying thought. Less than a second later his fast-weakening body, still strapped to the ejector seat, disintegrated amid the icy waves of the North Atlantic.

"Forget the radio," screamed Dzerzhinsky. "Get me a damage report." Kasparov checked in the other members of the crew on his intercom before switching on the ice light for the starboard wing. The light, usually reserved as a night-time means of checking for ice accretion, now picked out the fluttering mass of damaged metal beyond the outer engine.

Kasparov turned towards Dzerzhinsky. "The wing! Beyond the number four engine . . . it's gone . . . there is nothing."

Dzerzhinsky, fighting against the buffeting controls, had already decided the damage was in that area. The flying controls on the giant Tupolev Tu-95 was servo-assisted; and when you lost the servos on an aircraft cruising at approximately five hundred mph, everything had the feeling of having locked up solid. The fact that the control column was buffeting even so was proof of the extremely severe damage inflicted on the flying control surfaces. Dzerzhinsky said through gritted teeth, "Is that all?"

"Isn't that enough?"

"Doubtless it is enough for some men, my young comrade . . . What was it hit us?"

"Another aircraft, I think."

"Probably military then . . . a routine interception gone wrong."

Kasparov said nervously. "So what happens now?"

"Now? Now we check fuel and range . . . and perhaps shut down the number four engine—it might ease the vibration . . . Also we stay in the line of the storm and become invisible."

"What about the aircraft? Will we be able to land?"

"You tell me . . . what would you do?"

"With sufficient height for recovery I would reduce power and check the stall speed; then we know the minimum safe approach and landing speed."

"When would you do that?"

"When we get back . . . over the Motherland. If I'm going to die anywhere I would rather it was there."

Dzerzhinsky smiled briefly. "I was right. A fine gift . . . but long overdue."

"Long overdue . . . ? I do not understand."

"Never mind, you will; now take over. My arms are already tired."

Kasparov took the controls of the damaged Tupolev and slid the aircraft silently away from the UK radar network. Over two hundred miles away over the North Sea a pair of Royal Air Force Tornadoes had cancelled their search for the possible hostile when it had suddenly disappeared from the radar. It would be some minutes before it was realised that the vanishing hostile had been nothing more than a decoy missile running out of fuel and dropping into the black sea below. In the same way it would also take a number of minutes before Squadron Leader Maudsley's absence was noted. And by then Dzerzhinsky's crippled Tupolev would have merged into the thunderstorm clutter on its long and hazardous journey to North Cape and Murmansk.

It was 2300 hours. The last hour of Tuesday night, October 21. Kinloss, as were most parts of northern Scotland, was suffering the torrential rain that orographic lifting gives to an already active cold front. The grounded sea air rescue crews remained on readiness, waiting for the front—and its associated hurricane-force winds—to pass through before taking their Sea King helicopters out to search for the missing Blackhawk One.

In the main operations room an impassive Colonel Hood had carefully reconstructed Maudsley's intended flight path, from take off to rendezvous with the tanker west of Shannon and on to Keflavik where he confirmed with them the exact time, heading and estimated speed the Blackhawk had departed the Icelandic control zone. Right down to what had to be considered the deployment of the decoy missile. The area immediately northwest of Stornaway seemed—logically at least—the only place where Maudsley could have crashed.

Hood had considered all the angles; from Maudsley simply getting his sums wrong and mis-timing the pull-up from his high-speed descent, to structural failure of the aircraft. Maudsley was a good man. An experienced flyer. Had anything gone wrong he would have followed his briefing instructions and broken radio silence. The fact that he hadn't, pointed to one thing. Instant disaster. Which left the unconfirmed radar sighting—possible target moving northeast along the line of the storm. The clutter on the screen caused by radar returns from heavy precipitation had negated a confirmed sighting. Even so, Hood had his doubts. He swore for the hundredth time and went over to the wall map.

It had been his decision to leave the VIC system "off-line." His reasons—discounting what he had said to Maudsley prior to the flight—had been nothing more than bloody-mindedness . . . which he now regretted. A fighter controller monitoring the VIC system would have known exactly what had happened. Would have followed the fatal flight mile by supersonic mile. Would have known the where, the when, and the how.

Hood shrugged. It was too late for regrets. He was now faced with troubles of his own. The signal from Air Vice-Marshal Southgate-Sayers had been quite specific. If he couldn't come up with something pretty dramatic he was in for the high jump for having disregarded it.

Picking up a chinagraph pencil, he marked in the estimated line of the cold front—for a period two hours earlier—on the fablon-covered map. The unconfirmed pop-up traffic had been observed tracking towards Stornaway at the same time the Icelandic controllers had painted Maudsley sweeping out of their overhead. Hood now drew a second line—the track of the unconfirmed traffic. Extending that line through Stornaway it continued into the arctic circle and stopped above the northern tip of Norway—the North Cape. A few hundred miles slightly south of east would put the traffic overhead Murmansk.

Hood dropped the chinagraph, hurried over to the central desk, and picked up the red scrambler phone: the direct link to strike command headquarters at High Wycome, Buckinghamshire. A Norwegian air force interceptor would be able to confirm a Redstar aircraft en route to Russia—if such an aircraft existed. But even if it did, and even if they could locate it, had it been responsible for the disappearance of the Blackhawk? And if so, how? Hood decided he would cross that bridge when he came to it.

Air Vice-Marshal Southgate-Sayers did not take kindly to being awoken at three in the morning. Once the text of the telephone message had registered in his sleep-dulled brain, however, his attitude changed. He showered and shaved in seven minutes; dressed in another seven; drank half a glass of Perrier water and ate a slice of dry bread (he never went out on an empty stomach), and was waiting at the end of the short driveway to his house by the end of the third seven minutes.

The gleaming black official Mercedes collected him at exactly 0322 hours, hurtling its VIP passenger through the outskirts of Mons to the SHAPE building. Southgate-Sayers, who had fitted in deep breathing exercises during part of his twenty-one-minute timetable to leave the house, was now wide awake. First time out and it had happened, he thought to himself. First time! It was too good to be true. He just hoped that Foulkes had been good to his word and ensured the national press were aware of what had happened. There was a smile of satisfaction on his face when he thought of the government. Now perhaps, after their constant back-pedaling, they would be convinced. Now they would have to listen to his advice on Space Strike.

The Tupolev ran out of the storm two hundred miles east of the Faroes. The waxing moon, into its third quarter, shed a brilliant metallic light on the sea below. Dzerzhinsky checked his charts. Nine hundred miles to run to the turning point above the North Cape. Nine hundred miles—then another two hundred and fifty on a curving flight path into Murmansk. 1,150 miles total. 1,150 miles in a shaking aircraft which was threatening to come apart at any second. Dzerzhinsky had shut down the number four engine shortly after the incident. His prognosis had been correct. By stopping the huge Kuznetsov turboprop engine, the vibrations had lessened. There was of course a penalty incurred in closing down twenty-five per cent of your available power. In the Tupolev's case you were switching off the equivalent of 14,795 horsepower; which all added up to a lower, slower ride. Even now Dzerzhinsky had his doubts that they would get back.

He offered a silent prayer to the airmen's God and turned to Kasparov. The young lieutenant's flying suit was black with sweat as he fought to maintain the 18,000 feet altitude towards the distant North Cape waypoint.

"Did I ever tell you about Svetlana?" Dzerzhinsky said conversationally.

Kasparov, eyes unwavering from the instrument panel before him said: "No . . . not that I remember."

"She came from Arkhangel'sk. She had long black hair, like silk. A real beauty." Kasparov said nothing; he was only half-listening. His arms were slowing giving out with the concentrated effort and resultant pain of keeping the control yoke steady. "Her figure," Dzerzhinsky went on, "had to be seen to be believed . . . of course I should have married her."

Kasparov, suddenly realising he was expected to make some sort of comment, said: "Why didn't you?"

Dzerzhinsky smiled sadly. "She didn't like my mistress. As simple as that."

Kasparov checked a sudden jolt as the Tupolev ran through a patch of clear air turbulence. "Simple? You had a mistress . . . Christ, I would have thought it anything but simple."

"You misunderstand, Comrade Lieutenant. My mistress is also your mistress." He waved a hand towards the star-hung curve of sky.

Kasparov's peripheral vision caught the movement. "Ah, I understand. You never thought of swapping one for the other, then?"

"Only when it was too late. And by then she has sucked you dry ... tricked you with her lies ... filled your life with past regrets and future fears." Dzerzhinsky paused, searching for more words. When none came he looked once more towards his young lieutenant. "You want me to take over?"

"No, it's not a problem. After North Cape perhaps ... I wouldn't like to try the landing."

It was one hour and twenty minutes later when the Tupolev's radar operator reported high-speed traffic moving northwest—possibly out of Bodo.

Dzerzhinsky checked their position. One hundred miles west of the Lofoten Wall. "Norwegian air force," he said casually. "Probably an F-16."

Kasparov, whose arms were practically numb from the effort required to fly the damaged aircraft, said: "What do they want?"

"Routine interception ... nothing probably."

"Routine? Not out here surely!"

"A training flight then. Either way it's of no importance." Dzerzhinsky turned the instrument panel lights down to minimum intensity. Then he leant forward, looking across—past Kasparov—waiting for the dark shape in the moonlight.

The F-16 drifted into formation less than one minute later, its pilot jockeying the small fighter around the massive Tupolev like a bloodhound sniffing a wild animal. The Russian crew remained at their stations keeping radio silence. After what seemed an endless scrutiny the F-16 waggled its wings and broke away—its afterburners pushing it heavenward at the speed of sound.

CHAPTER FIVE

The official Mercedes cleared the security check at the main gates to the SHAPE complex at 0349 hours. Seven minutes later Southgate-Sayers entered the SACEUR (Supreme Allied Commander in Europe) office on the first floor. The inner door of that office led to the boardroom. Foulkes and Greenaway were sitting at the long conference table, waiting.

"Who got the news?" Southgate-Sayers said, joining the two men at the table.

Foulkes looked up. "I did."

"Amazing. I was just thinking on the way in. First time out and it happened."

Foulkes said: "Something's not right."

"Not right? The Blackhawk, you mean?"

"It's disappeared," Foulkes replied.

"As we thought it might . . ."

"No, Alister. This one vanished somewhere near the Outer Hebrides, no one knows how or why. One minute it was being tracked over

Iceland ... sometime later it was approaching Stornaway ..."

"And then it crashed, you mean?"

Greenaway joined the conversation. "It seems the VIC system was not in use, Alister. The aircraft was being flown manually. There's a Lieutenant-Colonel Hood running the operation and he's not saying much. However, George and I have since ascertained that the Norwegian air force were called in at some stage."

"The Norwegian air force?" Southgate-Sayers exploded. "The Norwegian air force? What the bloody hell has it got to do with the Norwegian bloody air force?" The two men remained silent; they were used to the air vice-marshal's outbursts. The answer was to leave him alone; let him stew in his own juice. It always worked.

For a while Southgate-Sayers drummed his fingers impatiently on the table. He stopped quite suddenly and looked across the table at Foulkes. "So how did you here, George?" The voice was quiet, controlled.

"My RAF regiment contact at Kinloss. As he's covering security at the base it was easy enough to check the movements of the flight. When it didn't return and the SAR crews were put on alert he knew something must have gone wrong."

"And he phoned you?"

"As planned, yes. He also sent a telex through a hotel at Aberdeen airport to the *Telegraph* ... anonymous of course. Not that I think it will help much with the D Notice in force. But it should stir things up."

"How did you find out about the Norwegian air force? More to the point, why were they involved?"

"Sent a signal to Kinloss, using your security number, of course. This chap Hood replied that strike command were contacting the Norwegians to intercept a Redstar aircraft en route to North Cape."

"And that was all?"

"He said he would keep you informed."

"A Redstar aircraft. That's promising . . ."

Half an hour later the signal arrived from Kinloss. The sender: Lieutenant-Colonel Jason Hood.

"A mid-air collision!" Foulkes said disbelievingly.

Southgate-Sayers sat in silence for a few seconds, elbows on the table, fingers laced together beneath his chin. "The conclusion seems inescapable," he said at length. "A Norwegian F-16 intercepted the Tupolev—apparently a Bear F—somewhere west of the Lofoten Wall. Its starboard wing was badly damaged. One engine shut down."

"And that's all?"

"It seems enough. Anyway," he picked up a copy of one of the signals on the table and checked it was the right one before continuing, "this earlier signal from Hood says it all. 'Blackhawk missing on manual flight. SCH liaising with Norway to intercept Redstar believed en route North Cape. Hood. Message ends.' So whichever way we look at it the VIC system could not have been responsible."

151

Foulkes frowned heavily. "But you did order it to be used on last night's operation?"

The slight inflection of tone, the implications, were not lost on Southgate-Sayers. "I did." He paused. "Nevertheless, the primary request was to test the northern defence chain."

"So who the hell gave this Hood chap the authority to take out the computer?" Foulkes replied angrily.

"I'll find out first thing this morning. Not that a prolonged post-mortem is going to help us very much, because whichever way you look at it the plan has backfired."

Greenaway, who had been sitting quietly with a worried look on his face, stood up and excused himself, making an unfunny joke about having a weak bladder as he left the room.

Foulkes waited until the door had closed before turning to Southgate-Sayers. "He worries me," he said in a low voice. "I get the feeling he's making notes or tape recordings for the fateful day."

"You may be right, so what do you propose?"

"You recall at our last meeting you said the flight recorder from the October the second crash hadn't been found?"

"Yes."

"Nothing new then; it's still missing?"

Southgate-Sayers nodded. "Go on."

"What if it somehow ended up in Russian hands?"

Light dawned in the air vice-marshal's eyes, "And all the right people got to know about it, you mean? Yes . . . no matter what it was found to contain, that would certainly make the government look pretty silly. Only problem is, the flight recorder's still missing; the chances of it being found are getting less every day."

"I don't believe that. It's got to be there somewhere. You must push, Alister. No use farting around over here. You must get back to London and push."

Southgate-Sayers let out a small laugh. "Easier said than done, George. Firstly we need to get hold of the Blackhawk flight recorder. Secondly, we have to pass it on to the Soviets with no fear of implicating ourselves."

Foulkes was quite unruffled. "You take care of the first part," he said evenly, "I'll look after the second."

The door opened at that moment and Admiral Greenaway re-entered the room.

Erica Macken was exactly five minutes into what was scheduled as a thirty-minute training flight. Hood's show was going on. His 0545 hours briefing had underlined that fact. "As you by now know," he said, "we lost Bluestar Two last night. As the mission was classified no details are, or will be, available. I can add, off the record of course, that any flight involving level six thunderstorms can be extremely hazardous." The cold, even tone continued. "As any of you who have played blackjack—especially in my former home of Las Vegas—will know, the deck is always stacked against you . . . dealer, house and odds. In our particular game we ought to get about the same return. Last night we were short-changed, that's all. Okay . . . so let's get out there and kill!"

Erica made a slight course correction by vocal command. The Blackhawk's synthesised voice acknowledged and responded with instant accuracy, maintaining its low-level run towards the target. Then Maudsley's fate was on her mind again. Much as she had disliked him in life she could not do so now. She had long since analysed her reasons as nothing more than his immaturity. Married, with a family, he would have become like all the other older officers. More confident, and therefore less aggressive. Except that now he would never be married. He would be like Gene, a young man smiling somewhere from a photograph, trapped in a silver frame. Never becoming anything more than a good fast jet pilot. And for all his faults he had been a good pilot. Too good for her to believe in Hood's flip reference to thunderstorms—as if Maudsley had let the aircraft break up in violent weather. Maudsley would never have made such a basic mistake.

She cleared her mind then and concentrated on her primary target—a mock sea-to-air missile platform. Coming up to it she talked the Blackhawk into a high-g twisting climb—into a "wheel" above the target. From the top of the wheel, at 6,000 feet, she ordered a wingover. The aircraft went into a steep dive. On the electronic head-up display a line projected down from the aircraft's path indicator, and at the bottom of the line was the "death-dot"—a small circle positioned continuously by computers which calculated the trajectory of bombs, based on the weight and aerodynamics of the bomb and on the current movements of the aircraft—which indicated where the bomb should hit.

Erica ordered: "Position death-dot on target." The VIC system took on the complicated task with consummate ease; tracking the constant motion of the HUD markings; holding the target in the dot.

It was so easy. She looked round, scanning the sky for defenders. The old-fashioned manual way required the pilot to fly the death-dot for at least three seconds on final before releasing the bomb; compensating for turbulent weather conditions at the same time. Therefore all concentration had to be poured into only one aspect of flight at the critical moment when the enemy was opening fire with everything he possessed; and the air-to-air threat of enemy planes was always present.

The practice bomb left the aircraft as the computer, responding to the pilot's vocal command, pulled the aircraft back up into the wheel. Erica's eyes, distorted by the high-g loading, had a passing glimpse of the phosphorous charge exploding directly on target. She levelled off at 6,000 feet and set course for the secondary target. All thoughts of Maudsley were now passed. Her training had taken over, blending pilot and machine into a single weapon. Now, approaching the speed of sound, she was in command; checking instrument readouts on the CRTs, monitoring radio transmissions. It was all second nature, giving her time to re-think a trick she had learned on more conventional aircraft. It involved diving at 500 knots towards the target and then pulling up into a forty-five degree climb; at the same time releasing a 2,000 pound bomb. The effect was to toss the bomb forward four and a half miles, with an error factor of 300 feet.

Erica Macken wanted to find out if the VIC system could perform the task with zero error. Four minutes later the trick succeeded. It was a trick which one day would save her life.

Away beyond the damaged right wingtip Lieutenant Kasparov observed the distant passage of the northern Norwegian coastline. Hammingberg, Vardo—south of that would be Kiberg, and further south still, over the icy sweep of Varangerfjord, Grense Jakobselv. The border. He coaxed the damaged Tupolev further right until the early morning sun had reduced his eyes to screwed-up slits. He glanced right again, willing the Motherland into view.

By now there was no feeling in his hands and arms. His shoulders, like his upper torso, had also passed that stage of crucifying pain caused by prolonged physical effort. He had wanted Dzerzhinsky to take over as they had approached North Cape, but had decided that the ageing captain would need all his strength to pull off their landing. He had therefore chosen to fly the aircraft on. He knew that once he relinquished the control he would be unable to take over again.

Dzerzhinsky glanced over at Kasparov. He saw

an ashen face, covered in a thin film of oily sweat. Anatoly had done well, had battled uncomplainingly through a long and arduous night. Anatoly had brought them home. Dzerzhinsky went back to the radio, sending messages on their damage status, then checking-in the five other crew members, telling them to be standing by for emergency evacuation after landing.

The great silver Tupolev slipped in over Motovsky Zaliv; then they were coasting-in. Running down the white landscape of Russia. With forty kilometres to run Dzerzhinsky slapped his huge bear-like hands onto the vibrating control yoke. "I have control, Anatoly," he barked. "Sit back and enjoy the landing."

Kasparov collapsed into his seat. His hands, like his arms, were still twitching, their uncontrollable spasms corresponding to those of the control column. He managed a weak smile. The first time he has used my given name, he thought. Yes, I was right. To gain a command is not important. I will serve with this man forever. He supposed it was like a marriage. Only the good ones survived. And only the very good ones knew the excitement of perfect mutual understanding.

Dzerzhinsky was amazed at the violent oscillations of the Tupolev's controls. Watching Kasparov through the long night they had appeared nothing more than a slight continual juddering. Now he knew differently; his thick arms, too long without exercise, were already rigid with the pain great physical exertion brings. Where had Anatoly found such strength? He was after all such a frail young man. Humanly it did not seem possible. Dzerzhinsky's thoughts were interrupted by the white winding line of the fjord's eastern shore. Then through the light blowing snow the runway lights, flickering a distant welcome. This was the moment. He reduced power fractionally and lowered the undercarriage. The approach speed was fifty per cent higher than normal. It was too fast. He chuckled to himself; too fast be damned. It could never be that. Besides, that cunning old bitch the sky had taken care of him too long to let him go now.

The airspeed hovered delicately on the 375 mark. He was tempted to reduce power even more. But the stall checks abeam North Cape had been very convincing—at 365 kph the aircraft would stop flying. His senses sharpened. A feeling as if of running along a tightrope filled his head. Too high a speed and he would smash through the platform at the end of the wire, falling to certain death. Too slow a speed and he would lose his balance and plummet to the circus ring below. There was no safety net. Just blind faith; a gut feeling of being right. The razor-edged balancing act continued.

Black outlines of trees flashed beneath. A violent tremor tramped through the aircraft. Dzerzhinsky's right hand increased the power to the operating three engines. The speed inched agonisingly forward. His final action was to press the intercom switch and shout, "Brace—brace," to his crew. Then the giant Tupolev was pulling up; holding off slightly too high. Dzerzhinsky snapped the column forward and back. The main wheels slammed into the packed ice of the runway. It was only a brief contact, the excessive flying speed relaunching the aircraft into the air.

"Come on, you whore . . . stay down," Dzerzhinsky yelled. "Down . . . down."

With the damaged right wing he had long ago ruled out the use of flaps. Even if the hydraulics were working sufficiently well he could not be sure both sets of flaps would lower. And if they didn't they would be left in an asymmetric condition. His right hand reached out and pulled the power back to ground idle. Still twenty feet up, the Tupolev screamed past the runway midpoint intersection, giving him a high-speed glimpse of crash trucks and flashing lights. Then the grey-white ice was coming up again. The wheels struck the runway firmly this time as Dzerzhinsky pulled the two inner engines into reverse. The Tupolev lurched sideways, then back; careening down the last third of the runway at an impossible speed.

He stood on the brakes. The red lights of the crash barrier were coming up too fast. The deceleration was never enough. The Tupolev, still travelling at over a hundred kilometres per hour, smashed through the erected barrier and out onto the snow-settled overrun. The rough uneven ground claimed the left undercarriage first, the massive four-wheel bogey snapping like a matchstick, sending the aircraft into a wild, metal-tearing pirouette to the left. The noise was deafening.

159

The sounds were dying when a voice started screaming: *"Pahzhahr! Pahzhahr . . . pahzhahr!"* Fire, fire, fire.

Kasparov looked across at Dzerzhinsky. He wasn't moving. The lieutenant shouted out to the flight engineer, who stumbled forward, choking on the smoke which was already filling the fuselage. The man reached down towards the co-pilot. "Not me . . . the captain . . . help him out. I'll follow."

The flight engineer pulled the stunned Dzerzhinsky from the left seat and dragged him aft towards the escape hatch. Once they were there other hands pulled the two men away from the burning aircraft.

Dzerzhinsky's first clear recollection was that he was being dragged through fresh clean snow. He opened his eyes slowly; they were still blurred from the smoke. Somewhere ahead were figures. His crew. He struggled to bring them into focus. One . . . two . . . three . . . four . . . five. He counted five. And he made six. And the crew compliment of the Tupolev was seven. He searched the row of faces again, giving each a name. Mikhailovich, Stanislavovna, Charushnikov, Gavrilin, Ivanovna. No Anatoly. He looked around desperately. No Anatoly . . . He pulled away from the helping hands, was half-running, half-stumbling towards the blazing aircraft; crying out over and over again: "Anatoly . . . he's still inside. . . . Anatoly."

It took five burly crash crew members to hold Dzerzhinsky back, to prevent him from entering the white-hot inferno.

In the right-hand seat on the Tupolev's flight deck Anatoly Kasparov had watched Dzerzhinsky being dragged towards the escape hatch. He wanted to be sure the older man was safe. Nothing must happen to him. Once Dzerzhinsky had been pulled clear Kasparov reached down to unclip his seat harness. He found he couldn't. There was no feeling in his hands, in his arms, in his entire upper body. No strength. The fierce heat of the aluminium fire, fanned by the fresh morning wind, grew steadily nearer as he struggled against his waist and shoulder straps. It was impossible.

Tears of frustration flowed down his cheeks. Already the searing heat was scorching the back of his head. He called out to Dzerzhinsky, now . . . and to his mother. But it was too late.

In London George Hinchcliffe was facing the beginnings of a trying day. Wednesday already, he had thought earlier that morning, driving in to the ministry of defence building in Whitehall. Half the bloody week gone and he hadn't even moved last week's paperwork.

He had been in the process of doing just that when Morriss, his secretary, had entered his office with the news of the Blackhawk's disappearance in northern Scotland, plus the information that its pilot had been Squadron Leader Maudsley, and that he was missing, presumed killed. Hinchcliffe was badly shaken. He had quite liked the young man. And as for the

Blackhawk itself ... A large vodka helped, and since Hinchcliffe considered it was medicinal, he had a second before returning the bottle to the drinks cabinet.

Feeling a little steadier he put Morriss on to chasing up the full story on the previous night's crash. Northern Scotland and night operations sounded ominous. Too much like the last one. God forbid that it should be. Hinchcliffe had hardly regained his composure when a call from the editor of the *Daily Telegraph* was put through to him. They had reports that a Blackhawk aircraft had crashed the previous evening; location unknown. Did the ministry have anything to say? Hinchcliffe said they did not and reminded the editor that there was a current D Notice out on that issue. The editor, unperturbed by Hinchcliffe's manner, then said that no D Notice could hold for ever, and besides he had received further independent information relating to the October 2 accident. Someone, it appeared, had irrefutable proof that the aircraft involved had been a Blackhawk, and not a MiG-25 as claimed by the ministry of defence. Hinchcliffe managed to control his anger and said he would personally look into it and call the newspaper back; if not later that day, first thing Thursday morning.

He turned back to his desk and pushed the remaining paperwork aside. There were more important issues at stake.

He pondered the question of irrefutable proof. Some air ministry document? It was of course possible that there had been a department leak.

Someone photocopying an official report and selling it to a newspaper. But he thought not—they'd tightened up on that sort of thing pretty successfully in recent years. He returned to the notes he had made at Yeovilton earlier that month. Air Vice-Marshal Southgate-Sayers had said they had not retrieved the black box—the flight recorder. Would that be irrefutable proof? He made a note for Morriss to follow that possibility up when he had finished his current investigations.

Air Vice-Marshal Southgate-Sayers arrived, unannounced and unexpected, ten minutes later. Hinchcliffe was almost pleased to see him.

"Glad you're here," he said, waving Southgate-Sayers to a seat. "All sorts of hell seem to have broken loose this morning."

"The Blackhawk crash last night, you mean?"

Hinchcliffe moved around behind his desk and sat down. "Yes. Perhaps you could fill me in on the details."

"What have you heard?"

"Next to nothing."

Southgate-Sayers shifted his tall frame in the uncomfortable chair before outlining the previous night's operation. It was a short, well-organised speech, which mentioned only lightly the surprising fact that Lieutenant-Colonel Hood had directly countermanded his orders.

Hinchcliffe noticed this but made no comment. He listened attentively until the air vice-marshal had finished, then leant forward, placed his elbows on the desk and steepled his fingers before his chin. "So it looks as though it was a mid-air collision, is that what you're saying?"

"More or less. We do of course have to wait for the air-to-air photographs from the Norwegian air force; but I'm quietly convinced."

"Thank God." No, thought Hinchcliffe—thank this Lieutenant-Colonel Hood. A little insubordination sometimes works wonders. "I had visions, Air Vice-Marshal, of that computer being at the root of the problem."

"Not this time, Minister: though I had tentatively suggested that we might use it."

"Was there a particular reason why we didn't?"

Southgate-Sayers replied very smoothly. "The man on the spot felt it was too soon for it to be used on night ops. As it's only just been put back into service, pilots need a little more time to get used to it. I agreed with him, of course."

That's not quite what you said just now, thought Hinchcliffe. But he didn't blame commanding officers for sticking up for their own men. He changed the subject. "Any more news of the pilot, by the way? I hear it was young Maudsley."

"Nothing since I left Belgium this morning. I'm afraid it looks pretty bleak."

Hinchcliffe glanced at his watch. "That's really a shame. He was a nice chap . . . Anyway, Air Vice-Marshal, you'll have to excuse me—I'm afraid this is going to be one of those days."

Both men got to their feet and moved towards the door. "You'll be over this side of the water for some days, I take it?" Hinchcliffe said.

"In all probability, yes; the enquiry, among

other things. Which reminds me—the flight recorder from that first crash, you wouldn't have heard anything, I suppose?"

Suddenly Hinchcliffe was wary. First, the *Telegraph* editor, and now this. He did not like Southgate-Sayers. But now, if for no very good reason, he did not trust him either. "The black box? My dear fellow, not a word. You're the chap I rely on in these matters."

"Of course." The air vice-marshal smiled unnecessarily warmly. "I'll keep you posted of any further developments, then."

"Do that, will you? One likes to be prepared, in case of awkward questions in the House."

Hinchcliffe reached for the door handle. "Oh, before I forget; I'm seeing my tame boffin this afternoon, the one who cleared the Blackhawk computer. I put him on to your satellite theory. I'm afraid he honestly doesn't think there's much in it."

They shook hands. Hinchcliffe closed the door and returned to his desk. The way things were going, the air vice-marshal's Space Strike project was out. And so, sooner rather than later, was the air vice-marshal. He checked his diary. "Lunch David 1230. Professor Blakeley 3 pm." He pencilled in a note to question Blakeley on the Blackhawk's flight recorder after he'd confirmed their earlier telephone chat about satellite interference. As for the *Telegraph*, it could have a long wait. He didn't like being blackmailed.

In the meantime Blakeley had already cleared the VIC system and British Aerospace were looking into the aircraft itself. His problems seemed to have lessened considerably when Hinchcliffe left the ministry of defence building shortly after midday.

He had chosen the Grill Room at the Ritz for no other reason than the generous spacing of the tables, which—if one spoke in moderate tones—prevented eavesdropping. David Courtney, assistant director-general of MI5, dressed in a charcoal-grey suit, white shirt, and dark-blue knitted tie, was sitting opposite him.

Hinchcliffe waited until the waiter had taken their order, then raised his glass. "To the department," he pronounced.

Courtney's face broke into a rare grin. "Bullshit, George. You're after something. You don't invite me to the Ritz every day. And when you do there are always strings."

Hinchcliffe leaned back in his chair and laughed. The two men got on well together, even though their backgrounds were poles apart—Oxford being the only common link. Hinchcliffe, educated at a grammar school in Sheffield, had won a scholarship to Balliol at the same time Courtney had won his place from Shrewsbury. Both had read English, and both had emerged with second-class honours degrees. It wasn't until many years later that they ran into each other again; when they became members of the same London club. By that time both men had climbed high on their different ladders.

"Right, lad," Hinchcliffe said, putting on his

thickest Yorkshire accent. "I've got a job for you."

"Not on the lines of the last one, I trust?"

"Ah—speaking of that, have we found out anything of interest yet?"

Courtney put his hand into his inside pocket, withdrew Karolyov's slim unmarked manila envelope, and slid it across the table. "Arrived on Monday."

"You've read it, of course?"

Courtney glanced around, before saying in a low voice. "Looks a little on the official side, George . . . I mean, it should at least be copied to the PM."

"In good time, David, in good time." Hinchcliffe had removed the contents of the envelope and was scanning the pages. Immediately he was troubled. Confused. Blakeley had assured him that the computer on the Blackhawk was impenetrable. And now, here was a document which had originated from Murmansk in the USSR and which indicated that the Soviets *had* penetrated it. Had caused the crash. There were even photographs. Infra-red, taken from Tupolev Tu-95/Serial No. 1883313. He pushed the document and the photographs back into the envelope. His hand was shaking slightly as he put it into his pocket. "Where did you get this . . . I mean how reliable is the source?"

"As reliable as anything in our line of business," Courtney said flatly. He brightened. "You mentioned another job?"

Hinchcliffe forced a smile. It seemed now that the missing black box was more important than ever. In a hushed voice he outlined what had happened since the crash of Major Kitrell's Blackhawk on October 2. The one-sided conversation came to its conclusion over the sole bonne femme.

Courtney's eyes fixed on Hinchcliffe for a moment. "And you think the reporter who passed the information through to the *Telegraph* could have found the flight recorder?"

"It's possible. Think about it. Someone witnessed the crash and correctly recognised the aircraft type at night—that makes him something of an expert, wouldn't you say? He passed the details to the paper, who immediately push the ministry for an explanation. We counter with a suitable press release . . . and then a few weeks later the same person, out scouring the mountains, finds something which proves the aircraft which crashed was indeed a Blackhawk."

"But surely it doesn't have to be the flight recorder? There must be other bits that are unique to that type of aircraft."

"True. Except that the flight recorder has never been found: that and a bit of fin, I gather. The sums add up, that's all."

"So why not send the air force security people in? It is their department, after all."

"Boys to do a man's job, David? Christ, you know better than that." Flattery, he hoped, would disguise his sudden distrust of all things air force. "Besides, I need a very discreet undercover job. If this reporter hasn't got it, and his story's so much bluff, I don't want alarm bells ringing all over Scotland."

"And if he has?"

"Difficult question. I don't know who he is, but what he's got is top secret. It also belongs to us, and we want it back . . . You decide the best way to handle it; your line of country, after all."

"As you wish, George," Courtney said equably. "I'll put someone on it right away."

Hinchcliffe picked up his starched white napkin and dabbed in gentlemanly fashion at his lips. "Not just someone, David . . . the best."

It was later, as David Courtney left the Ritz, that he remembered the Boris Gleb report. Perhaps he should have mentioned it. But he had his own career to think of. Ministers liked to hear what they liked to hear. The Karolyov papers were bad enough—though he strongly suspected them of being cooked up to look far worse than they were. But the Boris Gleb report was something else . . .

For one thing, it was criminal neglect on his people's part that the construction work it described had got so far without being spotted. And for another thing, its political implications were enormous. Soviet laser beam sites in the Kola Peninsula, for Christ's sake—and in an advanced state of construction! Nobody in the present government, not one single soul, would welcome the man who brought them such information. In fact, there was a tradition stretching right back to the Greeks that unpleasant things were done, sooner or later, to the bearers of bad tidings.

No. Courtney decided he was right to wait. After all, with Kristiansen taken he was the only man who knew, so there was no risk. And the coming election could make a world of difference. A change of government and he'd have a defence minister all gung-ho for Britain's own Space Strike, and then the Boris Gleb report would be just what the doctor ordered. And there were only a couple of months or so involved. So until then . . . well, he'd put someone on to the Scottish affair at once. Not easy. He couldn't very well go through normal channels on this one. But he did have Karolyov out of a job. Alexei Karolyov, *alias* Arild Hansen, the Norwegian insurance broker.

CHAPTER SIX

It was two evenings later, Friday, October 24. Paul Kitrell was waiting in the lobby of the Athenaeum Hotel. He had in fact been waiting for over an hour, sitting in a chair opposite the porter's desk, watching the ebb and flow of guests. Mainly American. Funny that he should be one of them and feel an outsider. But then home had to be more than a father's place of birth; an entry of an official form. Home was the country which had moulded you. Year by painstaking year.

He looked up and checked the clock by the reception counter. Eight p.m. She wasn't coming. It was as simple as that. Even so he left a message with one of the porters before walking out through the main doors into Piccadilly. He turned right and right again, into a small side street. Opening the door marked number ten he went up the narrow staircase to the first floor apartment. The building itself served as an annexe to the main hotel. Kitrell preferred it. It was altogether private and featured—apart from a large double bedroom and comfortable sitting room—a small and well-equipped kitchenette. In true bachelor fashion he had gone out earlier and purchased a few supplies; things for his breakfast mainly. Now he busied himself preparing eggs and bacon and a pot of coffee. Not quite what he had intended, but he was too tired to bother with restaurants; especially by himself. Cities, he had long ago decided, were not built for single people.

Of course it was possible that her flying duties had been extended. But then she would have telephoned—surely? No, you've got to face it, Kitrell, she's stood you up. Your age, for one thing. Besides, she's surrounded by pilots. Far more reasonable for her to stick to her own kind. People need common ground.

He went through to the bedroom and returned with the orange-painted box: the Blackhawk flight recorder. Something to occupy his mind. He placed the recorder on the bar top which made the division between kitchenette and sitting room, and went back to fixing the eggs and bacon. From time to time he shot a glance at the so called "black box". It was almost as though he disbelieved its presence. He reached out once and touched it, reassuring himself.

It had been an amazing stroke of good fortune. In one way at least. In another it was a disaster. Like the poor man being offered the million dollar banknote, with the proviso he could not spend it. Jamie Finlay had offered little help, other than that the Farnborough boys would have something to plug it in to. Paul had laughed, saying he could hardly appear at the gates of the Royal Aircraft Establishment and ask them to run the flight recorder for him. Jamie had countered with: "Why not go to the heart of the matter? The Blackhawk squadron itself. They'd have the right equipment, for sure. And the right weaknesses." Paul didn't need a picture painting. At a conservative estimate, nine out of ten people would accept a bribe. Of course it was a risk. But if he didn't want to take it he would be back where he had started. With one exception. He now knew for certain that Gene had been flying a Blackhawk.

It was much later. He was dozing in front of the television when there was a sharp knocking on the door. He started as the knock was repeated. He was halfway across the room when his eye caught the flight recorder sitting amidst the clutter of unwashed dishes on the bar top. He removed it and stowed it in an empty sideboard. Then he answered the door.

She was wearing a black velvet cloak, the hood of which rested on her shoulders. He stood there, transfixed. It was as though the breath had gone out of him. She was even more beautiful than he remembered. Her vivid green eyes were bright, her face was flushed. She had been running.

"My penalty for being three hours late!" she said breathlessly. He looked confused until she added, "Keeping me standing at the door."

"I'm sorry," he said quickly. "Come in, come in."

She smiled and went through to the sitting

room. "It should be me apologising," she said. "I do have an excuse though."

"You do," Paul took her cloak.

"Flying late ... then I thought I could still make it with a clear run. I got a puncture the other side of Basingstoke. And if that wasn't enough I found the spare was flat ... and England after six in the evening is of course impossible. Took me over an hour to find a garage who would come out ... I should have phoned of course, but you know how it is. Problem upon problem."

"Never mind, you're here now." He checked his watch. It was just after ten. "We can still go out for a meal. Never too late in this town."

"Do you mind if we don't? I feel at death's door ... tired."

"Coffee then?"

"That would be lovely."

"I can run to bacon and eggs if you like."

She smiled tiredly. "No thanks. Just the coffee." Her eyes settled on the writing desk by the window. "Do you mind if I use the telephone?"

"No, not at all."

"I usually stay with an old girl friend of mine when I'm in town. I said I'd call her at some stage to let her know when to expect me."

He plugged in the percolator. "Where does she live?"

"Near Swiss Cottage."

"Long way. You can always stay here," he offered. "Save you another drive. The bedroom's through there," he indicated the other side of the kitchenette wall. "I'll take the sofa."

174

"If you're sure it's not too much trouble," she said. "Except I'll take the sofa."

"It's not too much trouble and you'll take the bed," Paul said firmly. "Besides, I usually write late into the night, and the typewriter is in here."

"I'd better get my bag from the car then."

He poured the coffee and took the cup to the side table near the sofa. "No need, I'll get it. You sit here and enjoy the best cup of coffee in London."

She was smelling it appreciatively as he took her car keys and went out of the room.

When he brought up her hold-all and put it in the bedroom she was curled up in a corner of the sofa. "Well," she said as he came through to the sitting room, "Did you have any luck in Scotland?"

He walked across to the writing desk and perched on the corner. She was wearing a dark-green knitted dress with a high neckline and long sleeves which were flared at the wrists. The hem had ridden up above her knees. He couldn't get over her beauty. "More than that," he said. "Gene was definitely flying a Blackhawk."

Her eyes widened. "How do you know?"

"Finlay. The reporter I told you about in Scotland."

"He told you?"

"More than that." Kitrell went over to the sideboard and took out the Blackhawk flight recorder. "Ever see one of these?" he said.

She reached out, her feet swinging abruptly to the floor. "Where did you get it?"

"Scotland . . . Finlay. It's from the Blackhawk."

"I know. I also know that you shouldn't have it.

175

It's top secret . . . have you told the authorities?"

"Authorities? Which authorities had you in mind? Not the ministry of defence, surely? They told Fleet Street it was a MiG-25. They apparently haven't lost a Blackhawk."

"You mean, they're not saying they have. There's a subtle difference."

"Maybe. They're claiming pilot error too, and that box of tricks is going to tell me if that's just another of their subtle differences."

"How? I mean how do you propose to transcribe the contents? It's a highly specialised job."

He pushed his hands into his pockets and paced across the room. "I was hoping you would help me."

"Oh, Paul, you know I can't. Please don't ask me."

He spun round, his voice sharp with emotion. "I thought you loved Gene!"

"I did, you know that. But this . . ."

"No Erica, but nothing. My brother was killed in a flying accident. An accident that's on the record as his fault. And if it wasn't, and this is all a cover-up, with Gene carrying the can for something he didn't do, then I want to know about it. All I'm asking you is for help to get the flight recorder transcribed. Once that's done I'll return it to the air force."

She looked down at her hands, folded in her lap. "I don't know, Paul . . . I just don't know. Do you mind if I sleep on it? It's been a very long day. Perhaps I'll see things in a clearer light tomorrow."

He went over to her, took her hands and

raised her to her feet. "Yes," he said gently. "Tomorrow will be fine."

She found him in the sitting room the next morning, at the desk by the window. The only sound in the room was the gentle patter of raindrops on glass. She crept up quietly behind him. It was only when she neared the back of his chair that she recognised the deep breathing pattern of sleep. In front of him, on the desk, was a battered portable typewriter. She leant carefully across him and began to read what he had typed.

"On the other side of the moon it was as the traveller had said. The naked body of the Indian woman was as blue as the open sky. Her sari, stained with dried blood, lay in the dust nearby. Overhead, suspended in the desert's heat, the ragged wings of vultures were urging MacKinnon on. Back to Mombasa. Back to Fort Jesus. Better the imprisoned life of a barefoot infidel with water, than a free man without. It was later, when the brassy sun had reached its zenith and his swollen tongue filled his mouth, that he again met the traveller . . ."

Paul suddenly stirred and rubbed his eyes. Erica straightened, then stepped away. "Good morning," she said softly.

It took him a few moments to shake off the sleep which filled his eyes. He was at his worst in the morning, preferring at least one hour of solitude before he faced the day.

"Coffee?" she offered, instantly identifying his problem. She moved towards the kitchenette. "I read the page in the typewriter, by the way. It's good . . . what is it? A part of the book?"

"Perhaps. Something I remembered from a long time ago."

"Who was MacKinnon?"

"MacKinnon?"

"The man in the desert. The man who met the traveller."

"Nobody new. If you believe the writer's credo that nothing is original, then MacKinnon, the traveller, the Indian woman, even the plot—if there was to be one—have all been done before." He moved bleakly towards the short hallway which led to the bedroom. "Give me five minutes to shower."

"How do you like your eggs?" she called after him.

"No eggs. Just toast."

It was half an hour later, after breakfast, when he broached the subject of the flight recorder again. "Have you thought any more about what I said last night?"

She walked across to the window and looked out at the rainswept morning. "I think it might be better to leave it alone, Paul. Gene's dead. Nothing we can do is going to bring him back, is it?"

"No. It's just that I failed to honour a promise . . . I have to go through with it."

178

She turned. "A promise? Who to?"

He steeled himself. There was no easy way to tell her. "Our parents died in a fire. My father instantly, my mother later in the hospital." He went over and joined her by the window. A car moved silently up the wet grey street. "We used to have barbecues at the house. I came back late one night with some friends, my parents had gone to a party, and we decided to charcoal some steaks. Only problem was I couldn't get the charcoal to light. I went to the garage and found a can of paraffin to try to get the fire going. The only problem was it wasn't paraffin, it was petrol. The barbecue was one of those portable affairs. You could move it about on wheels. I'd put it near the house to be out of the wind. The house was built of wood . . ." his voice trailed away.

"And the house caught fire?"

"My parents were inside. Not that I knew. They'd come back early from the party and gone to bed."

"Oh my God, that's terrible." Erica closed her eyes. "Where was Gene? Was he with you?"

"No. He was staying with friends . . . it was vacation time." He was silent for a number of seconds, then he said: "My father was dead on arrival at hospital. My mother died the following morning. She spoke to me before she died . . . asked me to take care of Gene. Or Eugene as she always called him. She was very fond of him, you know . . ."

She turned towards him. So much guilt. At least she could understand why Gene had never

179

mentioned his parents' death. "But you couldn't be expected to watch over him forever, Paul. Besides, you told me once that an aunt took him back with her to live in the States."

"I tried to go with them."

"Is the fire the reason she didn't take you?"

He smiled sadly. "I don't know ... certainly something drove a wedge between us."

"And there you have it. How could you possibly be expected to look after Gene under those conditions?"

"I didn't. I failed him then and I've failed him ever since. But I was with my mother when she died, and I promised her. That's why I'm going on with this." He turned and placed his arms gently on her shoulders. "I realise I should never have asked you. I had no right to put you in that sort of position. I'll sort it out myself." His hands dropped and he turned back to the window.

"More coffee?" she said, walking across to the kitchenette.

"Why not?" he answered.

"And then you can tell me exactly what you want me to do."

It was noon in Murmansk. A cold Saturday in late October. Sergio Dzerzhinsky was at the military cemetery ten kilometres from the air base. A bitter wind blew sleet into his already frozen eye sockets. He remained totally still. The burial service was over; had been over for twenty minutes. Lieutenant Anatoly Kasparov had been laid to rest with full military honours. Alone now, Dzerzhinsky gazed down at the coffin, deep in its freshly dug grave. "It is a poor exchange, Anatoly," he said softly. "No sun, no moon, no stars; no more cloud palaces to roam. No more sky. Perhaps you were right after all; the Bolshoi would have been better . . . that way there would have been no kingdoms to lose. That way you would have stayed closer to the earth. To your mother and your children's mother."

Fumbling with gloved fingers, he unclipped the row of medals from his left breast and, kneeling down beside the grave, tossed them onto the coffin. His voice was little more than a whisper when he said: "If there had ever been a son, my young friend . . ." He climbed unsteadily to his feet, took one pace back and saluted. Then he turned and walked slowly through the silent ranks of other timeless soldiers.

It was only when he reached the gates of the cemetery that he paused and threw a glance up at the dark brooding sky. His eyes were full of anger. Once again she had stolen someone he had loved.

The Sabena flight from London touched down at Brussels airport shortly after six the following Monday evening. Air Vice-Marshal Southgate-Sayers was met in the terminal building by Major-General Foulkes.

"Well, Alister? How did it go?" Foulkes asked as the two men walked towards the exit.

"It didn't," Southgate-Sayers said shortly. "Not

a trace. I had five square miles of moorland combed. Took half a regiment to do it. And not a trace."

"Jesus Christ, I don't believe it. Where's the bloody thing gone, then?"

"Search me, George. Local gossip pointed to some aged local reporter, but he didn't have it. I spoke to him myself—clearly half-witted and didn't know what the hell I was talking about."

Foulkes managed an ironic smile. "If the Soviets weren't keeping so very quiet I'd say they already had it themselves . . . So what happens now?"

Southgate-Sayers followed him out through the electrically operated doors. It was already dark. Daylight saving time had ended four weeks earlier—Monday, September 29. "Well, as far as I can see, not very much; until November the third at least."

"The exercise, you mean?"

"Rolling Thunder, yes. As things stand the computer systems are now fully operational. I therefore suggest we can safely sit back and await results."

"And if nothing happens?"

"Negative thinking, George. Unlike you. Anyway, when I was back in the UK I went over the crash tapes again and I'm more convinced than ever. In fact I'd bet my life the Soviets were responsible. There's no other explanation."

"Four days more then, Alister."

"Four days more, George."

It was as they were walking towards the car park that Foulkes said, "A bit of good news at this end; or at least good news as far as what you were just saying is concerned."

"Which is?"

"Intelligence report in via Finnmark, Norway. A place called Kirkenes. Some Russki dossier giving their version of the crash. Photographs. Every lurid detail. *And* claiming full responsibility."

Southgate-Sayers stopped in his tracks. "I bloody knew it. Exactly what we've been saying all along. So what's happening?"

"Usual, I imagine. Our cabinet will push it over to the DPC in Brussels who in turn will push it over to our committee. Only problem is, if the Reds are really so confident, why aren't they going public? Just think of the propaganda value."

"Perhaps they're planning to do it again."

The two men walked on. Then, as they entered the car park, Southgate-Sayers dropped his briefcase. It was only the noise of it hitting the ground that alerted him. His eyes went first to the case, then to his right hand. There was no feeling in it. Nothing.

Foulkes stooped down and picked it up. "You all right, old man?"

"Fine, George, fine. Do you mind carrying it for me? Feel a bit tired . . . it's been a long week." Damn, what was happening? This was the worst it had ever been. Even his feet felt somehow

numb. And he couldn't remember being this
tired in years. Not since Korea.

Paul Kitrell had left the underground at Piccadilly Circus so that he could walk the last
mile or so to the Athenaeum Hotel. Walking
helped him to think. He had left the Blackhawk
flight recorder in good, if expensive hands. It was
nearly 7 p.m. Friday. The last day of October. He
hadn't heard from Erica for two days now. But he
had the information—or at least a part of it. The
radio technician at Hurn airport, Bournemouth,
had been very helpful in that department. One
thousand pounds in used notes had of course been
a key factor.

The lead had come from Erica, who had made
discreet enquiries via Yeovilton. There was a unit
at the naval base known as FRADU—Fleet
Requirements and Development Unit—which
was essentially a military operation manned by
civilian pilots and ground-crew. All were ex-
military. Erica had found out that the unit had
originally been based at Hurn airport. Following
the unit's move to Yeovilton, a number of technicians who had settled in and around the
Bournemouth area decided to find jobs with civil
companies at Hurn, in preference to moving their
entire families to Somerset.

The ex-corporal, whom Paul had visited that
day, had been one such person. A gaunt-faced
unshaven character with hollow eyes and greasy
black hair, he had been a good choice. He worked

184

for an aircraft maintenance company located in the corner of the airport, and permanently complained about the long hours and poor pay, saying he had been better off in the RAF. His name was Johnny Stubbs.

But whatever Stubbs's shortcomings in personal appearance and company loyalty might be, he was a brilliant technician. He had rigged up the necessary computers and leads to a test bench and had partly opened Pandora's Box. Following an initial flood of information Stubbs discovered that he needed to get hold of more specialised equipment to help him extract the rest. Or so he claimed. Anyway, unable to argue, Paul had paid him the first thousand pounds with the promise of another when he could come up with the missing part of the transcript. Stubbs gave Paul his home telephone number and told him to stay in touch.

After that Paul had gone to the main terminal at the airport and placed a phone call to Jamie in Scotland. He wanted to tell him they had found out the "how" if not yet the "why." There was no reply to his call.

Now, walking down Piccadilly, past the Royal Academy, Paul retraced the story he had so far assembled, from Erica's outline of the Blackhawk VIC system to Stubbs's devastating summation—or at least part summation. Devastating because it showed that the vocal interface command system had somehow locked the aircraft in a high-speed descent. The "why" element of the transcript was yet to come; but Paul knew from his discussions with Erica that the fail safe system

185

had not failed safe. On the contrary it had taken his brother to his death. It didn't need a genius to arrive at the conclusion of sabotage.

When he opened his front door his first thought was that the apartment had been burgled. Things had been moved, not a lot but noticeably, and there was a strong smell of Aramis aftershave. Finding nothing missing, however, had created another possibility in his mind. Ole Renterre's footprints told stories other than simba. They translated surprisingly well from bush to city. He went over to the writing desk and again telephoned Jamie in Scotland. This time it was answered; but by a voice he did not recognize.

"Can I ask who's calling?" the gruff Highland-accented voice said.

"Mr. Kitrell. Paul Kitrell."

A brief crackly silence. "I'm afraid it's not possible to speak with Jamie Finlay just now . . . he's been involved in an accident, you see."

"Accident!" Paul caught his breath. "Who am I speaking to?"

"Inspector Preedy, Inverness constabulary."

"What sort of accident, Inspector?"

"I canna go into that just now, Mr. Kitrell . . . may I enquire where you're calling from?"

"London."

"London, you say . . . just a moment." Kitrell picked out vague distant snatches of conversation. "Mr. Kitrell." Preedy was back.

"Yes, Inspector?"

"Enquiries, you understand, but were you in Scotland last week. More particularly, were you

186

in Brora?"

"I was in Brora, yes."

"And you left when?"

Paul paused and worked back through the days. It was a silence which would be misconstrued. "Last Thursday, Inspector. A week yesterday. I took the morning flight from Inverness."

"I see. And you haven't been back since?"

"No, I've been in London."

"Aye, well, that's all for now, Mr. Kitrell, except perhaps if I could have your telephone number. Routine, you understand . . . we may need to contact you again."

Paul passed the number, then added, "Is Jamie Finlay dead, Inspector?"

Preedy's voice registered surprise. "Dead, Mr. Kitrell? What makes you ask that?"

"Your line of questioning. It follows a known path."

"In that event, Mr. Kitrell, I'll leave the conclusion up to you. We may talk to you again, then?"

"Yes, Inspector. Goodnight." The telephone clicked distantly, leaving Paul with his doubts, and Inspector Preedy with his first and therefore prime suspect in a murder case.

It was five minutes later when national pride gave way to police logic and Preedy placed a long-distance call to his contemporaries at New Scotland Yard, London . . .

Paul was packing when Erica arrived at the apartment. He impulsively kissed her on the cheek and drew her into the room. "I wasn't expecting you."

"I was expecting to be here, but the weekend flying programmed was scrubbed, so I took a chance and came . . . I did try to phone earlier but there was no reply." She stopped talking as her eyes were drawn to the half-packed suitcases visible through the door into the bedroom. "You're leaving?"

"Changing address, that's all."

"Why? Has something happened?"

"I had a visitor today."

"A visitor?"

"A burglar . . . except that nothing was stolen."

Her confusion deepened. "I don't follow . . . you're not making sense."

"I think it was someone looking for the flight recorder; fortunately it wasn't here. They left their mark, though. It has to be a warning. These men are quite capable of coming and going without a trace. So presumably I'm supposed to get rattled and bolt for cover . . . if I've got what they're looking for, that is. They naturally follow."

"Then what?"

"Then," he said, "they deliver the little speech they've been saving up. If I was as naive as they supposed I was, I should hand over the goods; and finally they say goodbye . . . forever."

"Do you mean, kill?" she said.

"Not a tasteful word, Erica, but if you like . . ."

Her eyes flashed with a sudden anger. "My God, Paul, what are you doing? You know all this and yet you're playing right into their hands. If you leave, won't that prove to them that—"

"But you see, I know what they're doing. And if they're professionals they will not expect me to. Newspaper people are supposed to move in different circles. Therefore the element of surprise will be on my side."

"But ... you said professionals. What chance have you got against them?"

He took her hands. "Come and sit down ... over here." They sat facing each other. "Do you know how to track a lion?" he said.

"No."

"No, and neither do they? But I was trained by a Masai warrior a long time ago in Kenya. It's an exercise in patience, in self-control, in thinking not only for yourself but for the animal you're tracking. A lion, you see, works to a set formula. The pattern rarely changes. He's an arrogant beast who leaves the actual hunting to the female of the species. She—the lioness—stalks and manouevres the prey into the ideal place for the strike. It is only in the final scene that the lion appears and steals the plunder ... Basically that is what is happening here. The lioness is pushing me out—to more favourable ground. The lion, of course, is waiting. He may not even be on the lioness's side. But my salvation lies in knowing the rules in advance. He will not be able to find me. And if he does, I won't have what he requires in my possession."

Erica considered the man as if for the first time. She had thought him reserved, a man happiest among books and words. And what he was saying now did not fit that image. She decided to try him.

189

"It sounds too dangerous, Paul. Why not leave it? You've done all you can. Gene's gone—nothing you or I or anyone else can do is going to bring him back. All right, so you didn't keep your promise. Such things do happen."

He raised his eyebrows. "And maybe I ought to grow up? You could be right. But now there's something else." He told her then about his train journey to Bournemouth, and about the provisional transcript ex-Corporal Stubbs had produced from the Blackhawk flight recorder.

The colour drained from her cheeks. "Sabotage?" she interrupted, her challenge to him forgotten.

"Hypothesis only," he replied. "But you did tell me that when the primary computer fails it should automatically transfer the controls to the manual mode?"

"Yes, but . . ."

"And should the power controls which enable the aircraft to be flown manually also fail they hand control to a ground operator who remotely flies the aircraft back to wherever and lands it . . . is that correct?"

"More or less."

"Okay. So the transcript from Gene's flight recorder showed the aircraft never left the primary computer mode. It was still working from his voice-prints . . . why would he put it into a descent and forget to pull up?"

"I didn't know that was how it happened," she said quietly. "Pilot incapacitation. He could have had a heart attack."

He paused, choosing his words carefully. "But he didn't. So it has to be sabotage."

"How do you know he didn't?"

"According to the flight recorder he ejected four seconds before the crash."

"Ejected?" Surprise. Shock. "He could still be alive then, couldn't he?"

"I've already thought of that. He was very low. It seems unlikely."

"Unlikely, hell!" she said sharply. "It's been a cover-up from first to last. One lie after another—you said that yourself."

Paul moved through to the bedroom to finish his packing. "I agree," he said. "But a thing like his survival would be very hard to hide. Especially when they had Jamie Finlay on the spot to reckon with. And what would be their reason?" He checked, remembering that now Jamie Finlay was dead . . . He cleared his throat. "Whatever really happened, Erica, we'll find out. As soon as the rest of the black box transcript comes through we'll find out."

He snapped the suitcase shut and, stepping round it, kissed her lightly on the cheek. She stiffened. Then suddenly she was in his arms. They kissed again, parting only when it was necessary to draw breath.

"So what happens now?" she said.

Unsuitable as the moment might be, he felt enormously happy. "First off we get out of here. I've a friend from way back we can stay with. Guy with the oddest name—Winter." He hesitated, watching her reaction. "Wint's only got the one spare room, though."

"I don't see that as a problem." Quietly she met his gaze. "Do you?"

He released her. "How long can you stay?"

"Only until Sunday. The squadron leaves first thing Monday morning for Norway."

"Norway?"

"NATO wargames. The code-name is Rolling Thunder. It's no big secret—you'll hear about it every day on the news."

"How long will you be there?"

"It's planned to finish on Christmas Day. An unseasonal way to end the year . . . but, as one of the squadron pilots remarked: 'Scrooge still lives—except now he runs NATO!'"

Paul managed a weak smile. "Is there any way I'll be able to contact you? Stubbs must come up trumps before too long."

"They have very tight security on these exercises. It won't be easy. I could try and phone you, though."

"No good. I may be on the move again."

"For what help it is, I'll be at Trondheim," she said. "Do you know any newspaper people there?"

"Not off-hand, but I could check." He picked up his briefcase and took her arm. "Let's go then."

"What about the cases?"

"I'll leave a message with the porter to come and get them. He can get them at reception for the moment. If I have to take off again I'd rather travel light . . . and I'll leave my car too, for obvious reasons. We'll take yours. Okay?"

He opened the door and ushered her out. A last

glance round the room and he switched off the light.

At hotel reception he had the choice of two night porters for the honour of his tenner. He chose the shiftier-looking man, on the principle that he must therefore almost certainly be the more honest. It was not, as things were to turn out, a good choice.

Ten minutes later, in Erica's Ford estate, he eyed the rearview mirror calculatingly. Then he made up his mind. A BMW had been with them ever since they had left the hotel. It could take Erica's car any time it wanted. Turning into Vauxhall Bridge Road, he said: "The car is taxed, isn't it?"

She gave him a curious look. "Of course, why?"

"How about your insurance . . . does it cover any driver?"

"Yes . . . I think so."

He switched off the car's sidelights. "Let me know if you see a police car; and when they stop us leave the talking to me."

"The BMW is still following, I take it?"

So she had seen it too. "Yes; but not for much longer."

The blue-and-white Panda car picked them up before they reached Vauxhall Bridge. Paul wound down his window, watching the dark-coloured BMW cruise silently past. It pulled discreetly into the kerb a good two hundred yards ahead.

"Now, sir," said the policeman, bending down towards the opened window, "do you realise you're driving without lights?"

Paul feigned shocked surprise, and also an accent somewhere between Bronx and Springfield, Missouri. He reached forward and switched on the lights. "My apologies, Officer. I thought I'd just killed the headlights when I came into town. Must have accidently knocked them all off."

The officer suppressed a sigh and said in a resigned voice, "You're an American, I take it, sir?"

Paul produced his press card. "That's right. With AP—Associated Press—just came in from New York . . . we er, seem to be lost. We have a reservation at the Athenaeum Hotel, Piccadilly."

The officer smiled. "You've just driven in from Heathrow airport, is that right, sir?"

"That's right, Officer."

"You've just missed it then. You must have turned right at Hyde Park Corner." The policeman pointed back the way they had come.

"That wouldn't be the big rotary about half a mile or so back?"

"A bit further than that, sir, but yes."

"And the Athenaeum Hotel?"

"Instead of turning right at what you call the big rotary, sir, you should have gone straight on. The Athenaeum is approximately two hundred yards down on the left."

Paul took his press card back from the policeman. "I take it you'd like to see my licence and insurance?"

"That won't be necessary this time, sir. But if you could pay a little more attention to your lights?"

194

"That's real nice of you, Officer. One last thing, how would I get back to that Hyde Corner you mentioned?"

"Hyde *Park* Corner," the policeman told him. "Strictly against the rules, sir, but if you watch for my directions you can make a U-turn right here and go back the way you came."

Paul beamed at him. "Wish we had your sort of guys in New York, Officer . . ."

The policeman, with twenty years of the Metropolitan under his belt, managed a bland smile before he walked away. When it was all clear he waved the Ford back in the direction of Victoria station.

Erica let out a long breath and laughed. "Of course, he could just as easily have booked you," she said.

Paul eased the accelerator down, watching his rearview mirror at the same time. The BMW was nowhere to be seen.

"Always helps to be a foreigner," he replied.

They went around Hyde Park Corner and headed north up Park Lane.

Erica said: "You still haven't told me where we're going."

"Winter le Cheminant in Westbourne Gardens. He's a Guernsey man. And he really does work for AP."

"Is it far?"

"No. Off the Bayswater Road. About two miles from where we were staying."

*　　*　　*

At the same time as they arrived at Westbourne Gardens a police car pulled up outside the Athenaeum Hotel. The detective-sergeant, who had been despatched from New Scotland Yard to follow up enquiries in the murder case of one James Finlay, was seventeen minutes too late.

CHAPTER SEVEN

The sound seemed to come from every direction at once. It was vaguely reminiscent of a creaking gate, or a distant marching band, or barking dogs. Erica looked up: great arrows of geese seemed flung out against the sky, beating a southerly path through the cold arctic air.

A last glance at the vast whiteness of the Norwegian airfield, then she turned and activated the red entry button. The solid steel doors opened; the outflow of warm air soaking over her as she stepped into the pressurised operations building. The fifth day of the NATO exercise, Rolling Thunder had just begun.

In the briefing room Major Stray held the floor. Before him the pilots listened intently. Arctic survival briefings rated on a par with enemy tactics—real or otherwise. Stray, a Norwegian air force major in his forties, moved across to the demonstration single-man dinghy. "Your body's thermostat is located in the front of the brain," he said in excellent English. "Just behind the bridge of the nose in an area called the hypothalamus. This piece of tissue is a temperature that varies no more than a couple of degrees from its optimal 98.6 degrees Fahrenheit."

Stray adjusted his half-moon spectacles. "Which is just as well," he continued. "For the body can only function properly within a very narrow internal temperature range. That range is 97 to 102 degrees. Which brings us to this!" His right foot tapped the dinghy. "Now, because you will be wearing immersion suits do not be fooled into thinking you have guaranteed survival. You don't. And as the majority of operations will be over water we will look at that aspect first." Stray glanced quickly along the rows of listeners.

"So, we have ejected from our aircraft, and successfully parachuted down to the sea. Now we are in the water and it's bloody cold. The dinghy has automatically inflated and we are bobbing happily beside it. Happily! Remember that word. Our happiness is gone in thirty seconds. Remember the thirty seconds. That is the time we have to pull ourselves into the dinghy." Major Stray held up his hands. "These, you will recall, are outside your immersion suit—as is most of your face. Now, the brain's first response to dropping temperatures is to chop off the circulation to hands and feet. Our feet are fine, they're inside the suit. Our hands are not. Therefore we lost all sensation in them very quickly. Failing to get into that dinghy rapidly—especially at this time of year—can prove very inconvenient." Stray spread out the fingers of both his hands. "As you see, I have lost two fingers from my left and one from my right. I ejected from a Hunter some years ago and failed the thirty-second test. The result was frostbite and amputation. So, gentlemen, I speak from experience." He laughed. "Needless to say— in my own defence—I was already at that time in pilot terms an old man. Not as fit as you." Stray lowered his hands. "Now we continue with what happens once we are in the dinghy . . ."

Erica, sitting near the back of the room, was listening with only half of her attention. The other half was back in London, thinking of Paul and their last weekend. Unlike him, she did not believe in guilt. Responsibility, which was constructive yes; guilt, which was corrosive, no. And guilt towards the dead she considered particularly unreasonable. And Gene was dead—in spite of his ejection there was no doubt of that. So for her to fall in love with his brother was no betrayal; it was in fact an affirmation. An affirmation of life. They were so alike, yet so amazingly different, and she loved Paul as much for his differences as for his similarities . . .

She turned her full attention back to the arctic survival briefing. Although she had been raised in the frozen wastes of northern Canada she didn't imagine that she knew it all. That way lay complacency. And death.

Two hours later all pilots were on readiness. The pretend war was about to begin.

The threat of chemical and bacteriological warfare was the reason for respirators. It was also the reason for the pressurised operations building, which would safeguard its occupants should threat become reality. The airfield itself, tucked away up the winding Trondheimsfjord, gave the appearance of a peaceful agricultural area nestling in the shadows of the surrounding mountains. The buildings, scattered in no apparent order, were disguised as farmhouses and barns. The tracks which linked the farming community were in fact taxiways and runways. During the summer, without the camouflaging effect of snow, the long take-off runways were literally painted and broken up with temporary fences so that from the air their appearance was of dirt-rutted farm tracks.

As for aircraft, none was visible. The barns were in fact small hump-backed hangars. Each one held a single aircraft. Each one was lead-sealed and bombproof. It was inside one of these Erica was now standing, counting off the minutes, breathing uncomfortably through her respirator. The smell of rubber was slightly nauseating. She checked her watch, ducked under the aircraft's wing, and went towards the two technicians. Like other ground-crews from other wars they were playing cards on an upended oil drum. Unlike their predecessors they had the appearance of rubberised robots with great frog eyes. The wiring from their mouthpieces was connected to the walkie-talkie radios which were hooked to their belts. She signalled the time and they dropped the cards and moved silently into action. To call for start clearance, due to the screening effect of the hardened shelter, one of the technicians went through an electrically operated side door and climbed the metal steps fitted to the side of the building before activating his walkie-talkie.

Erica, strapping into the Blackhawk, began reading down the checklist on the CRT. Apart from the basics of seat and parachute straps; oxygen supply; radio lead connection; and the removal of the upper and lower seat pins, everything was done by vocal command. The time-saving was self-evident, as was the cancelled-out error factor.

As the pilot read down the screen, each item on it, having been electronically activated, disappeared. Any malfunctions would be instantly reported by flashing red lights on the central alert system, and by written messages on the miniature television screens.

The start-up itself was somewhere between shock and delirium, even with the hard hat and the glycerine-filled inner ear pieces. Even though the heavy steel armour-plated door had commenced its twenty-five-second opening cycle, the double explosion halfway down the fuselage seemed literally to shake the concrete foundations. The thunderous shock waves, steadily building, set up a gentle rocking motion in the aircraft. Behind the aircraft's jet pipes, in the hangar wall, vast chutes had opened, venting smoke and flames into the sub-zero arctic air.

A ground-crew member signalled her out, and with a last look at the CRTs she ordered fifty-five per cent on the power and brakes off. The deadly black shape, carrying a full load of air-to-surface missiles, rolled out over the folded-down shelter door. Erica flicked down her dark visor against the sudden blinding flash of snow and then checked in with ground control.

She met up with L'Estrange's plane and followed him onto the runway. At the briefing he had been designated leader on the Blue team's shipping strike. Afterwards he had laughed nervously, saying that the job should have gone to her. She, after all, was the better pilot. Unfortunately, he had added, the choice wasn't up to him. It was up to the boss of the Blue team, Squadron Leader Thomas; a wiry little Welshman. And Thomas had a chip on his shoulder. He himself was still flying the older Tornadoes when he considered he should have been one of the first to be transferred to the new Blackhawk squadron. Apart from that, he did not like women flying fast jets; any jets come to that. It was as distasteful as the thought of the Anglican church appointing women ministers.

The two aircraft left the winding fjord at a sedate 400 knots, avoiding the possibilitiy of a wirestrike—caused by the hazardous power and communications cables strung out across the fjord—by flying underneath them. They swung right then on a northeasterly course, running up the coast, dodging the multitudinous scattering of small flat islands. Their height—fifty feet. Their problems started abeam the coastal town of Osen, four minutes later.

"Four, this is Two, do you read?" L'Estrange's voice, slightly tense filled Erica's ears.

"Affirmative . . . go."

"Electrical problem . . . INS off line."

"What about standby systems?"

"Nothing showing . . . no failure indications, but everything seems to be winding down." L'Estrange's voice advanced and receded against a background of static. She wondered what he meant by *everything winding down*.

"Your transmission fading, Two."

"Roger, breaking off . . . I'll eyeball it back . . . see you later." The bonedomed head swivelled towards her and she raised a gloved hand, then the other Blackhawk was pulling up and breaking gently left.

Now she was alone with the Blue team's reserve plan. She rapidly analysed the relevant information. Wargame rules applied. That meant she would run up the coast to Vikna before turning left onto a westerly heading. She had the coordinates of the Red frigate which lay two hundred and fifty miles out in the North Atlantic. Remaining at low level over the sea to avoid radar detection, she would attempt to avoid the Red Harriers and press home a missile attack.

The attack itself was closely linked to the Blackhawk's fuel range at low level. According to the wargame rules, since the nearest diversion airfield was 150 miles away, she had to have 300 miles diversion fuel remaining on return to base. The changeable winter weather made diversions an almost daily occurrence. It was because of those rules that she knew the reserve plan wasn't going to work. The Red team, being fully aware of the Blue aircraft's range capabilities and the fuel reserve contingency, could concentrate their aircraft and radar into a known area. And that was why she changed the plan, increasing her risk factor by something like a thousand per cent, taking the Blackhawk inland on a 300-mile detour.

A solid layer of grey damp cloud clung to the mountains as she swung the interceptor inland. With her vocal command of 150 feet ground separation and 500 knots fed into the computer, and the new waypoint at Krokstranda programmed into the inertial navigation system, she sat back and waited for the mountains and their valleys ahead.

The roller-coaster ride would last for eighteen minutes. Eighteen minutes of gut-churning violence. Eighteen minutes of bone-jarring transference from high positive "g" to high negative "g". Of near blackouts and near redouts. Of body-bruising contractions of the anti-g suit as it attempted to keep pace with the frenzied pitch changes of the aircraft. Even experience took a back seat on this ride. This was the tirp where primeval instincts screamed for their freedom. The pilot was nothing more than a passenger. A breathless voyager caught up in a kaleidoscope of near supersonic cloud—impossibly fast images of swirling greys and whites; of milli-second breaks filled with granite blackness. While speeded-up soundtracks of rain, snow and hail, drilled brief and erratic passages over the canopy, and the blurred automated movement of controls maintained the minute capsule on its heart-stopping nine-miles-a-minute journey towards Krokstranda. For Erica her mind juggling fuel figures and navigational problems, it was not the time to be considering the consequences of her actions. First she had to achieve the objective.

Two hundred and fifty miles west of Trondheim the Red frigate radar operators were sweating away the final three minutes. On her bridge the captain, Commander Farnwell, an individual with large ears and an insufficient chin, was concluding that the strike had been aborted. Neither radar, nor the Harrier pilots had reported any "incoming". He checked his watch. Two minutes of the operation remained.

He turned to his number one. "I think we can throw it away then ... don't you."

"I have the feeling they have something up their sleeves, sir."

"What the hell are you talking about, something up their sleeves? We know the endurance figures and we have covered all incoming areas." Farnwell smiled complacently. "I suggest you retrieve the Harriers."

Lieutenant Retallick, a Cornishman who had been raised on the sea, reluctantly nodded his acceptance and moved away. He had a gut feeling about this one, but you didn't talk to Commander Farnwell about gut feelings. If it couldn't be written down it didn't exist. Simple as that.

There were three seconds remaining as the first Red Harrier approached to "land on". Farnwell, hands clasped behind his back, watched from the bridge, mentally chalking up the Red team's first victory of the exercise. Blue team probably got lost, he thought. Or perhaps—his thinking was shattered in the final second as a Blackhawk appeared, virtually in the ship's rigging, travelling at over 1,000 miles per hour. A black shape, no more, gone in an instant, leaving only the terrible thunder of its passage, a roaring in Farnwell's ears that seemed to increase as dizziness swept over him. It would be some seconds before he pulled himself together. Then he would realise they had been "sunk" by a lone rogue aircraft.

Erica had left the frigate, emergency operational power pushing her Blackhawk skyward at over four times the speed of sound. Nothing would catch her now. Nothing except lack of fuel. If her sums were wrong she would never get back. She selected "stud one" and called for recovery, at the same time passing on her weapons state. The sweat was in her eyes as she dropped towards the fjord. The low fuel warning had been flashing for the last twenty seconds. How many miles of flying time were left? How many? She stayed high, waiting for the engines to flame out. Then she would be down to the "one for one": one mile's worth of gliding distance for one thousand feet of altitude and the virtual certainty of running out of height while still among the mountains. But her figures had been right after all; the airfield came up seconds later; and then all that remained was a rapid sequence of landing checks before ducking under the overhead cables and slamming the Blackhawk down on the snow-covered runway.

The refuellers were waiting as she rolled the aircraft to a halt outside the hardened shelter. She motored the canopy open, feeling the sudden rush of freezing air.

The smell of hot engines and kerosene filled her head as she climbed down the steps. Then, removing her hard hat she turned and walked away from the aircraft. That was when the mechanic, who had been hovering nearby, approached her. "Excuse me, ma'am. You heard about Flight Lieutenant L'Estrange, I take it?"

She stopped and turned towards him. "Heard? Heard what?"

The mechanic shuffled his feet uncomfortably in the snow.

"Wirestrike I think, ma'am. Went down in the fjord."

She was appalled. "Did they pick him up ... did he get out?"

The mechanic shrugged. "Don't know."

He knew very well, she thought, as he motioned towards a jeep parked by the shelter. "I can run you over to ops. though."

She was sitting in the locker room. A slumped, white-faced figure, eyes red with burst blood vessels. The flying suit, stained with dark patches of sweat, hid the bruises of a thousand collisions with the seat harness during her low-level flight through the mountains. It didn't matter how tight the straps were, they could never be tight enough. Not that she felt any pain. Not physical at least.

L'Estrange had been killed shortly after leaving her to return to base. The visibility in the fjord had dropped, and no radio call was ever received—which tied in with his report of the electrical problem, everything winding down. *Everything winding down* . . . it didn't make sense. Not that they would be able to retrieve the wreckage and ascertain the cause. The aircraft, with the best part of its take-off fuel load remaining, had exploded on collision with the high tension power cables. A scattering of fragments. Nothing left.

She looked down the rows of lockers. It was all very neat and modern; unlike the dingy British bases which had stood for the best part of half a century. It was also very quiet. Too quiet. The silence became a nagging reminder of his cheerful laughter. She hadn't known him well, but his casual good humour had brightened the wardroom. And now he was dead. First Gene, and then Maudsley, and now L'Estrange. Perhaps there was a pattern. If so, then she wondered whose turn it would be to die next.

At that moment in London, Paul Kitrell had problems of his own. Winter Le Cheminant had been gone too long. It was nearly midday. Paul shivered and went over to the gas fire. Presently, when the heat had softened his chill, he stood up and moved back to the window. There was no sign of Wint beyond the black wrought-iron railings. Nothing but the clutter of parked cars and the grimy sweep of terraced town houses huddled around the tiny park which was the focal point of Westbourne Gardens. Not that November offered much to look at. The stunted trees appeared arthritic with the cold. The coarse grass was as grey as the leaden sky. Unlike the tall magnificent African sky, this one was mean and dirty. The looking-glass of too much human misery. Paul shivered at his imagination and went back to the fire.

He sat in Wint's rocking chair, trying to control his impatience. The last piece of the jigsaw puzzle to be fetched from Bournemouth: a simple enough job. He should have gone with Wint. Ignored the AP man's advice.

"Seven days," Wint had argued. "It's a full week since you arrived. Erica left last Sunday and you've been holed up here ever since. Why throw it away now? You get picked up and what have you got? Nothing. Nothing except some cock and bull story without an ending. On the other hand you do have a valuable item of military equipment, which just happens to be so bloody secret it's not true. Of course, in wartime they'd shoot you . . . come to think of it, they'll probably do the same in peacetime."

"So what are you suggesting?" Paul had replied.

"I'll go. I'll ring Larsen in Trondheim first, with a pecker-up message for Erica, and then I'll go."

"Now way, Wint. You've done enough . . ."

"I've done nothing, Paul. Nothing except give you a bed and pick up a couple of suitcases; which if you think about it implicates me anyway. And if I'm going to hung for a lamb . . . or however that silly bloody saying goes."

Paul had known the old Guernseyman for a long time. It had been one of those spasmodic friendships. Meeting up in different corners of the world; covering wars, political coups, famines, more wars. Each meeting had been spaced by years. Sometimes one, sometimes two, sometimes three. Each space terminated by mild disbelief as he witnessed a telescoping of the ageing process. In the main he put Wint's down to his endless consumption of cigarettes and whisky; that and a two-finger aptitude for typing which had burned more midnight oil than the North Sea had produced. Even so, Wint had always been a cautious man. This foolhardiness was out of character.

"I get the idea you're enjoying this?" Paul ventured.

The straggled eyebrows, which curled upwards at the corners, tilted in mock concern. "Enjoying it? We've been in the game too long, Paul. It's like copulation. The first time blows your head off. After twenty years all you've got left is a damp squib and post-coital depression." The concern

210

dissolved into a faint smile. "Perhaps I'm looking for one last big explosion."

Wint returned shortly after one o'clock. His nose and his ears were bright red from the cold. He was breathing hard, as though he had been running. He slumped exhaustedly into the chair by the desk.

Paul prompted him. "What happened?"

Wint looked up. Still wheezing, he pointed to the sideboard. "Whisky," he gasped. "Get me a whisky."

Paul poured a generous measure and handed it to him. The older man knocked it back in one, shook violently for a second, then slammed the glass down on the desk. "Happened?" he said at last. He put his hand into his raincoat pocket and produced the early edition of the *Evening Standard*. "Not much ... except that you've just become famous. Or infamous, depending on your point of view." He tossed Paul the folded paper.

The photo had been taken a few years earlier, in Afghanistan. Sun-bleached hair, heavy sun-tan, sweat-stained bush shirt. Even so, there was no mistaking the man as a marginally younger version of Paul Kitrell. Or the caption: HAVE YOU SEEN THIS MAN?

Wint pursed his lips. "I assume the murder enquiry is to do with the guy Finlay you told me about ... I mean you haven't been knocking off anyone else, have you?"

Paul ignored the remark. "What about Stubbs

211

in Bournemouth? What did you find out?"

Wint pulled a number of sheets of folded paper from his pocket. "It's all here," he said. "Quite unbelievable. A kind of metal fatigue in the electrics. Apparently induced by prolonged low temperatures . . . metal contraction, that sort of thing."

"He's sure, this guy Stubbs? Not sabotage—just this . . . metal fatigue?"

"Absolutely positive. All the answers came tumbling out of the black box and he's written them up in plain English for you . . . I stashed the recorder in a lock-up at Waterloo, by the way. Here's the key."

Paul took it, dropped it thoughtfully into his cupped left palm. He looked up suddenly. "You did say fatigue induced by prolonged low temperatures?"

"It's down here in black and white."

"Christ! and the planes are in Norway. November thereabouts isn't exactly tropical . . . we'd better do something, quick."

There was a heavy silence before Wint said, "I think we might already be too late."

"Too late? What do you mean too late?"

"When I was in Bournemouth I telephoned Larsen—he's our stringer in Norway I told you about. Apparently a jet fighter crashed this morning near Trondheim."

A cold wave of dread washed over Paul. "Erica! Did she contact him . . . Larsen, I mean?"

"When she first arrived, yes. Nothing since. But

212

don't go getting yourself all screwed up. We don't even know if it was a Blackhawk."

Paul moved over to the desk and picked up the phone.

His friend said: "You're not thinking, Paul."

"Certainly I'm thinking! If we don't tell someone fast, then—"

"Correction, Paul, you *are* thinking, but about the wrong thing. Your young lady is clouding your judgement."

"She's not my young lady, Wint, I've already explained that."

Wint smiled wistfully. "You know something, I shall forever regret belonging to that lost generation of National Servicemen and ration books, and knickers, any access to which required promises of marriage; while only a few years later . . ." He shrugged. "I digress. What I was going to say was—the phone call you are about to make is presumably either to the police or the ministry of defence. What you seem to have forgotten is that someone else is on to you—hence the charming visitor back at your apartment."

Paul replaced the telephone receiver. "So? Probably MI5 . . . or the CIA . . . as I'm an American citizen."

"Or the KGB?" Wint spread his hands. "Anyway, I think it would be prudent to map out some sort of strategy before we call anyone. At this moment you are a liability. An embarrassment to the government. For all they know you could be a Russian agent; and as you have a very valuable

213

piece of their equipment in your possession, and as you have given them the slip for the past seven days, they might be forgiven for shooting first and asking questions later. And even if you're on the level, can they afford to have *The Times* leader writers making you a *cause célèbre?* Good for you maybe, but it's going to send high Richter scale vibrations throughout Whitehall."

"A fine speech, Wint. So what are you suggesting?"

Wint jabbed a forefinger at the electric typewriter on the desk. "Copy, Paul. Copy. Two thousand words should do it. Beginning to end; as you two told me over the weekend. From the funeral at Cambridge . . ."

Paul interrupted. "And get it notarised, so that once I've handed it over nobody's going to play about with it. Yeah, I'm with you." He paused as a thought struck him. "You do realise that by doing what you suggest I'll be implicating Erica? No, Wint, I can't . . . she's signed the Official Secrets Act. I'd be throwing her to the wolves."

"Maybe, maybe not. But better that than the death sentence. You're stalling, Paul, and there isn't the time. If you start now we can have those aircraft grounded by tomorrow."

The typewriter was already clattering as Wint left the room and went to the kitchen to make coffee.

Unseen by both men, a pale blue Ford Fiesta

214

had entered the opposite end of Westbourne Gardens a few minutes after Le Cheminant had arrived back at the house. There was one man in the car, Alexei Karolyov alias Arild Hansen, recently returned from Inverness. At fifty years of age his continuing success and survival had been due to an uncanny sixth sense. That, and a generous amount of guile and good fortune. He had latched on to Le Cheminant two days earlier at the Athenaeum Hotel.

The hotel porter Paul had chosen to leave his suitcaess with had proved to be both a lucky and an unlucky choice. Lucky because he had once done a three-year stretch in Wormwood Scrubs, and therefore had a criminal's hatred for the police, so that when the detective-sergeant had arrived to question Kitrell the previous Friday evening, the porter had made no mention of the luggage he had in his possession.

Paul's choice had been unlucky, also, however, because the porter was still, when the opportunity arose, criminally inclined. Easy money only; nothing too difficult—the job at the hotel was after all his bread and butter. Thus, when Karolyov, seeking Kitrell, had booked into the Athenaeum for one night under the name of Arild Hansen and had started asking him discreet questions, followed by an envelope stuffed with five-pound notes, the porter unhesitatingly told him all he knew. Mr. Kitrell, he said, had left the hotel in something of a hurry. He had been accompanied by a young lady. The police had arrived shortly after that, wishing to speak to Mr. Kitrell. And finally, Mr. Kitrell would very soon be arranging for his baggage to be collected.

It was all so easy. Karolyov watched the man with the thinning grey hair—Le Cheminant—arrive at the hotel and collect the bags. He followed him back to Westbourne Gardens and watched him unload the car. Following that he arranged to have the house staked out. Kitrell was bound to show up sooner or later. And when he did Karolyov would have the flight recorder from the Blackhawk. Whether he would give it to Starling or to his friends in Moscow was something he had not yet decided. As for Kitrell and his elderly accomplice, they would both be dead. Suspected foreign agents warranted little else. The guns in their hands would show they had been desperate men.

It was as Karolyov was parking his Fiesta and preparing for a long wait that George Hinchcliffe, at the ministry of defence, was recovering from the initial shock of a telephone call from Southgate-Sayers. The words "Blackhawk crash" had brought him out in a cold sweat. It wasn't until the air vice-marshal had explained about the wire-strike that Hinchcliffe's heart rate subsided. The call complete, he sank back into his chair and breathed a sigh of relief.

Ever since he had received Blakeley's assessment of Courtney's report he had been back in the poker game. His luck, it seemed, was holding out.

Contrary to first appearances, the Murmansk document had in fact been satisfactorily vague in its findings.

"Tupolev—NATO code-name Badger—aircraft based Murmansk. Reduced crew compliment of 7, due experimental computerised operation. On night October 2 Badger returning home base detected infra-red presence exiting Arctic Circle. Computers confirmed infra-red footprint belonging to latest NATO interceptor—Blackhawk I. Badger computers working on one million interrogations/second 'clobbered' buffer seventeen seconds into search pattern, re-programming plus six point eight seconds. Blackhawk tracked in continuing descent mode. Infra-red photographs indicate flight termination time 2239 zulu. October 2. Position: NO58:09:15 WOO3:50:00."

Blakeley had scrutinised this report and its two accompanying pages of closely typed technical jargon, and his usual long-winded ramblings had been communicated to David Courtney at MI5 in one word: "Inconclusive."

Following that, a curiously reluctant Courtney had agreed to try to obtain more information. In the interim George Hinchcliffe remained joined with him unwillingly in a three-handed poker school, the third player being a newcomer and possible Soviet agent: name, Paul Kitrell. The black box had still not been found, a retired

Scottish newspaper reporter was dead, and Kitrell appeared to be the connecting link. A brother of the pilot who had died in the first Blackhawk crash, apparently. And a veritable Houdini, if his present disappearing act was anything to go by.

By now a third Blackhawk had crashed, and a third young pilot had died. Hinchcliffe sighed. He wondered if they were all getting things wrong somewhere. The trouble was, in this game everyone played their hands so confoundedly close to their chests.

CHAPTER EIGHT

The squadron leader's office was clinically clean, much the same as the locker rooms had been. It was also sparsely furnished and centrally heated. After the sub-zero outdoors the dry heat picked uncomfortably at the back of her throat. Squadron Leader Thomas had lost a pilot. But he was more concerned, it seemed, with a woman who hadn't precisely obeyed his orders.

". . . There are rules and regulations after all. In war games—even in war itself."

Erica's eyes were fixed on the wall map behind Thomas's head. She was still wearing her flying suit. The sweat stains had now dried, leaving white edges around the discoloured patches. Her face reflected weariness. Operational flying had that effect on pilots. It was a game for the young and fit. It was funny, she thought, how flying had been enjoyable with her father. Even on the bleakest of days there had been an element of fun, a sense of easy-going adventure. But those aircraft had not carried guns, and missiles, and bombs. As for the petty rules and regulations, they were a long, long way away; filed neatly behind some desk in Ottawa or Montreal. In the bush there were only three enemies: the elements, the machine you flew, and yourself. The first you regarded with unfailing respect; the second called for thoroughness in checking before flight; and the third, yourself, if you survived your inexperience, the odds against you crashing, at your own hands, were good. Good until the years had rolled up sufficient familiarity for complacency to take a hand . . .

"... It is inconceivable to me—with all my years of service, you understand—that one of my pilots should blatantly disregard a briefing and jeopardise one of Her Majesty's aircraft, not to mention ships, with such a foolhardy stunt . . ."

It had been the year before her father died. Summer. They had just landed from an aerobatic detail in a Stearman. She was feeling pleased with herself. It had gone well; really well. The book on aerobatic flying she had borrowed from one of the local flying instructors had helped a lot. Of course her father didn't know about that: he would think that the stick and rudder precision was due to her natural aptitude. They were walking away from the aircraft when she turned to him. "How was I?"

"Precise," he had replied. "And that's the problem. It was all so precise."

"So what's wrong with that?"

"Nothing, if you intend to be a driver. Being a

pilot, honey, is altogether something else. A pilot feels the aeroplane, becomes a part of it. The result is natural grace rather than a mechanical study in perfection." They walked on in silence towards the wooden shack, which served as office, briefing room, coffee shop for the aviation fraternity of Sept Isles, and general meeting place to shoot the breeze when the days flying was done. Too mechanical, she thought. Too mechanical! But it was exactly as the book said. What else is there?

"... thirty seconds of fuel remaining. Thirty seconds! And what if the field had been clamped. What then?" Thomas's question was clearly rhetorical. "I mean if we all went round behaving like Casey Jones we wouldn't hack it, would we? This is the Royal Air Force, after all ..."

They went into the shack and she said to her father: "So you're saying the book isn't any good?"

He smiled, his eyes creasing into a multitude of sun spokes.

"Of course I'm not. The book is excellent ... to a point. What you must remember, honey, is that we live in a progressive age. We are moving forwards all the time. In doing that we must keep rewriting the rules, looking for things which do not yet exist. Don't forget, there will always be a better way. A truer way. It's up to us to find it and pass it on down the line to the next generation of flyers. Progress, Erica my dear, progress." He had pointed towards the stove then. His way of asking for coffee. And as he had told her a thousand times before, the first step in becoming a pilot was the ability to make a good cup of coffee.

". . . So I think that wraps it up. How long you will be grounded I can't really say. Depends upon the enquiry, you see. Is there any thing you wish to say?"

The images of Canada faded and she looked at the Welshman as if for the first time. He was still smiling in his self-satisfied way. "To say?" she repeated. "Not really." She climbed wearily to her feet.

"Good," he said. "I'll let you know about the enquiry of course. As soon as the powers that be decide, that is." He laughed as if to cover up a feeling of embarrassment.

"There is one thing," she said as she reached the door.

"Yes?"

"Doesn't it ever strike you as inconceivable that we won the last war? I mean, with so much red tape flying around it's amazing we didn't succeed in strangling ourselves before Hitler had even reached Paris."

Thomas sat open-mouthed as she left the room.

At Murmansk the cold disc of sun was three finger thicknesses above the horizon. Fifteen minutes a finger. Three-quarters of an hour of daylight remained. A cold bitter wind ran down the flight line of Tupolevs as Sergio Dzerzhinsky—hands thrust deep in his greatcoat pockets—made his way towards his replacement aircraft.

Once inside he secured the door against the

elements; rubbed his face briefly to generate warmth, and went forward to the flight deck. He couldn't be sure his plan would work. Could he fly the plane alone? Twenty minutes on a simulated dry run would give him the answer. Then, for all her beauty, for all her promises, for all her seductive glances, for all her icy passion, he would slap her in the face. Would scream abuse at her. Would make sure that she, the sky, his ageless lover, took no one else from him.

By the second rye and dry Erica had loosened up considerably. It was early evening when she arrived in the officers' mess. She walked through the anteroom and went down the stairs to the bar. Like other buildings on the base this was also sealed and bombproof. The underground bar was a brightly lit room, tastefully furnished in the Scandinavian manner. The walls were hung, appropriately, with pictures of aircraft. Norway, being a socialist state and more democratic than most, gave senior NCOs the same messing facilities as officers. A few of them were present when she arrived.

She was considering a third drink when Major Stray, who had spoken to her once or twice before, joined her. "Good evening; and how is the war going?"

Erica considered the question for a long moment before saying. "Is that a serious question?"

"If you wish it to be."

"What do you think, Major? It's your country

223

after all. What would happen if the Russians decided to move in on Norway?"

"I think we would stand little chance."

She turned the empty glass in her hands. "Why do you say that?"

"The weather more than anything. The cold. The art of surviving while still fighting. Scandinavians know of these things as do the Russians. But how many of your people do?"

"I think we are aware of the hardships, Major. We do have lectures and training on arctic survival."

"Ah, lectures and training. But the Russians are born to it. Like breathing, they *know* . . . but how many American marines are aware? I say Americans, because they would supply the weight of numbers in a real war. I'll tell you what every Russian soldier is raised on. He knows that, as core temperatures reach ninety degrees and lower, the brain may become so chilled that it loses control of the heating mechanism. Shivering ceases and the brain seems to give up. Then the real enemies arrive: apathy and drowsiness. As often happens the victim may simply lie down, drift off to sleep . . . and never wake again. It is understanding these things deep inside that gives you the edge on surviving. And if you can survive by instinct, then you can fight with total concentration. But for the man who works it the other way around . . ." Stray raised his arms in a gesture of defeat.

"But with all the right survival gear—"

"You must remember that equipment has a

nasty habit of detaching itself from its owner. Especially in a war zone."

"But that must apply to the Russians as well."

"Yes. Except that they put as much importance in their survival gear as in their rifles. They will die trying to recover it, knowing that if they don't they will die anyway."

Colonel Hood arrived as Major Stray was leaving. He pulled up a stool and without preamble said: "You realise the shit has really hit the fan, I take it?"

"Today's op., you mean?"

"Yeah. Just what the hell were you thinking about?"

"That is just the point, sir. I was *thinking*. Not just rushing blindly into a carefully planned trap. It seems to me that wargames are no more than jolly fun. They have no value, because everyone knows what everyone else is doing. I somehow doubt that in a real war the Russians would be as accommodating as that."

Hood didn't bother to hide his approval. "As the boss of the Red air force I shouldn't be intervening in this," he said. "But I am. As of now you're back in the air."

The glass slipped from her fingers and rolled across the bar. "Back flying?" she gasped. "How? I mean . . ."

Hood slipped off the stool. "Never mind the hows and the whys and all that other crap. I did one or two things in Vietnam which were against the rules. The difference was I survived. Doing it their way I'd have been dead."

She looked at his stern face, trying to find a way past it. "Thank you—" she started.

"I don't want your thanks, Lieutenant. They're about as worthless as you are. Just remember I didn't do it for you. I did it for me. I trained you. It's my reputation at stake . . . okay?"

She nodded. "Sir."

"One last thing, get your ass out of this den of iniquity. My pilots don't drink . . . not unless they want a desk job."

He stalked out of the bar, taking his anger with him. Unknown to Erica she had probably got closer to him than anyone else in a long time. His wife and children had been killed in a navy transport plane. The plane had crashed in Hawaii, and it was found that its pilot had been drinking. From that day on Hood had hated the navy. Especially its pilots. The news that Flight Lieutenant Macken had wiped out a Royal Navy frigate single-handed had brought a bitter smile to the iron man's face. Squadron Leader Maudsley would have known the reason, gleaned from a tour of duty on secondment at the colonel's home base in Nevada, but few others did.

It was nearly 3 a.m. when Paul Kitrell finished typing his report. Even then he had his doubts. It all appeared too easy. Too crude. Wint had reasoned that that might well be the case. The engineers who had built the Blackhawk could only have gone so far with testing; time and money were limited, especially when it came to cold-weather trials.

Paul sat back and rubbed his eyes. He didn't understand all the technicalities, but he knew enough to see that metal fatigue in the Black-hawk's starter system could induce a total power-down. And when that occurred, obviously it took away the electrical power required to activate the second stage of the fail-safe programme. There-fore Gene would have been in a situation of having commanded his aircraft to descend, and the computer having acknowledged and placed the aircraft in the descent mode when the failure occurred. No power. No power to activate the switch to manual. No power to rescind the command. No power even to recognise a known voice-print. The aircraft would be trapped, de-scending until it hit the ground.

Paul took a small cigar from a packet and lit it. He inhaled deeply, and reached up with his free hand to massage the back of his neck and a portion of his right shoulder. Too long at a typewriter.

Wint came in at that moment carrying a tray and two mugs of coffee. "All finished, then?" he said, putting the tray down on the edge of the desk.

"More or less. I still don't understand it. I mean how the hell can something like this get past the experts . . . the people who build them?"

"Don't ask me, Paul. Been going on since Daedalus though. You see we can even go back to Greek mythology and find a flying accident. Icarus flying too near the sun. Just as complex in those times as what we've got here. Of course the classic case was the de Havilland Comet, back in the early fifties. They were flying passengers and falling out of the sky ... nothing changes, my friend—except the degree of complexity, perhaps."

Paul stifled a yawn. "So when do we get this thing notarised?"

"Now."

"Now? Do you realise what time it is? Twenty past three in the morning."

"It's late in Norway too."

Paul thought of Erica. She might be flying a Blackhawk at this very minute. Sleep could wait. "You're right, of course. So what's the plan?"

"Coffee first. Then I'll get my solicitor out of bed ... make him earn his money for a change. After that we'll pick up the flight recorder from Waterloo."

"Then what? The police?"

Wint rubbed the stubble on his chin. "No, I think not. We'll go directly to that man Hinchcliffe."

"The minister of defence?"

"Unless they've reshuffled the cabinet since dinner."

Thirty-five minutes later both men left the house, driving off in Le Cheminant's car. Unknown to either of them they had a tail. The streets were deserted, and he kept well back. One man in a pale blue Ford Fiesta. An expert. Alexei Karolyov. The Russian adjusted his spectacles and afforded himself a rare smile. The rats were entering the trap. His right hand slipped inside his jacket and touched the handle of the sheathed knife with an almost erotic pleasure, as his eyes held the distant rear lights of Le Cheminant's car. At last the waiting was over.

Erica Macken was at the briefing at 0400 hours local time. The room was filled with sleepy-eyed pilots, some drinking coffee, some smoking. All of them wishing they were still in bed. Squadron Leader Thomas was in full flood. "This morning's objective is the main Soviet Backfire base in the Kola Peninsula." He addressed the wall map with a long cane. "For our purposes the Kola Peninsula is now here—at Bodo, just inside the Arctic Circle. There will be four flights; one Blackhawk, three Tornado, supported by tanker aircraft during the mission. Not all attacks will be low level, Reindeer and Lapland aircraft will go in at medium level with a shield of electronic counter-measures and a high-speed dash to the point of release for their stand-off weapons. There will be a Tornado CAP (combat air patrol) and tankers forward in your area. Their role will be to deal with an expected heavy MiG force on your way back. Right . . . lights!" The lights dimmed and the projector buzzed into life. "Latest intelligence gen by satellite . . ."

The briefing continued for another twenty minutes. The weather conditions, actual and forecast, were good for the target area. A cold front with associated heavy snow showers was currently passing through Bodo. By the time they arrived the target would be visual. The report that Bodo was experiencing its coldest day of the year at 30° below freezing at the surface held little significance for the aircrews, other than a triple check of their aircraft's heating system prior to departure. But for the Blackhawk it was another step nearer power-down. Another inexorable step towards disaster.

Le Cheminant drove away from Clapham Common slowly and carefully.

After a while he said, "You must have been imagining it."

"No. It was there. A blue Ford. Small. One occupant."

"So where is it now?"

"He could have attached a small magnetic radio bleeper to your car while we were in the house." Paul paused. "Your solicitor guy didn't seem too happy, did he?"

"Stewart? Well, would you? Under the circumstances?"

Paul looked across the darkened car at his friend. "What circumstances?"

"The leggy blonde falling out of the black dress."

"He said she was his daughter."

"I know what he said, but he'd obviously forgotten that I met his daughter about eighteen months ago. Plain little mousey thing. No, that's his 'my wife's gone to stay with her mother' present to himself."

Paul looked back, checking for headlights.

There was nothing. One or two cars going the opposite way, but no tail. Definitely no tail.

"What are you thinking?"

"I'm thinking, Wint, of an old Masai . . . I'm also thinking that collecting the flight recorder from Waterloo may prove dangerous."

"I still say you're imagining it. There's been no blue Ford, or anything else come to that, since we left Stewart's place."

"I don't think there has to be. Is there a quicker way to Waterloo . . . than this one I mean?"

"Sure to be if you're familiar with the back streets. Especially at this time of night. Why do you ask?"

"How does this sound? The man in the car goes to the house after we leave. Extracts information on where we've gone from Stewart. Then hotfoots it to Waterloo to act as reception committee."

"Preferred your magnetic bug idea. Lot less hassle."

Paul said: "When we get to the station I want you to pull up outside, in a place that's well lit. Keep the engine running and your foot on the accelerator. I'll go and collect the box. Should anyone approach the car while I'm gone get to hell out of it. Not Westbourne Gardens though, I have the distinct impression they know about that."

Wint smiled crookedly. "I'll say one thing for you, Paul, you're not without a sense of drama. So where do I go? Back to Stewart's place?"

"No. If they're waiting they've already got to Stewart—as I said before. Best bet might be the AP offices. Safety in numbers and you'll instantly

231

recognise a strange face."

"And you'll follow?"

"With the flight recorder, yes. Then it will be up to one of us to drag George Hinchcliffe from his bed and convince him we're not a pair of escaped mental patients."

Both men fell silent then, each with his own thoughts. Paul thinking of Erica. The red hair, the green eyes, the curve of white shoulder . . . No, damn it. Two nights were all they'd had. He should give her time. Time to get over Gene. All the time she needed. And then at the end of that time, if she still wanted him . . .

Wint swung the battered Audi into Waterloo station. The car braked gently to a halt at the bottom of the wide expanse of steps. "Give me two minutes," Paul said, opening the door. "And keep your eyes open."

Apart from two taxis and a British Rail van the station forecourt was deserted. He checked his watch, 5 a.m., then hurried up the steps into the station. A figure moved suddenly out of the shadows, weaving unsteadily towards him. Paul stopped, his body tense. A scruffy army greatcoat tied at the waist with string formed the bulk of the man. The remainder: dirty white hair falling in waves over his collar, a puffy purple face, and washed-out pale-blue eyes full of emptiness.

"A quid for an old soldier, guv'nor." The tramp held out a filthy hand.

Paul looked around. His uneasiness was still there. He felt in a pocket, grabbed a handful of coins, and stuffed them in the old soldier's hand.

Two minutes later he had the red plastic bag containing the flight recorder and was trotting back to the car. The tramp had disappeared. The station was completely deserted. The bloody lioness! He broke into a sprint. The old man was the lioness. Setting up the prey. Him? Or Wint? Or both? He skidded to a stop at the top of the steps. Nothing had changed. The two taxis, the British Rail van and Wint's Audi—engine still ticking over smoothly. He descended the steps cautiously, looking carefully to left and right as he did so. Too much imagination, he thought. Seeing things that didn't exist. He grinned sheepishly at his caution and slid into the passenger seat. "No problem, Wint. Seems you were right after all." His friend made no reply. "Wint?" Paul turned, and for the first time in the darkened interior he noticed the hands clasped tightly at the throat. As though Wint were trying to strangle himself. Paul reached across and touched the hands, recoiling instantly at the sticky warmth of blood pulsating weakly through his fingers. Now, as he shrank away in horror, Wint's hands slid down his chest to his lap, exposing the bloody fatal wound. His throat had been cut, severing both carotid arteries.

It was as Paul fought against the momentary shock that a dark shape moved up silently behind the car. With the element of surprise on his side, Alexei Karolyov was about to strike for the last time. His bleeper had done its job, the Fiesta was waiting out on the road. He crouched, choosing his moment. That was when the wretched figure of

233

the tramp staggered drunkenly from the station and teetered at the top of the steps. Paul, catching the blurred movement at the edge of his vision and assuming it to be the killer, leapt from the car, confronting Karolyov as he did so. He couldn't make out the face; it was lost in the shadow. Both men froze for a surprised second. Then the Russian was lunging forward, knife hand extended. Paul sidestepped, bringing the plastic bag and the weighty flight recorder round in a sweeping right cross. It connected on Karolyov's left shoulder, sending him sprawling against the car. Seeing the second man coming down the steps toward them, Paul took his chance and ran.

The weather state was *red*. A silent invasion of fog had knocked out the air base as effectively as any Soviet strike. Now it was down to waiting. Running over the briefing, eager to be airborne, ears full of wingmen, fighter controllers, ground intercept controllers, audio indication of nearby ground-radar sites, and one's own missiles' audio chirps which in plain language were saying, "I'm locked onto a heat source, fire me now." Fingers poised over switches which would drop flares to confuse a heat-seeking missile coming towards the aircraft, and containers of chaff to draw away radar-guided weapons.

Erica Macken, strapped into her Blackhawk, restrained herself from calling down to the ground-crew to check the weather state again.

She would be told if it changed. Boredom crept into her brain. She cursed, checked the time and realised she had been strapped into the aircraft for nearly an hour. Her eyes, seeking employment, ran across the instrument panel and down the consoles beside both legs. They paused on a switch labelled "Nuclear Consent" on the lower left console. Pressing that was one action which still had to be performed manually, and even then the switch was only one part of an elaborate coding and protection system designed to ensure that "nukes" were released only when, and by whom, intended. And the awesome need to keep control of all of this while under attack, and flying at speeds up to one mile a second, was now second nature to her.

It was twenty minutes later that the operation was scrubbed. The met. office had decided the fog was in for the day. Erica descended the steps from the cockpit, patted the aircraft affectionately on the nose, and made her way towards the green-lit exit door at the side of the hangar.

She had removed her respirator and now breathed in the freezing fog of the early Saturday morning as she waited for the crew bus. For the moment the cold didn't worry her. She had been thinking of Paul. She had managed, late the previous evening, to put a call through to Larsen, Wint's staffer in Trondheim. Le Cheminant, he told her, had contacted him that very morning. The message was short: "Positive news on the orange box. Action within twenty-four hours. Please contact me or Paul through Larsen soonest."

235

Erica had explained to Larsen the difficulty in making overseas telephone calls from the base—local ones were difficult enough.

"It is not a problem," he had said. "Can you get off the base?"

"It's possible . . . at night."

"Good. Phone me tomorrow and I will arrange to pick you up."

Now, a lonely waiting figure in the swirling mists, she realised it might be possible to get a pass out earlier than tonight. Then, at last, she could find out what had caused the Blackhawk crashes. Discounting L'Estrange's crash as possibly only an unfortunate wirestrike in poor visibility, she was left with Gene's and Maudsley's. Both had crashed in northern Scotland. Both had crashed at night. Somehow night had to be the key factor. As the Blackhawks here in Norway were not carrying out night operations, Erica felt reasonably safe. Yet still L'Estrange's phrase, *everything winding down*, haunted her.

A horn sounded thinly through the fog, followed shortly by the yellow headlights of the Volvo crew bus doing the rounds of aircraft shelters. The air-operated doors opened with a hiss and she joined the unsmiling faces framed by windows.

It was during the long slow drive around the remainder of the dispersals that she learned of her nickname. One she had acquired since her arrival in Norway. The young Norwegian pilot with sandy hair had told her for no other reason than making conversation.

"Ice Princess?" she exclaimed. "Well, it's an improvement on some of the names I've been called . . ."

The young man's voice faded as she turned to the window and the vague black shapes which appeared from time to time through the grey-white fog beyond it. Ice Princess . . . It had never occurred to her before that she might give people that sort of impression. But then she *had* decided right from the beginning that she would not get the name around the squadron of an easy lay. Still, cold? If so, then it was the snobberies of the British that had caused her to behave so. A memory came to her: nothing unusual—the poster for a forthcoming show being held in the NAAFI. And the wording at the foot of the poster, the wording that had been the invitation, had read: ". . . officers and their ladies, NCOs and their wives, and airmen and their women." It had rankled in her mind. It still did.

Suddenly the thought of being a military pilot made her feel almost claustrophic. It had been seven years after all. Seven years of uniforms, of orders, of necessary and unnecessary restrictions. And, in her case, of distorted ambitions.

To analyse a problem you needed experience. Experience was a by-product of years. She was now beginning to understand. You do not cage eagles, her father had once said. His words had been an oblique reference to bush pilots. They belonged to the sky as much as the wind and rain. For them—for seat-of-the-pants aviators who needed nothing more than fabric-covered wings and the song of wind in the wires—freedom. Perhaps after Christmas she would go back.

At that same moment in Murmansk two old men were sitting together drinking. And it was still not yet noon.

"Two girls," Rokossovsky repeated. "High class . . . quite clean."

Sergio Dzerzhinsky winced, as though someone had pulled a molar without first administering anaesthetic. "Thank you for the thought, Milhail, but the winter is in my bones just now." He slid the half-empty bottle across the table. "Perhaps in the spring, my friend. Love is always nicer then . . . even if you do have to buy it."

Rokossovsky laughed. A harsh crackly sound. Like an old crone. "My great, fat, sad, philosophical friend! Love? Whoever said anything about love? I'm talking about sex. Lurid, exciting . . . the stuff you can't get from your wife."

Dzerzhinsky drained his glass. "I'm not married," he said simply.

"I know you're not married. You were too clever for that." Rokossovsky leaned forward and winked. "That's why I've always admired you, Sergio. You were always everything I wanted to be and never had the skill or the guts . . . or whatever it takes."

Dzerzhinsky eyed the gaunt-faced man with the baggy eyes and grey complexion. "Admired? Me? What am I, Milhail . . . the oldest captain in the Soviet air force. No home. No wife. No

238

children. No friends . . . except for you, that is. What is there to admire in that?"

"You miss the point, you bear. You are free. You are a giant. People move out of your way. You speak your mind and get away with it. Me if I had tried but few of the things that you have done . . . a work camp, long ago." Rokossovsky refilled his glass and returned the bottle to Dzerzhinsky.

"You are wrong, Milhail. You are the lucky one. You are the one to be admired. You have a wife and a home and grown-up children. People to miss you when you are gone. People who may need you while you are here."

"Ahh," Rokossovsky dismissed the words with an angry wave of the arm. "It is not good to speak to you when you are this way. Come, we drink. That way you forget your philosophy and I forget my wife."

Dzerzhinsky smiled weakly, climbed to his feet and went over to the wood stove. Whenever he visited it was always the same. Rokossovsky supplied the bottle while he arranged for more wood to be brought to the briefing office. He threw a few damp logs into the cherry-red interior now and listened with satisfaction to the hissing sound. A sound which was company in winter. He looked casually at the untidy room as he returned to his chair by the table. That was something else that was the same. Piles of papers in no apparent order. Yellowed notices pinned to an entire area of wall. It wasn't, Dzerzhinsky had remarked on more than one occasion, so much a filing system as a system of filing. The secret was that Rokossovsky could put his finger on any one item within seconds. To try and change the system would therefore be folly. It would also throw the entire crewing schedule for Murmansk into turmoil.

"My crew," Dzerzhinsky said, lowering himself into the chair. "For the next flight . . . who are they to be?"

Rokossovsky was attempting to light a cigarette. The hand with the lighted match was weaving drunkenly. "Over there," he said, tossing the match at the stove. "On the counter."

"Usual time?"

"Of course. When does anything change in this place?"

Dzerzhinsky put his elbows on the table and leaned towards Rokossovsky. "I want you to notify them that departure time will be two hours later," he said quietly.

Rokossovsky took the cigarette from his lips and screwed up his eyes against the tobacco smoke. "You know I cannot do that, Sergio . . . I need authority."

"You can have mine."

"But that is not procedure. It is . . ."

"To hell with procedure, Milhail! There will be a technical problem on the aircraft. You will make sure the crew do not arrive for those two hours. I plan to leave without them. Furthermore, you will tell no one of this. You understand?"

"Ah, Sergio, what are you saying? How can I do these things? I need the proper authorisation. The colonel, at least."

"I will get it for you then." Dzerzhinsky pushed his chair back and stood up. He went over to the counter and shuffled through the clutter of papers until he found an internal memo signed by Colonel Vorontsyev. He folded the paper neatly, slipped it into his tunic pocket and returned to his chair.

Rokossovsky's gaze seemed to penetrate and question. The rheumy eyes with the baggy folds of skin beneath them suddenly narrowed in understanding. "You are going to forge the order!" The words were spoken in hushed disbelief."

"Forge, Milhail? Forge! What do you know of these things?" Dzerzhinsky picked up the vodka bottle and filled both glasses. "You know, my old friend, you were right."

"Right? Right about what?"

"Love and sex . . . what better way to spend a bitterly cold winter's night?"

Rokossovsky laughed. "And you too were right, Sergio. Forgery . . . I am but a simple man. What do I know of such things?"

CHAPTER NINE

In London that Saturday afternoon it was raining. A fine misty rain that clung and soaked through to the skin. Courtney was sharing Hinchcliffe's umbrella as the two men made their way down Shaftsbury Avenue.

"A bloody mess then," Hinchcliffe said savagely.

"Not irretrievable though, George. We'll get him."

Hinchcliffe snorted, a sound of disbelief. "This other chap that was involved . . . the one who was killed earlier this morning . . . what was his name again?"

"Le Cheminant. He was a staffer with Associated Press."

"Yes, yes. Le Cheminant. What was he? French?"

"Channel Islander. Originated from Guernsey."

"And you think he was involved in this matter?"

"Had to be. He'd been hiding Kitrell for nearly a week. According to his solicitor chappie in Clapham Common!"

Hinchcliffe sidestepped two girls as they ran laughing out of a side street. "Speaking of him, what happened exactly?"

Courtney smiled. "Oh not much. We threw the Official Secrets Act at him and the promise of twenty years in the tower. He'll stay quiet. Funnily enough he was more concerned about his wife finding out what he'd been up to. Anyway he told us enough, don't you think?"

"That's what I find so puzzling, David. Why would this Kitrell bother to make a statement and get it notarised? Assuming he's a Soviet agent, why not simply take the goods and run?"

"Cover, George. Everyone needs a cover. Also bear in mind he didn't have the flight recorder at the time. When he wrote that statement, it was still locked up at Waterloo station. Should he have been picked up before he collected it he had the perfect cover story. From what he told Stewart about it, it was clearly pretty sensational stuff."

"But this Kitrell took it with him from the solicitor, you say?"

"No problem, George. We'll get it back."

Hinchcliffe felt anger rising inside him. "How long then?"

"For what?"

"Catching this spy of yours!"

The two men were approaching the bustle of Piccadilly Circus. "Not long, George; my chap should be checking in today ... wouldn't be surprised to find he's got Kitrell with him."

Hinchcliffe plucked at Courtney's sleeve and brought him to a halt. "And this one, David," he

244

said quietly, "make sure he's alive. We need to know what kind of network they have in the RAF." The defence minister held up his hand and hailed a taxi. "Give you a lift somewhere?"

"No thanks . . . I'll keep you posted then."

Hinchcliffe called his address in Eaton Square to the cabbie, lowered his umbrella, and opened the door. "Make sure it's not too long, David; I'd like to have a few days of peace before the family descends on me for Christmas."

Courtney stood in the rain and watched the taxi pull out into the traffic flow. Alive, George had said. In that case he prayed to God that Karolyov had not already found him.

Erica stood there in the bar, trembling, rooted to the spot. It was as if whenever she received news it was always of another death.

They had left the military base over one hour earlier, she almost happy to be out of uniform, content to sit back and enjoy the forty-five-kilometre drive around the fjord to the city of Trondheim. Larsen, a tall studious-looking man with short white-blond hair, had chatted comfortably throughout the journey. Even his fast driving through the foggy conditions had not unnerved her. He was a very competent driver. Also, he had pointed out, the Volvo was built like a tank. Even if they hit anything there would be no problem. Unless, he added with a laugh, it was another Volvo.

As for news from Paul, there had been nothing.

245

They would try again when they reached Trond-heim.

Larsen had suggested lunch. She had wanted to phone Paul first. They had compromised and gone to a small hotel behind a tall black church. The hotel was run by a friend of Larsen. He sat her in a small red-furnished bar with a brandy and the menu, and went off to the reception area to make the telephone call. He was away for nearly fifteen minutes and when he had returned his eyes were clearly troubled.

"You got through?" she'd said, standing up and walking towards him.

"A man called Le Cheminant!" he replied. "Did you know him?"

"I stayed at his house in London with Paul for two nights . . . Why do you ask?"

Larsen said disbelievingly, "He's dead. He . . . he was murdered last night . . . the early hours of this morning."

It seemed a long while before either of them moved, then Larsen steered her gently to a seat. He called through the red velvet-hung archway which served as the entrance to the bar, and when no one came he went behind the bar and poured two large brandies.

"Drink this," he said, settling down on the stool opposite her.

She took the glass mechanically and put it down on the table. "Murdered? How? What about Paul . . . what's happened to him?"

Larsen swallowed half his brandy at one gulp. "I couldn't get through to Le Cheminant's house. I

246

called the AP office . . . difficult on a Saturday as I said earlier . . . skeleton staff only. Anyway I managed to get hold of someone in the end. They said the police had been there all morning. It seems they are looking for Paul Kitrell."

"The police! Looking for Paul . . . I don't follow."

Larsen said: "I think they call it wanting him to help with their enquiries."

"You mean they suspect Paul. That's ridiculous."

"I am sure it is," Larsen replied with a small sad smile. "We also have the same police. The same problems."

"What else did you find out?"

Larsen outlined what he knew, which was precious little. One fact it appeared had been ascertained; a man who fitted the description of Paul had been seen running from the scene of the crime.

Larsen took a plastic pouch of tobacco from his pocket and began rolling a cigarette. "Perhaps," he said, putting the thin cigarette between his lips, "perhaps you should tell me exactly what is going on. I think this friend of yours, Paul Kitrell, may need some help."

At first she was uncertain. How did you trust one man in a city full of strangers? How did you dare confide in this one or that one? It was stark necessity, which eventually convinced her, the memory of talking to Paul in London. Someone had been looking for the flight recorder. Much as Paul had thought, someone, it seemed, had even been prepared to kill for it. Except that they had killed poor Wint. Possibly by mistake. If so, then

247

they would now be after Paul.

It took the best part of an hour to outline the story to Larsen. Throughout it all he had listened attentively. At the beginning he had taken a notepad from his jacket pocket. But the pen in his right hand had never moved. It was when she had finished that he put the pen and the notepad away. "It would be wiser," he said, "if nothing is written of this."

She looked at his quiet grey eyes. "What do you think . . . is there anything you can do?"

Larsen shrugged. There was doubt in his voice when he said: "I think it is not possible, Miss Macken. Playing games with governments can be dangerous. You understand that what you have told me can be construed as espionage? In Norway it can still be the death penalty for such a crime."

"But don't you see, we have been trying to uncover the truth? It's the government themselves who are suppressing it."

"Perhaps. But they have the right. They are the government. They are the people who make the rules."

Erica's eyes flashed. "Are you saying you won't help?"

"Not exactly. I said it is perhaps not possible to find an answer. But I will try." Larsen finished off his brandy. "So, I think our first task is to find your Paul Kitrell."

"How do we do that from here?"

Larsen tapped the side of his nose with his forefinger. "Easily, I think. We are in the information business, after all. I will call London straight away." He stood up and moved across towards the archway, and the corridor which led to the reception desk. "Something I meant to ask you," he said stopping and turning around. "The crash yesterday . . . in the fjord. Was that a Blackhawk?"

Erica looked up. "Yes, but it was a wirestrike, and in daylight. It couldn't have been connected with the other two. As I explained, they crashed at night."

"And you think the night is a key factor?"

"That, and possibly northern Scotland, yes. What else is there?"

"Perhaps something . . . perhaps nothing. We will see." Larsen turned and went through the velvet-draped archway.

Forty-five kilometres away, in an aircraft shelter named "Delta 5," Erica's Blackhawk maintained its dark secret. Laden with its full complement of bombs and missiles the black interceptor looked nothing less than what it was, a messenger of death. From its delta wing form and small canard foreplanes, to the thickening fuselage which ran aft of the cockpit and housed two side-by-side F404 engines, and the two fins which angled up and slightly out from the twin jet pipes, it was the killer of the future. A technological leap into the twenty-first century. A marriage of carbonfibre, tomorrow's electronics, superplastic-formed titanium and aluminium-lithium.

Its undiscovered Achilles heel lay in a single

complex piece of metal weighing less than a hundred milligrams—and in the aircraft's cold-weather trials, or lack of them. Behind schedule from the first year, corners had been trimmed, if not actually cut. Kitrell and L'Estrange had therefore died because of a government department timeframe. A timeframe with no room for sufficient high-altitude cold-weather operations. A timeframe which now had resulted in the almost human fraility of NATO's latest inter-ceptor: susceptibility to prolonged and extensive cold.

The icy feathers of swirling fog continued to cling to "Delta 5"; a premature shroud as if sensing the death within. But it would not be yet. The Blackhawk with the legend *Flt. Lt. Macken* stencilled neatly beneath the canopy had three hours of flight remaining—one hundred and eighty minutes. One hundred and eighty minutes in which to die of cold.

It was Sunday. London's Gatwick airport was early morning busy. Crowds of package tour holiday-makers lined the check-in desks. The annual winter migration to the sunshine. Paul Kitrell, suffering from the debilitating effects of fear and lack of sleep, blinked at the almost painful glare of neon lights in the building. He kept walking. It was as if that one simple act would make him invisible. To pause and look confused might draw attention. He had thought about invisibility for the last twenty-six hours.

Ever since Wint had died.

The house in Westbourne Gardens had of course been out of question as a refuge. So had Stewart's place on Clapham Common. Which left the AP offices. Too late; the police would have identified Wint, would have started their systematic enquiries. And he, Paul, was still wanted for Finlay's murder.

He didn't know the answer. For once he seemed totally uncertain. All he did know for certain was that, with Finlay dead, and now Wint, he had an icicle's chance in hell of reaching the cabinet minister, Hinchcliffe. He had to stay invisible. And he had to get out. Where to? The answer to that was surprisingly simple. It came without reasoning. Norway. He had to get to Trondheim. He had to find Erica. Warn her. Warn all the Blackhawk pilots. He would take the flight recorder with him as well as the statement. That was the proof. Larsen would help, of course, and between them they could surely do something. Surely to God they could do *something*?

He rounded the corner of a row of check-in desks and saw the SAS sign immediately. Scandinavian Airline System. And SAS flew to Norway. He walked past the counter, checking for police presence. It took a minute or so to negotiate his way through the crowded check-in areas; then, around the far corner, he picked out the dark uniformed figure of a police constable standing by the door marked DOMESTIC DEPARTURES. He turned away and walked slowly back to the SAS desk. His scalp was tingling by the time he got there. He touched his forehead lightly and found he was sweating. Fear. The airline clerk was on the phone, talking to someone about a computer being down. Paul shuffled his feet impatiently, expecting the policeman to stride around the corner at any second.

The clerk having finished his telephone conversation, replaced the receiver and turned towards him. "Yes, sir?"

"Oslo via Bergen," Paul said as casually as he could. His destination was really Bergen, but the Oslo ticket might throw any pursuer for at least an hour or two.

"When for, sir?"

"Today . . . the ten thirty-five this morning."

"Will that be one way or return, sir?"

Paul had already thought of that. "Return." Unremarkable. Just another business man.

"And will that be tourist, sir?" For the first time Paul noticed the accent. Scottish. Not unlike Jamie Finlay. The clerk repeated the question.

"Sorry," Paul replied. "Yes, tourist will be fine." He pulled out his wallet, extracted his American Express card, and slid it over the desk. The police might be looking for him, but he had to believe the credit companies still kept their data banks confidential.

Where to now? Paul realised he was hungry. And there were three hours to go before the departure of flight SK516 at 1035 hours. He stopped and pulled out his wallet. In it he carried his passport and jab records as well as credit cards and cash. And that was the next problem. No cash. He wondered if he could get a cash advance against one of the credit cards and decided against the idea just as quickly. Lengthy questions at banks might create suspicion. He delved into a smaller pocket of the wallet and found three folded-over notes. French francs. Three twenty-franc notes. Something left over from a stop in Paris many months earlier. He went to the first bank with a free teller and cashed the notes. Enough to eat with—four pounds and seventy-one pence. He almost laughed. There was nearly a thousand pounds of his money at Wint's house. He wondered whether he would ever get it back, or if it would be confiscated. Either that or one of Wint's distant relatives would be receiving an unexpected windfall.

Walking away from the bank he followed the restaurant signs and took the escalator to the next floor. A bookshop was directly opposite him as he stepped off. His eyes felt too tired for anything but sleeping, but a newspaper was an effective shield. From the bookshop he returned past the escalators, saw the gold lettering on the red background: London Pride Buffet and Bar. Reassuringly it was as busy as the rest of the airport. Easy, in such a place to remain invisible. It was following the cheese sandwich and the cup of watery tea that he again faced his final problem. The most difficult problem of all. How would he get on the aircraft without being spotted when all departure gates were being monitored by the police?

Two hours later Paul had moved out of the buffet area and was sitting on the balcony which looked down on the floor below. "God in heaven," he muttered, "there has to be a way." But there wasn't; he had known that for some time now. He had worked methodically through the options. It was impossible. Of course, the ideal situation would be an unofficial flight from a small disused airfield. But how the hell did you arrange that?

He went through the names in his address book. Each one seemed more distant the more he considered what he would be asking them. They weren't true friends anyway. Not the sort to go out on a limb for you. And this was a hell of a limb after all. Defeat was staring him in the face now. The Norway flight would be leaving shortly.

The same tannoy message was repeated for the third time in what seemed as many minutes. "Will the passenger recently arrived from Milan please collect their blue suitcase from the second floor." The female voice sounded bored. At that moment Paul almost envied her. Her only problem, it appeared, was worrying about a forgetful passenger's item of luggage. He went back to the seemingly insoluble equation of finding an escape route. Back to the beginning, he said to himself. Run through it again. But the warmth in the Gatwick main terminal was lulling him towards sleep. He fought to keep his eyes open. The beginning! Back to the beginning. The time of

Wint's death.

He had remained on the streets. At seven o'clock that morning he had found a small cafe open down near the embankment. He had loitered over a greasy breakfast as long as he could, then left and walked the streets again. A little later that morning he had gone into a travel agent, enquiring the flight times to Oslo. He had booked nothing; leaving the country would not be easy, he had yet to work that one out. Distracted and uncertain, he had paid no attention whatsoever to the thickset man, wearing steel-rimmed spectacles, waiting behind him at the counter.

At a nearby shop he had purchased a small suitcase, a shirt and underpants, and a raincoat. After that he had gone to Charing Cross station, washed and shaved in the public convenience, changed into the clean clothes, and put on the raincoat. Following this general freshening up he had packed the flight recorder along with the dirty laundry into the suitcase and taken the underground to Heathrow.

Most of the day he had spent checking out different terminals, hoping to find a way through. In the end he had decided against it. There were too many police watching the departure gates. It was late that evening when he decided to try Gatwick early the next morning. He took the train back to London, happier when he arrived there and was absorbed into the anonymity of streets.

He found an all-night cinema in Soho showing girlie movies and dozed there fitfully while a repetitive sequence of third-rate starlets did their unsuccessful best to appear sexy and appealing.

When daylight came he caught the first train out of Victoria and staggered into Gatwick airport at around seven o'clock on a dark and unbelievably cold Sunday morning. The train fare had taken the last of his money. He could no longer find any logical reason for his movements. His decisions were becoming totally irrational. Tiredness, hunger and cold, were all taking their toll . . .

The tannoy sounded again. This time a male voice spoke in "Berlitz" Italian, repeating the message about the passenger from Milan and the blue suitcase. About time, Paul thought. Even if the guy was an Italian national and didn't speak English, he'd be bound to turn up now for his luggage.

A young police constable moved across the edge of his vision; the range was less than twenty yards. Paul raised his newspaper. His stomach turned over. When he looked again there were three uniforms, a sergeant and two constables. One of the constables was tying a wide white ribbon to a pillar. The white ribbon was carried across the corridor out of Paul's field of vision. A knot of passengers was beginning to congregate now. And more police. Paul glanced nervously behind him, back towards the buffet. More inquisitive holiday-makers were drifting towards the hubbub.

He checked his watch. Ten o'clock. The crowd had grown considerably as he moved out from the row of blue and green chairs. Then through the bobbing heads he saw the long wide expanse of empty corridor beyond, now completely cordoned off. He chose a man with a sheepskin jacket and a friendly face. "What's happening? Any idea?"

The man, without turning his head, said: "Happening? Some joker's left a suitcase unattended. They," he indicated the army of police, "think it's a bomb."

A man beside them turned and said: "Why they don't have army blokes at these airports I'll never know . . . they're the experts after all."

Sheepskin jacket smiled in agreement. "I was army, once. Best years of my life."

"Me too. Out in Germany, were you?" The two men drifted off into an instantly familiar conversation, only made possible by their once having belonged on some crusty RSM's parade square.

It was going to be easy after all. Clearly every copper in the place would be up here on crowd control for the next half-hour or so. Paul went down the escalator and walked quickly to the men's toilets. One minute later he emerged, hurried across to the desk and handed over his suitcase.

"You'd better hurry, sir, the flight's already been called."

He thanked the young lady and, clutching his boarding card, ran to International Departures. Ten minutes later he was boarding Flight SK516, London Gatwick to Oslo via Bergen. The quickest way to get rid of the police! A bomb scare . . . why hadn't he thought of that? Why? He settled into the window seat, fastened his lap strap, and was instantly asleep, He didn't see the thickset man in

257

the slouch hat and round steel-rimmed spectacles who boarded the plane last of all.

Alexei Karolyov relaxed in a seat two rows behind him. His eyes were fixed on Paul. He was glad he had not reported in or asked for help. Everything had worked out perfectly.

There had been at least a hundred occasions when he could have taken Kitrell out, but he had been, in the great Russian tradition, patient. And as soon—after the travel agent—as he had known where the American was planning to go, he had only to wait. He had decided there was more in it for him if the flight recorder found its way back to Moscow. And Kitrell was doing exactly what he wanted him to do. Carrying it out of the country. If it worked, all well and good—he could collect it on the other side. And if not, if Kitrell was stopped, the Russian could always move in, flash his MI5 card, and make Starling happy instead.

The bomb scare idea was part of his KGB training. It never failed. And now his mission was over. Except for the execution, and after that the red plastic bag. The one now in Kitrell's suitcase. The plastic bag from the baggage locker at Waterloo station, which contained the Blackhawk flight recorder.

Flight SK516 landed at Bergen at 2 p.m. local time. Half an hour late. The delay had been due to fog and had given Paul a few anxious moments when he realised the flight might divert to Oslo. Time was critical. In getting to Erica every

258

second counted.

After what seemed an eternity of circling and one aborted attempt at landing, the Scandinavian pilot finally brought the airliner down. To Paul, his face pressed against the window, it seemed that the snow-settled airfield only came into focus as the aircraft's wheels thudded gently onto the runway. And even then the visibility appeared to be no more than a couple of hundred yards.

Leaving the flight was no problem, except for the SAS girl who insisted on altering his ticket to show the Bergen–Oslo portion was still in credit. After that he had found a pay phone, changed the last of his sterling into Norwegian currency, and tried to contact Larsen in Trondheim. His office said he was out but would be in later that afternoon. Paul had mouthed a silent curse. The girl on the other end of the phone had asked if there was any message. Paul said he would call back. He was reading the sign on the wall in front of him: "Bergen Air Services—Charter Flights."

Half an hour later he was strapping himself into the co-pilot's seat of the twin-engined Piper Aztec. His credit card again. The pilot, a pipe-smoking old veteran who had introduced himself as Arni, reached across and locked the aircraft's door. Paul turned and looked towards the terminal. The man in the slouch hat had gone. Even so the uneasy feeling remained. He had caught the man's glance as he left the terminal. Perhaps it was nothing. No one could have followed him from London. No one could have guessed his movements. But still it worried him. The eyes especially. He had seen those eyes behind their spectacles before. Quite recently. But he couldn't remember. He was still dog-tired—maybe his mind was going.

The flight lasted an hour and forty-five minutes. Arni—who wasn't given much to talking—sat hunched over the controls, pipe clenched between his teeth. Paul had tried to drag some conversation out of him, but had given up after the third monosyllabic reply. Long before they had reached the halfway point he was being lulled to sleep by the hot air from the aircraft's heating system.

It was dark when they landed and taxied up to the terminal of Trondheim's civil airport. That was when Arni became talkative.

"Do you have a hotel arranged, Mr. Kitrell?" he said.

"No. I have to phone a friend . . . he will make the necessary arrangements."

The fog had cleared completely now, and a bitter wind howled across the airport. Paul's ears were hurting long before they reached the terminal building. "God, it's cold."

"You get used to it after a while," Arni replied.

Paul forced a laugh. "I'd rather not."

The two men entered the oven-like building. "There's no happy medium, is there?"

"I do not follow."

Paul said: "Freezing outside, while inside you take a sauna."

Arni shrugged. "You get used to that also after a time." He motioned towards a row of public telephones. "Telephones . . . to call your friend."

Paul crossed to the telephones and dialled. "Mr. Sven Larsen, please."

"Who is calling?"

"Kitrell. Paul Kitrell."

"You wait one moment please, Mr. Kitrell."

"I'll do that." Phone pressed to his ear, Paul turned casually to look at the Sunday passengers. All, he observed, were dressed to cope with the arctic conditions. Something he needed to do at the first opportunity. Arni, he noticed, was waiting politely, just out of earshot.

"Hello . . . Hello?"

"Hello. Sven Larsen?"

"Yes. That is Paul . . . Paul Kitrell? Where are you?"

"At Trondheim Airport."

There was a pause as Larsen caught his breath. "You are here? But how . . . never mind. I will be there to collect you in twenty minutes. Where will you be waiting?"

"Is there a bar?"

"Yes, I think so."

"That's where I'll be then . . . you can't miss me. I'll be the only one dressed for a wet English summer."

Larsen laughed distantly and put the phone down.

"No problems?" Arni said, moving across to join him.

"All sorted out. He's on the way."

Arni inspected his pipe for a moment then stuck it between his yellowed teeth. "Good," he mumbled. "Perhaps you will let me buy you a

261

beer . . . after such an expensive charter it is the least I can do."

Paul accepted for no other reason than he was without any more hard cash. Credit cards might pay for charter flights and airline tickets, but you could hardly walk into an airport bar and buy a beer with one.

"You're going back to Bergen tonight?"

"I think so," Arni replied in between sips of beer. "Not much happening here." He noticed Paul eyeing his beer. "The young pilots only observe the no-drinking rules so that they may get as old as us. After that it is not so important."

Paul reached into a pocket and pulled out his pack of small cigars. There were only three left. He lit one and went back to his beer. "So how long have you been flying, Arni?"

"A long time," he said flatly. "Sometime I think too long. Good days and bad, like everything else." He checked his watch. "Will you excuse me a moment. I need to phone through to the weather office . . . make sure Bergen is still good, you understand?"

Paul nodded and watched him walk down to the far end of the almost deserted bar. He could just about make out the wall telephone. Arni removed the receiver and dialled three numbers. It was during his conversation that Paul had the feeling something was wrong. Arni turned from time to time to look back at him. As if checking to make sure he hadn't left. Paul glanced at his watch. Larsen should arrive in five more minutes. He finished the beer and stubbed his cigar out in the glass ashtray by his left elbow.

Arni returned as he lifted his small suitcase onto a barstool.

"You are going? But your friend is not here yet." Paul sensed tension in the pilot's voice.

"Any minute," he said holding out his hand. "Anyway, thanks for a smooth flight and thanks for the beer ... perhaps catch you again some time."

Arni took the proffered hand reluctantly. "When do you go back to Bergen?"

"Don't know ... why do you ask?"

Arni shrugged. "Oh ... just that it is sometimes possible we have an empty plane returning. Perhaps we could do you a special price."

"I'll bear that in mind," Paul said, and started walking towards the opening which led back to the passenger concourse. Arni followed. They literally bumped into a tall, blond-haired figure five paces later.

"Paul Kitrell?" the man said.

Paul hesitated. "Sven Larsen?"

Larsen smiled. "That is right. You said to look out for the wet English summer ... " They shook hands.

"This is Arni," Paul said. "Flew me in from Bergen."

"The weather is better now, I think," Larsen said, eyeing the pilot warily.

Arni nodded. "Yes, better." He turned to Paul. "Remember, Mr. Kitrell, should you want to return to Bergen, to phone our office."

"I'll do that, Arni ... be seeing you."

The older man slotted his pipe back between his teeth and walked slowly away down the concourse. "Strange guy," Paul said.

"Strange? In what way strange?"

"I don't really know, Sven. Just a feeling I had." A light twin-engined aircraft taxied up to the building at that moment, sending a sweeping shaft of white light through the tall windows.

Larsen turned away. "The car is just outside."

Paul followed. "Have you heard from Erica?"

"Today. I have seen her today."

Paul gave a sigh of relief. "Thank God, she's safe. Where is she now?"

"Back at the military base." Larsen held the door open.

Paul shuddered at the sudden blast of cold air. "Is it far to the base?" he shouted above the wind.

"Yes, quite far."

"We can phone her, though?"

"I don't know . . . The Volvo there is my car . . . she has always called me. It is possible perhaps. We will try from my house." He opened the driver's door. "The door is unlocked . . . a little stiff, that is all . . . this weather, you know."

Paul settled into the passenger seat as Larsen gunned the engine into life and engaged reverse. It was then that Paul looked back and saw the face of Arni pressed against the glass of the exit door. He couldn't be sure, but as Larsen pulled away Arni seemed to be writing something down.

"There is something not right, Paul?"

"Just that pilot . . . No, my imagination. I'm too tired to be thinking straight. Still, I'm here now.

Has Erica told you anything about what's going on?"

Larsen kept his eyes on the road ahead. "Everything. Today. It was after I heard about Winter . . . I told her, of course. She seemed to think you were in a lot of danger."

"She wasn't wrong," Paul said. "Did she tell you about Finlay?"

"The man in Scotland, you mean?"

"Yes. He was the one who found the flight recorder in the first place. And he's dead too."

Larsen drew in his breath sharply. "What was he? This man Finlay?"

"At one time a reporter, same as you and me. Also an ex-air force pilot. Something of an aviation expert."

Larsen raised his hand to shield his eyes. "Some drivers are not fit to be on the road." He flashed his headlights on main beam. The other driver dipped his. "Better. Now, back to our problem . . . you do not mind that I say *our?*"

"Definitely not. The more shoulders to the wheel on this one—"

"Shoulder to the wheel? Ah yes, I see. You have plans made?"

"Yes. Except I can't implement them. I'm a wanted man."

"So, I implement them for you. Is that what you mean?"

Paul looked across at the man he had just met. "I should warn you, Sven, it's dangerous. I mean, bloody dangerous. Whoever it is who wants the flight recorder back is stopping at nothing; you do

265

appreciate that?"

"Yes, I know what you are saying," Larsen said in a gentle voice. "So what else is new in our business?"

Paul smiled to himself and sank back into his seat. Once all of this was sorted out, he promised himself, he was going to sleep for a week.

CHAPTER TEN

It was Monday. The last of the engines' thunder died in the early morning light. The reds, oranges and whites of afterburners, the startling effect of shock diamonds, the quiet rustle of jet efflux down through the brittle dawn; all had gone. The wind picked up then and dispersed the remaining memory of kerosene and hot engines, before drifting loose snow into the telltale maze of tyre tracks. Five minutes later the military base was nothing more than a bleak, snow-swept coastal plain.

At twenty-four thousand feet the three-plane element of Blackhawks streamed white contrails towards the north. Erica Macken, flying number three in the Reindeer flight kept her eyes locked on the number two aircraft. The computer was flying deadly accurate formation, but even so she monitored. She always monitored. Directly in front of her the head-up display projected on glass carried comprehensive information; heading, pitch ladder, airspeed, altitude, g-loading, time to destination, slant range to target, computed bomb impact point, bomb fall line and current weapons state. Lower down on the right side of the cockpit the dolls-eyes flickered white and black in time with her breathing. She lifted her eyes briefly and saw the Tornado element high above. An umbrella of white streamers. The only change on today's operation was that this time the Lapland flight—the second element of Blackhawks—was going in at low level.

Bodo—today representing the Kola Peninsula again—was nine minutes away. Nine minutes and still no sign of defending fighters. She looked left and forward to the lead aircraft. Sanderson. Then back to the number two. Cox. Eight minutes thirty seconds. They too would be waiting for the missiles. This was the time when reality took over, when the game ended and the war began. Now you were in a fighter. Now you were the hunted. Now the missile could be sliding up the enemy's range bars towards you. Now you were face to face with death. Not simulated. Not pretend. But real.

Sanderson's voice: "Reindeer aircraft, buster power . . . GO."

She passed the order on. Simultaneously the three aircraft went to maximum power, leaving a trail of sonic booms echoing in the mountains below. The timing had been precise, coinciding with the Lapland flight's approach, hugging the terrain far below. Theoretically the deception would draw away the defenders' attention long enough for the low-level strike to hit the target. Especially as the higher level Blackhawks would continue to penetrate deep into the defenders' territory, suggesting a possible second target.

They were inland of the Lofoten Wall when Sanderson ordered subsonic cruise and descent. The three aircraft swept a giant curve of white vapour trails and picked up a reciprocal heading. Now they would hit that second target—the Backfire base—on their way home. No longer a game. Reality.

Cox called: "MiGs . . . eleven o'clock . . . high."

"Bloody callsign, Reindeer Two."

"Boss."

"One to Reindeer aircraft, one fifty feet . . . GO."

The three black delta shapes dropped down into the mountainous terrain east of the fishing town of Nordfold.

"One to Reindeer aircraft, ETA one minute and thirty seconds. Watch out for SAMS."

Erica's sense of panic mounted. She felt cold. Beneath her pressure suit the sweat was running freely, chilling her sides, her waist. She flicked her eyes up and checked the rearview mirror. No enemy aircraft. No missiles. Not yet. Sanderson in the lead aircraft ordered line astern. Attacking formation. Thick black smoke drifted up out of the horizon seconds later. The target.

She saw the missile launch as Cox's ECM equipment screamed in her ears. "Reindeer Two . . . Three . . . missiles four o'clock."

He knew from his training that there was one slim chance of avoiding heat-seeking missiles. A sudden and dramatic change in direction. A devastating high-g manoeuvre. It was not guaranteed, and you needed to time any evasive action right down to the last possible second. Cox, out of inexperience, was too early. The words "missiles four o'clock" had hardly been received before he was ordering maximum power and climb from his computer. The aircraft rocketed skywards in a zoom climb intended to make the missiles overshoot. Instead the pair of SA-7 Grails, with time in hand, remained locked on to the heat source.

Sanderson's voice was curt as ever. "Still with you, Two ... one mile ... check your mirror. Chop your throttles and reverse when they're on your tail. Reindeer Three close up."

Erica took the number two slot, following the lead aircraft into the target. Cox was gone now. If the missiles hadn't got him the MiGs would.

The flat expanse of airfield suddenly filled the windscreen. Aircraft, hangars, smoke, a barrage of AAA fire, figures running.

"One pulling up ... GO."

One thousand ... two thousand ... she followed her leader, releasing her bombs at the same time. Then it was maximum power and run. But the MiGs were waiting. Six of them. Sunlight glinting off perspex in the tall blue arena. It was the classic manoeuvre, out of the sun. Before either pilot knew what was happening the lead MiG had hit at Reindeer One. They were at twenty-eight thousand feet as she watched Sanderson hurtle from the sky, executing an aileron roll as he did

so. She tried, as any good wingman, to stay with
him, but it was futile. She realised that as the MiG
drifted into her mirror. The Blackhawk flicked
violently over and down, pulling plus nine g's. Her
vision tunnelled to the point of blackout. Her eyes,
mouth, entire face, sagged painfully down, the
face mask trying to rip away from her lower jaw.
Easing off, she drifted onto the MiG's tail and held
him for four seconds. The aircraft was out. But
she was outnumbered, five to one, and cannon
shells were exploding against her tail. She
waited, timing her final action with cool precision. Waited until the tracers flashed again.
Waited until the enemy was calling "Guns . . .
guns . . . guns." Certain of his kill. Then she
flipped the Blackhawk onto its back and tumbled
out of control towards the mountains below. The
forces in the cockpit were pounding her body into
insensibility. She hung on, waiting for the final
second when her aircraft dropped behind the
rugged screen of mountains and was gone. Then
the MiG pilot, kill apparently confirmed, pulled
up to rejoin his formation. It was only as he
reached thirty thousand feet that he saw a distant
vapour trail climbing away towards the south.

For once in her life, the game now over, Erica
was thankful for the low ambient temperature
which left vapour trails at lower levels than
normal. They would all see she had tricked them.
At a speed approaching five times the speed of
sound they would never catch her.

The battle sequence was still in her mind as the
radar controller talked her on to final approach.

"Maintain three thousand feet, stand by to commence descent. Weather state is Blue."

"Roger Reindeer Three . . . range check."

"Nine miles . . . cockpit checks for landing."

"Stand by." She ran automatically through the pre-landing check list. The speed remained unchanged. That was when she noticed the VDU readout. Hydraulic failure. She checked for three greens—undercarriage down and locked. Nothing. It was still up.

"Reindeer Three, commence descent now to maintain three-degree glide slope. You should be leaving three thousand now . . . your heading is good."

"Reindeer Three, stand by. We have a hydraulic problem."

"State intentions."

"Reindeer Three, we'll climb to the west and run through the emergency procedure."

"Roger Reindeer Three, so cleared. Maintain seven thousand feet and remain on this frequency."

Erica fed in climb power and pulled the Blackhawk up into a gentle left turn. The time was 7 a.m. and she had been airborne for one hour and forty-seven minutes. Of her plane's ultimate in-flight life seventy-three minutes remained.

The next fourteen minutes were consumed with checking and rechecking the hydraulic system before commanding the computer to use the CO_2 bottles to "blow" the gear down. The last three minutes belonged to a low and slow approach and, with faulty hydraulics a landing with no brakes.

"Barrier up . . . cleared to land Reindeer Three."

"Roger, Three."

The runway drifted up in the early morning sunshine. Selecting dark visor down she monitored the approach speed at 150 knots. Power back . . . lose a little height . . . steady . . . hold it . . . speed 140 reducing . . . down . . . down. The runway loomed nearer, merging into the waters of the fjord. 130 . . . lower . . . power back . . . hold it . . . steady . . . speed 120 . . . lower . . . speed 110 . . . power off . . . land. The wings rocked, then the Blackhawk thumped onto the runway. Engines off . . . the dying whine continued as the aircraft careered down the runway. Ninety . . . eighty . . . seventy . . . sixty . . . she could see the crash barrier rushing towards her . . . fifty . . . forty . . . she braced herself and waited for the rapid deceleration as the Blackhawk's momentum was absorbed by the maze of nylon and rubber.

It was harder than she had imagined. From twenty knots to zero in less than a second. Her upper torso seemed almost to break through the seat harness. Then all was still. Quiet. She had survived, and the Blackhawk also.

But with one difference. The in-flight life expectancy of the aircraft had now been reduced to fifty-six minutes.

It was four hours after Erica Macken's emergency landing that Sven Larsen was killed. The red plastic bag he had carried to his car through the thickly fallen snow that morning had been the signature on his death warrant. His failure to contact Erica the previous evening, Sunday, had been the first link in this disastrous chain of events.

Paul had been angry. "What d'you mean, you can't get through?"

"I think they call it red alert." They were in the living room of Larsen's small but comfortable third-floor apartment in Trondheim. "Simulated war conditions, you see ... Anyway, it's not a problem," he went on. "She will phone tomorrow. I left a message asking her to."

"What if they're flying tonight?"

"They're not. Day operations only, that's what she said. I told you on the way here."

Paul rubbed his face tiredly. "You're right. I'm sorry, Sven. It's been a long day. It's just that after coming so far, I ... you understand?"

"She means a lot to you, I think?" There was a sparkle in Larsen's eyes.

Paul dropped into the chair by the television set. "It's that noticeable, is it?"

"Yes ... I saw the same look in her face today when she asked about you." Larsen went to a small angular bar made of ornately carved wood, with the lower panels covered in red leather. "You will have a drink?"

Paul stood up and joined him at the bar. "The same look? How do you mean?"

"Cloudberry wine. Have you tried it?"

Paul shook his head. "No."

Larsen poured two small glasses. "I think," he said, "she had suddenly realised how much you mean to her."

Tired though he was, Paul had slept badly that night. The thought of being so near and yet so far kept nagging at his mind. He dozed off finally, and then he dreamt he saw Erica crashing. He was standing watching her go. Somehow, in the dream, he had been unable to move. Able only to feel the violent pain of a broken heart. Waking, he peered at his watch: the time seemed to be around five thirty.

Eventually he slept again, total exhaustion claiming him, and woke late. Larsen was up and about and the smell of coffee drifted through the apartment. Paul dragged on the dressing gown his host had loaned him and hurried through to the kitchen.

"Has she called?"

"No. But I managed to get through to security and leave another message for her to call this number."

"When will that be?"

Larsen smiled. "Patience, Paul . . . it will be all right. Now, would you like coffee?"

"Thanks."

"What about breakfast? We usually have sardines and cold meats and bread. I can fry you some eggs though."

"Just the coffee, Sven, thank you."

Larsen poured two cups and slid one across the breakfast bar. "So. What are we going to do about the flight recorder?"

"Who do you know in television . . . here in Norway?"

"One or two people in Oslo."

275

"Could we get them to run this on the news?"

Larsen frowned. "Maybe. But I think they will first contact the minister concerned with the air force or NATO, to get a clearance."

Paul shook his head. "That's no good. He'll have to contact his opposite number in London. That'll take hours—days, even. And there's a D Notice running there."

"What about America? I know a man in Oslo who is a stringer for the *Washington Post*. It is possible that they would break the story."

"It's worth a try. I'll give you a copy of the report I had notarised."

"You do that." Larsen finished his coffee. "I will go down to the office now, and call Oslo. And if Miss Macken phones you will contact me. Yes?"

He went through into the living area and picked up a small white hold-all. "And on my way I will take my clothes to the laundrette. There is a nice young lady who does it for me. Then I collect it on my way back. Do you have things that need washing?"

"It's not any trouble?"

"If it was I wouldn't offer. No, it is no trouble."

Paul went through to the bedroom, took the flight recorder from the red plastic bag and replaced it with his dirty laundry.

"That is all?" Larsen said, taking the bag.

"The rest is in London . . . I didn't have time to collect it."

"Of course." Larsen dropped the white hold-all into the larger red bag. "Good. I will see you later then. Help yourself to food and drink."

276

"Thanks, see you later."

Alexei Karolyov was waiting for Larsen. It had been easy enough. He had watched Kitrell leave Bergen with Larsen before going to the air charter company's office. His British Intelligence cover, especially with the ID, had worked as well as it always did. They called up their pilot on company frequency and made sure that the pilot was the only one wearing a headset, and the passenger could not listen in. Karolyov had then passed the message to Arni that the man he was carrying was a dangerous criminal, wanted for murder by the British police. He had advised the pilot to say as little as possible until they arrived in Trondheim. Once there he was to attempt to detain the man as long as possible, pending his— Karolyov's—arrival in a second aircraft operated by Bergen Air Services. Should the passenger wish to leave the airport immediately, the pilot was to find out where he was going; or if being met, by whom. Following the radioed instructions, Karolyov had placed a telephone call to operations London and left a message for Starling. It was comprehensive. "Arrived Bergen 1400 local. Am following up the purchase of Scottish artifacts. Mr. Merrick, by the way, was made unavailable at Gatwick airport, hence could not complete the deal your side. For what it's worth I suggest you send Merrick back to the company sales school."

The name Merrick referred of course to the

Special Branch. Throughout the UK, tannoy messages paging the Merrick representative at any airport constitute the code for the plain clothes Special Branch. Karolyov made no mention of the bomb scare. Starling would find out soon enough that every security man in Gatwick had converged up on the floor near the Gatwick Village and left the departure gates clear for Kitrell to escape. Karolyov had exposed the hole; Starling would plug it and claim the credit.

The pilot had done a good job. Not only had he obtained the name of Kitrell's contact in Trondheim, but his car type and registration as well. It had taken Karolyov less than half an hour to find out Larsen's address. Using the guise of the local Volvo agent he had telephoned all the S. Larsens in the directory; the pretext being a minor defect on the new 244 model. Karolyov struck lucky on the twelfth call. The man was a relation of Sven Larsen; he knew Sven had just bought a new Volvo, and although he couldn't be sure of the model, felt certain it was the Larsen he was looking for. He gladly passed the phone number and address, saving the Russian another possible twenty-one telephone calls. After that Karolyov hired a Saab from Avis and drove to the address in Trondheim. It was in a quiet side street, and Larsen's Volvo was parked outside, less than fifty yards away.

From then on the job had been straightforward surveillance.

*　　*　　*

Shortly before eleven thirty Larsen left his apartment building and walked along the pavement to his car. Karolyov intercepted him. The red plastic bag Larsen was carrying was Karolyov's reason.

The street, in the heavily falling snow that Monday morning, was deserted. Karolyov approached rapidly, and in total silence. Then the practised sweep of cold steel, the severing of the windpipe and the major neck arteries. Larsen's body fell to the ground, twitching, and Karolyov rolled it quickly half-under a parked car. As he picked up the bag and hurried to his Saab, snow was already settling on the blood-spattered pavement. He set off towards the railway station.

He was almost there when, certain now that he was not being followed, he reached his right hand across the seat, delving inside the red plastic bag. His eyes, staring through the wipers at the road ahead, widened in shock as his hand dug deeper. Then he was stamping the brakes, bringing the Saab to a skidding stop. Shirts . . . socks . . . pants . . . what was this? Karolyov flung the clothes into the back seat, muttering abuse at his own stupidity.

Think! He pounded his forehead with the heel of his palm. The apartment—Larsen's apartment. He would have to be quick now. Once the body was found the police would be all over the place.

The briefcase saved Paul Kitrell's life. In Larsen's eagerness to be off he had left it, and the

279

notarised statement inside it, on the table. It wasn't important—Larsen had made his own notes of everything Paul had told him—but when Paul spotted it a few moments later he hurried to the window, hoping to be able to call down as Larsen left the building. From the apartment he could see the street quite clearly. No one was about. Snow was falling in thick eddies. Perhaps Larsen had left from some back entrance. Apart from a line of parked cars the only traffic was a tram, virtually empty, which glided slowly up the centre of the street. Paul watched it until it was out of view.

He was about to return to his coffee when a Saab, travelling dangerously fast, breaked to a violent halt directly below the window. Briefly the snow flurries thinned. Paul saw a man jump from the car and look up. Then he was running into the building.

Paul couldn't be sure. Not absolutely. Even so he went to the bedroom, gathered up his suitcase and fled out into the corridor, grabbing a heavy fur parka and gloves from beside the door as he went. Behind him the telephone started ringing. He ignored it and ran towards the elevator. The lights were moving—one . . . two . . . three . . . a bell sounded and the doors sighed open. Paul, however, had gone, leaping down the stairs three at a time. The more he thought about it, the more convinced he became. The man from the Saab was the man who had watched him in Bergen.

*　　　*　　　*

Forty-five kilometres away, at the military base, Erica redialled Sven Larsen's number. That she had only just then received his message from security was due to her having spent a great deal of the morning after her crash landing in sick quarters, having chest x-rays; and when they proved negative, going through the uncomfortable chest taping procedure. Then the MO had wanted to ground her; she had fought against that and won.

Finally there had been a lengthy discussion with the engineering officer on hydraulic problems.

Larsen's telephone remained unanswered. She counted sixty seconds more. Swore softly. And hung up.

CHAPTER ELEVEN

In Murmansk, it was late evening. Sergio Dzerzhinsky was preparing for his last flight. He stopped, listening to the sky. He imagined he heard her weeping. He looked up. Of course she had dressed for the occasion. Black velvet and diamonds. He looked further across the heavens and noticed the thin wisps of silver gossamer. It was her best trick always. Whenever he was angry with her she would dress in his favourite dress.

Except this time she was too late. It had taken him a lifetime, but he had found her out. A woman with eyes as hard as the diamonds she wore. A faithless mistress who slept with every pilot, discovered their strengths and their most secret weaknesses. And from this knowledge devised for each man her cruellest betrayal. Only now he was getting out. She—the sky—had owned him for too long. He would cheat her now, just as she had cheated him.

Dzerzhinsky continued walking down the arc-lit flight line, his breath leaving his mouth in puffy clouds of white. The soldiers with the guard dogs patrolled the aircraft in sullen silence. He did not envy them their job; he had only been outside for a matter of minutes and already he could fell the aching cold in his feet.

"Pilots and their mistress," he whispered to himself. "That explains why so many have bad marriages. Yes." He smiled. "I said that once to Anatoly."

Dzerzhinsky dismissed her from his mind then went up the steps to his aircraft. He shuffled forward to the flight deck and switched on the internal power, before carrying out a methodical check of all the systems. The interior of the empty aircraft had looked quite normal as he had made his way forward. Banks of computers all hidden beneath green canvas sacks with zips and locks firmly in place. It was all set up for another trip over the Atlantic. One more day. One more routine-filled day.

Except that Dzerzhinsky was leaving early, and alone.

Suddenly floodlights stripped the area naked of darkness. Normally, no pilot enjoyed the prospect of flying out just before dawn, especially if the airfield was gripped by the crucifying cold of November; but for Dzerzhinsky it was summer. A day of blue skies and warming sun and cooling breeze. His last. Now, as he sat alone in the cockpit, he sensed the weights being lifted from his shoulders. One by one they went, leaving him almost light-headed. Almost young again. When did you last fly solo, Sergio? Yesterday? Last year? It didn't matter. He yanked open the direct-vision window and called for ground power. The litany began. Page after page of checklists. Mumbled incantations for the control tower's benefit, seeking responses from non-existent crew members. A bowed priest offering Mass to an empty church.

The Tupolev's engines burst into life one by one. Slowly the giant aircraft came to life for its last dress rehearsal.

It was the silence more than anything. And the cold. It must be nearly dawn. Tuesday? Paul frowned. Yes—Tuesday. A thin smudge of light was apparent in the lower eastern sky. Somehow that light made it colder. Now, the snow and ice and his steaming breath, all were visible. Did it actually become colder at first light?

Paul moved on, legs dragging tiredly through the deep snow. He had dispensed with the suitcase long ago, when it became more like a lead weight. But the flight recorder was tucked tightly under his arm.

The silence seemed to be challenging his sanity. It was a long time since he had heard another voice. Held a conversation. Sven Larsen had been the last one—no, it had been the girl in the car hire firm. He discounted that and went back to thinking of Larsen. What had happened to him? The man with the round steel-rimmed glasses perhaps? Yes, *he* was what had happened. In the same way as he had happened to Wint ... and Jamie Finlay? Paul shuddered at his reasoning.

"Survival," he said out loud, the sound little more than a dry croak. He said it again: "Survival," and again, "Survival," before clearing his throat. His lips had cracked with the movement and he sensed the sharp, stinging pain spreading to his cheeks. He stopped and removed a glove, then dabbed at his lips. They were bleeding. He ran his tongue automatically over the congealed mess, tasting the salt as he did so. "Not far now, Paul. What? Another three kilometres?" He shrugged. "At a guess. Then what?" He started moving again. "Find a way in?" He answered himself immediately. "And get arrested? Break in through the fence or whatever and walk straight into the arms of the military police ... then who's going to listen? Nobody. They'll drag you off to some quiet room and start questioning you. And while they're doing that the Blackhawks will be flying. And by then it could be too late ... it could already be too late!"

What was it Erica had told Larsen? High security on the gates; the usual passes with mug shots required. Inside the base, dog handlers and guard dogs on twenty-four-hour patrol. All service personnel save for the company who carried out aircraft refuelling; its staff were civilian. If he could locate the fuel dump, and borrow some coveralls, and find a layout of the base ... He pressed the back of his gloved hand against his lips in a futile attempt to suppress the pain. One

286

ticket in a lottery, he concluded. Too much of a gamble . . . but it was all he had.

He surged on with renewed vigor. If he could once get to Erica their troubles were over.

Squadron Leader Thomas sat on the edge of the desk and lit a cigarette before continuing with his briefing. "First bit of luck then to us. One of our Nimrods confirmed Red shipping at Point Snow-drop," he picked up his cane and tapped the wall map in the area directly west of the Lofoten Wall, "at time 0400 zulu. Six contacts in all. Radar photographs indicate three frigates, two destroyers and one carrier. The Nimrod carried out a creeping line ahead search further south . . . with negative results. However, bearing in mind that the Red navy is still smarting from Flight Lieutenant Macken's escapade the other day, you can bet your boots they have something up their sleeve."

Thomas stubbed out his cigarette. "We have a reconnaissance sweep under way at this time, so once confirmation comes through we'll move out. Similar pattern to the Kola Peninsula job. Tornadoes flying high level CAP. Reindeer flight medium level and Lapland flight low. Okay, any questions?" No one spoke. The tension was building. "Weather next, then," Thomas said, leaving the desk.

Twelve minutes later the pilots were boarding the crew buses outside the operations block. No one spoke, each preferring silence, and the constant mental gymnastics which were an integral part of the battle ahead. For now the game element was still alive. And once you were knocked out, you remained out. And no pilot wanted to sit out the remainder of the war in the control room. In much the same way they did not want to lose their aircraft to the Red team. They all knew that winning was down to their combat effectiveness, the rate at which they could mount sorties against the enemy. Start losing aircraft and your effectiveness is reduced; with morale suffering as a direct consequence. And suddenly you're staring defeat in the face. And no one accepts defeat . . . not without a fight.

Erica was the last but one to leave the crew bus. Thirty seconds before she did so she had been staring out of the window towards the white sweep of mountains. Had her eyes refocused down into the area of the wire perimeter fence, she might have observed a movement in the thin cover of dark firs. A man had been working at the wire, attempting to gain access to the base, when the sound of the crew bus had come to him. The man had paused; listening, waiting. Once he was sure it was coming his way he had scrambled back to the cover of the trees.

For Alexei Karolyov there had been moments of near panic. He had had the man in his sights, no more than a matter of metres away. "You cannot play against luck," his old KGB instructor had told him. "Instead you wait for it to change seats.

And what is important to remember, Alexei, is that it always does." But the memory had not helped him. Karolyov was different, neither a gradual planner nor a team player. He seldom had time to wait. He was a killer.

No, what had worried him most at the moment of Kitrell's escape had been his age. His eyesight had never been good: he had compensated for that with excellent spectacles. But how did you compensate for growing old? How did you compensate for making mistakes you would never have made a few short years ago?

It should have been a routine interception. There were two ways to get to or from Larsen's apartment on the third floor. One was the elevator, the other the stairs. One was adjacent to the other. He had reached into the elevator on the ground floor and selected three, then jumped clear as the doors hissed closed and the lift made its ascent. The entrance hall was deserted and as the elevator stopped at the third floor he pulled back into the shadows. If Kitrell had been watching from the window and suspected something he might try to run. And Karolyov had both exits covered.

The luck started running against him in that very second. A group of noisy young Norwegians burst into the building from the street and effectively covered the doorway to the stairs as they dusted snow off their clothes and jabbed impatiently at the elevator button. And that was the moment when Kitrell rushed down the stairs. Their eyes met for a brief moment; then he was gone into the street. The Norwegians had hampered Karolyov's exit, so that by the time he also had run out into the street, Kitrell had disappeared. Not a sign. Just large whirling snowflakes, muffling the sounds of the city.

Kitrell had escaped. And the bag he was carrying must hold the flight recorder. Karolyov's panic died, to be replaced by the voice of reason. The man is on foot. The weather is against that. Therefore he will be looking for shelter. Assuming no other contacts than Larsen, that would mean a hotel. Not a large hotel, though—fugitives always sought smaller, cheaper places. Their reasoning, anonymity. In that they were nearly always wrong, since smaller hotels had fewer guests and therefore their desk clerks were far more likely to remember a face, whatever the name used. And Kitrell spoke only English, another identifying features. Arni had told him that.

Karolyov drove to the nearest hotel, the Hotel Norge, bribed the young man on the desk with a handful of American dollars to make some calls around the other hotels for him, went into the hotel's small restaurant, and ordered a steak and a bottle of French red wine. He took a window seat and peered out from time to time through the gauze of white net curtain. Apart from the odd car slithering through the deepening snow the street was as quiet as the grave.

The hotel checking drew a blank. He still kept calm. He didn't know why this man was in Trondheim but, whatever the reason, now that he had been discovered he would probably try to leave. Karolyov had found out that there were no more flights out from the city due to weather. Which brought him to the hire car companies. He checked with Avis first and struck gold, using the flimsy story that he was Kitrell's brother and was supposed to have met him earlier, and would have done if his car hadn't broken down just outside Trondheim. The Avis girl became very helpful. Not only did she remember Mr. Kitrell hiring the car; she recalled giving him instructions on how to get to the military airfield forty-five kilometres away. She had, she said, advised him against such a journey as it had been late afternoon and the snow ploughs would not get to that region until early the next morning. Karolyov thanked her for the information and left the hotel.

He found the red Avis Volvo in a drift on a straight stretch of road twenty-five kilometres out of Trondheim. The car was empty and the engine was cold. He went back to his own car and sat in the comfortable warmth contemplating the next move. It had stopped snowing now and the wind had eased. Even so, twenty kilometres on foot, probably without a pocket compass or any other means of navigation, no knowledge of the road and the path it took, and sub-zero temperatures, meant only one thing. Death. Kitrell, he decided, was a fool. He, Alexei Karolyov, was not. He turned up his coat collar.

The snow plough arrived three hours later, its high searchlight and massive wheels giving it the appearance of some kind of moon buggy. Karolyov flagged the vehicle down and persuaded the driver to take him up in the cab. There was a man out there somewhere—lost. They had to find him.

The unlikely pair set off slowly. The farmer who made spare money by working the night snow-clearing shift as far as the military base, and the bespectacled killer who was already observing the operating controls and making helpful searchlight sweeps from left to right.

It was shortly before first light when the driver spotted the movement on the brow of the hill. Karolyov killed him ten seconds later. Getting rid of the body took a little longer. Having pushed it out of the high cab Karolyov climbed down and dragged the body off the side of the road. The blood was crimson on the white snow. The cascading snow from the plough covered all the signs, as it did the body.

Now, fifty minutes later, Karolyov was crouching in the sparse cover of firs watching Kitrell move towards the perimeter fence of the air base. Karolyov was closing silently on his target when the sound of a bus engine grew in his ears. And that was when Kitrell turned and scampered back through the snow. Back to the trees. Karolyov, knife in hand, was waiting.

Paul froze in his tracks, his eyes disbelieving what they saw. How? It wasn't possible.

Karolyov edged forward. "Mr. Kitrell?"

"Yes . . . and you . . . who the hell are you?"

"It is not important who I am, Mr. Kitrell. All that matters is the package you are carrying. We would like it back."

"We? Who the hell are *we?* MI5 . . . British Intelligence?"

Karolyov took another step nearer. "If you wish," he said tonelessly.

"Except you're not English . . . what are you . . . Russian?"

Karolyov's eyes were showing his impatience. "Nationality is not important in our line of work, Mr. Kitrell . . . just results . . . Now I will ask you again for the package."

"And if I refuse?"

The knife blade sliced sideways through the air. "You are either very foolish or very brave, I have yet to decide which. But either way you will lose."

"KGB . . . has to be . . . our people wouldn't murder innocent civilians."

Karolyov laughed. A dry humourless sound. "Wouldn't, Mr. Kitrell . . . wouldn't? Now to foolishness I must add naivety." He took another small step. Paul held his ground. "The flight recorder. If you please."

"And me?"

"You? You will be free to go."

"And I'm supposed to believe that, after what happened to Wint in London . . . and Jamie Finlay. It was you who killed him I presume?"

Karolyov said nothing. His eyes, cruel and unblinking, were fixed on his prey. In his imagination the blood was already spilling onto the snow beneath. He took another step forward.

"And Larsen?" Paul added. "Is he dead too?"

Two more steps and Karolyov knew he would be in striking distance. Two more short, careful steps. "If you like . . . yes. My job, you understand." His left foot slithered forward. "But for you and me . . . I think a truce. The package for your life. That is fair, is it not?"

As he took the last step the sound hit him with the force of a juggernaut. There was no thunder, it was too loud for that. It was a terrible cracking roar. An impossible assault on the eardrums. Karolyov hesitated, his eyes drawn to the smoke and flames belching from the small building one hundred metres beyond Paul's left shoulder.

It was in that split second of hesitation that Paul took his chance. He hurled the heavy metal flight recorder at the Russian's head. Karolyov, sensing movement, side-stepped instinctively, twisting his body as he did so. He was not fast enough. The flight recorder caught him a glancing blow to the side of the head. His spectacles flew off with the impact.

Temporarily stunned, he somehow maintained his balance. He felt for the side of his face with his left hand. It was covered in blood—*his* blood. Anger rose inside him as he staggered forwards. Before him in the cold grey dawn he saw two blurred figures, two hazy, wavering outlines. He could not focus. Without his glasses he could not focus. The knife came forward, sweeping from side to side. "A mistake, Mr. Kitrell . . . a big mistake . . ."

He continued his advance towards the slowly retreating figures. He squinted, trying to make them merge. He remembered the line from his old instructor in Moscow. "You cannot play against luck; instead you wait for it to change seats. And what is important to remember, Alexei, is that it always does." He wondered which seat it now favoured! It was a straight fifty-fifty chance. Everything he possessed on the figure on the left.

Paul was unprepared. One second the Russian was staggering drunkenly closer, muttering incomprehensively; the next he had leapt forward, quick as a cat. His knife sank deep into Paul's side. He gasped, as if in surprise. Then the knife was withdrawn. Then it was slamming into his body again. There was no pain, but he felt sick. Violently sick. The knife was being raised for the third time when, inexplicably, dogs started to bark.

His head rolled to one side and he vomited over himself and the snow. His face was burning now. Covered in sweat and burning. Jesus God, it was hot. And there was pain now. He dropped to his knees, then forward onto the snow. Too much pain . . . too much . . . he couldn't take it . . . He raised his head and saw the figure of the Russian scrabbling around in the snow, looking for his spectacles. Funny, the light seemed to be fading. It was early morning and yet the light was fading. The wavy, dark shape of the Russian was moving away . . . into the trees.

He reached for his left side, working his hand out of his glove at the same time. It felt bad. He didn't know how bad, but he'd seen guerilla fighters in Afghanistan with their guts falling out. He knew how long they had taken to die.

Stop the bleeding, he thought. Must stop the

bleeding. Carefully, and with what felt like great precision, he began to scoop small amounts of snow through the torn clothing into the wounds. Perhaps after a while he would feel better. Perhaps by then he could walk to the security gate. How far was that? One kilometre? Two . . . three. Whatever, it wouldn't be too far.

His eyes were closing as if in sleep when the jets roared overhead. He listened as the thunder faded and the silence returned. And he knew he had failed her. She had been up there. They had just said goodbye. The pain seemed to go then. It was almost as if it had never existed. Now he found warmth, and silence, and an undreamt-of-peace.

The pull-up built in a steady, relentless drive, pressing her deeper and deeper into the seat. An invisible iron hand clamping and squeezing her flesh. Her eyes picked up the readout. Five . . . six . . . seven . . . eight . . . nine. Nine times the force of gravity. She felt as if her entire body was being mashed into pulp. All fighter pilots were familar with the squeeze of g-forces. All fighter pilots took the pressure through the sitting posture of their spines, from the head to the tailbone. All knew the havoc being created in the circulatory system where the blood has become as heavy as molten lead and the heart is fighting a losing battle to supply the brain a mere twelve inches away. All had experienced the onset of tunnel vision as their angle of sight narrowed. All had seen the greyness and felt the racking pain before blackout.

Erica Macken ordered maximum power and thundered up towards the clouds. Colonel Hood was still up there. Trying to get a bead on her jinking Blackhawk. She disappeared into the clouds seconds later.

It had all gone wrong after take-off. The weather state at the base had been amber—instrument conditions. The Blue high-level Tornado CAP had failed to materialise, having been bounced by a Red flight, led by Hood, which had been waiting above them. For reasons which were as yet unclear this Red flight had not been picked up on radar.

Her own low-level Blue strike force of Lapland Blackhawks also failed, the two lead destroyers having put up a barrage of chaff rockets in a carefully designed pattern. During their trajectories the rockets had disgorged many millions of metallised glass-fibre needles, each thinner than a human hair, producing several false but radar-attractive targets to decoy the imaginary incoming missiles safely clear. Lapland flight, having failed in their objective, then turned for home, only to run into a dozen Red Sea Harriers. Only one Blackhawk had managed to get through. Reindeer Four. Erica's.

Now, climbing vertically through seventy thousand feet, she was fighting to stay alive. Also she had been airborne for forty-eight minutes. And, unknown to her, the aircraft would fail to respond in exactly eight minutes' time.

The sky was becoming a darker blue, merging

into indigo, as the Blackhawk, Reindeer Four, drifted ghostlike through 100,000 feet. The beauty, however, for once went unnoticed. Hood was still there, drifting from time to time through her six o'clock position. She had realised earlier, from his tactics, that he had to be out of missiles. All that remained were his cannon. And for them he had to keep her locked in his sights for a minimum of four seconds. So far he had failed.

Somewhere just below the roof of the world she kicked the aircraft into a violent spin. The dirt and dust floated up from the cockpit floor; a reaction to negative g. Then the height readout was unwinding, flashing out numbers in a blur. She checked her fuel state. Thirty minutes. The long climb with afterburners had been responsible. She had halved Reindeer Four's remaining endurance.

Hood was following her aircraft down towards the lower cloud deck when the message came: "Redstar One, this is Snowman. Break off engagement . . . unidentified traffic for you to investigate."

"Redstar One, roger . . . who's the Blue guy who just took me on the moon trip?"

"Say again, Redstar One."

"Forget it, pal, just identify the ship I've been chasing, will you?"

"Stand by, Redstar One . . . break . . . Reindeer Four, this is Snowman, acknowledge."

Erica eased her Blackhawk out of its spin. "Four's with you . . . go."

"Roger Four, team up with Redstar One. We

298

have identified fast-moving traffic ... possibly White Bandit ... stand by for coordinates."

Hood's Blackhawk drifted into her eleven o'clock position. "That's you I guess, Lieutenant Macken ... recognise that accent anywhere."

She smiled. His voice seemed almost human.

"Redstar leader, this is Snowman. Turn left, heading zero nine zero, descend two four zero; coordiates as follows." The controller read off the numbers as the two aircraft streaked towards the east. A White Bandit would be a genuine Russian intruder."

Hood said: "Snowman from Redstar One, what sort of range on the target, nothing showing on radar?"

"Range sixty miles closing, Redstar One."

"Roger One ... what sort of speed have you got on him?"

"Indicating four five zero, Redstar One ... reduce now to six zero zero, stand by for further vectors and say fuel state."

Hood swivelled his head towards Erica. "How's the gas doin', Lieutenant?"

"Twenty-six minutes, Lead."

"Er, Snowman from Red One ... twenty and twenty-six minutes ... got any altitude on the 'unidentified'?"

"Eighteen ... one eight thousand Redstar One ... right now, new heading one zero zero ... range two zero miles closing ... descend now to one eight zero."

"Roger. One hundred the heading and down to one eight thousand."

Hood cranked his bonedomed head back again. "You ready for this, Lieutenant?"

"Ready, boss."

"Okay, battle formation . . . GO."

Two thousand yards separated the Blackhawks' line abreast as they dropped down through a layer of high cloud. Holding speed and heading and rate of descent through the mild turbulence and light rain they broke out twenty seconds later, maintaining the same separation. Their height readout was 19,000 feet when she looked to the left and picked up Hood's aircraft.

They were at about four miles when Hood called: "Snowman from Redstar One . . . target twelve o'clock . . . Bear."

There was a silence as the last word sunk in. Tupolev Tu-95. NATO code-name: Bear. The controller's voice was full of disbelief when he said: "Redstar One from Snowman, confirm Bear?"

"That's a roger. Stand by I'll close up and take a look-see . . . you with me, Two?"

"Affirm . . . and contact the Bear."

"Kinda big, uh?"

Erica eased the Blackhawk across the sky and called out reduced power settings. She knew Colonel Hood well enough to be certain that he was enjoying every minute of this.

Sergio Dzerzhinsky sat quite still, flying the huge Tupolev calmly through the early morning. He knew they were there, had picked them up on his radar. He had of course expected them. He was just surprised they had taken so long. Of course he would have liked a little longer—a few more minutes of reliving the happier moments of his life. He smiled. And that was all it would take. A few more minutes. Over half a century condensed into a few more minutes. It was sad. Still, for the first time in his life he was free. Completely free. Free of the air force with its endless rules and regulations. Then there was the Motherland. He was free of her as well. Free of her rules. Free of those neat ledgers which recorded everything: how much vodka is imbibed as an average by the average citizen; how many engineers, ballerinas, revolving lathes, dogs of all breeds.

It was better this way, he had decided. Now that Anatoly was gone it was better. She, his mistress, the sky, had taken the only possession he had left for his old age. A son. Someone who would have visited him on weekends. Played chess, swapped stories. And even if flying duties had kept him away he would have telephoned. And he, Sergio, would have reassured the young man that he was still breathing and that he had a bottle of Dark Eyes in for his next visit. And they would have laughed about the cardboard sandwiches which had sustained them on their long night flights over the Atlantic.

Dzerzhinsky's eyes were drawn to the Blackhawk interceptor which had eased into close formation forward of his left wing-tip. He raised a gloved hand and waved. The fighter waggled its wings in response before breaking away gently to the left. "It is no use asking me to go with you my friend. My destination has no runways, no hangars, no people." He looked down at the fuel gauges. Thirty minutes left. Thirty minutes and the giant Tupolev too would find its final resting place.

The Blackhawk drifted back on station, close now and menacing. Dzerzhinsky smiled sadly. "Ah, *tovarich*, why don't you understand? I am not here to fight. I am an old man. I suffer from no specific ailment, simply a general wearing down . . . and perhaps a broken heart. I am like the bull elephant in Africa—I am going to my graveyard."

Warning cannon-fire from the Blackhawk angled across the front of the Tupolev. Dzerzhinsky maintained his heading. Hood's order to engage came two minutes later. By then he had dropped back to one thousand yards astern of the Soviet bomber. Erica was in formation to his right. Both had greened-up their aircraft; the prelude to *real* air warfare. Both had heard the growl in their earphones as the homing heads of their missiles had picked up the infra-red emissions from the Tupolev. Both now pressed buttons to lock-on their missiles, hearing the insistent *nee-nee-nee* sound confirming ready to fire.

Erica watched in horror as Hood's missile came off and guided to the target. The man was crazy. He couldn't have gained the necessary authorisations—there hadn't been time. And there was no immediate threat. Shooting down a Russian plane . . . this was the way World War III

302

got started. The man was criminally insane.

The plume of white smoke from his missile jinked once, then settled down. The missile impacted on the Tupolev's left side, near the wing root. There was an explosion, a fireball, smoke, debris floating back from the damaged aircraft. Hood's voice came over the radio, telling her to stand by. He sounded like a Southern US football coach planning out the last quarter. He was relaxed and happy.

The Tupolev reared up suddenly, disappearing momentarily into light cloud cover. What happened next must have surprised Colonel Hood as much as it did Erica.

Dzerzhinsky, badly injured in the explosion, was now flying by instinct. He had no way of remembering what had happened, he was in too much pain. His dying seconds were given to pulling the burning aircraft into a vertical climb. As he entered the cloud and neared the point of stall he kicked in full right rudder and put the bomber into a vicious spin. Then he fired a missile.

Erica saw it first, and then for only part of a second. The grey trail of missile hurtling from the cloud. It was too close to Hood for her to call. The words were still forming in her mind as his Blackhawk disintegrated. One second it was there, the next ... She looked frantically around for the Tupolev as the radio started asking questions. She ignored the voice as the blazing Russian aircraft suddenly filled her mirror. He was there. Behind her.

The missile left the Tupolev in a snaking white line as Dzerzhinsky fell forward on to the controls. His aircraft started breaking up long before it reached the sea.

Now in an inverted descent, Erica watched the missile gradually close the gap behind her. At the last moment she would push up in a high-g reversal. The missile would overshoot. But she had only five seconds left to execute that final manoeuvre. In five seconds' time the Blackhawk's computer would fail.

"Come on," she called. "Closer . . . closer." Her eyes were holding the image in the mirror perfectly still. And the missile was getting nearer. Its details were growing. It was white, with a long pointed nose; four stablising fins at the rear. Sweat was running down inside her oxygen mask. She could taste the salt on her lips. "Three . . . two . . . one . . ."

She gave the command. The word for escape. Nothing happened. She called again, grabbing the computer-locked controls, fighting to free them. She was too late. By less than one hundredth part of a second she was too late.

Her eyes still watching the missile in the mirror; her hands still fighting with the controls; her voice still screaming commands at a computer which would not answer, she continued down the grey sky towards the mountains of Norway.

It was in those last seconds that the pictures came back. She had never believed they did, but then she had never been here before. This close to death. And now they came, the pictures of past life. Her father. Canada. The Beaver on skis lifting off frozen lakes in the winter. The silver-framed photograph of her mother. He had never got over her death. She had sometimes caught him, late at night, sitting by the blazing log fire; listening to the howl of wind, staring intently at the photograph. Willing her back; or himself with her, wherever she might be. Then his funeral, and the mourning; and the careful packing of memorabilia. And Montreal. And England. And the Royal Air Force. And Gene. And Gene was gone too, now. That was when she had known there'd be no sepia-printed memories for her. Paul appeared last of all. He was more like her father than she had realised; given to quiet moments and pensive stares. As though he didn't belong. As though he was forever seeking shelter away from some violent storm. In her he would have found it. And if she was to save herself for him, now was the moment.

The Blackhawk was no more than five hundred feet above the white snow-capped mountains when the missile exploded. The orange fireball blossomed and died in less than a second.

Black, white, and dark grey clouds were fighting over Trondheim, one formation chasing the next one over the skies. The snow had just started again, blowing horizontally down the platform at the railway station. Alexei Karolyov stood, face to the wind, watching the approaching train. He had found his spectacles, one lens cracked but mercifully unbroken, in the snow by the air base. In a few minutes he would be on board the train and safely on his way to Bodo. Once there he would have to stay overnight as there were no connecting flights to Kirkenes until the following morning. He would of course send a coded message to Starling saying he had the Scottish artifact and was on his way back with it. That would give him the day he needed to fly to Kirkenes and make a night crossing back into Russia, taking the flight recorder with him.

There was a glint in his eye when he considered the second message he would prepare. He would ask for it to have a delayed transmission time from the Bodo post office; not being sent to London until the time when he was slipping quietly into the Motherland. The text of that message would simply say. "The tenth commandment." In the spy decalogue that was translated as—"You can do anything you want—if you can get away with it." And by the time Starling read it Alexei Karolyov would have done just that.

CHAPTER TWELVE

It was a year later. A year to the day. November the tenth. The small yellow biplane drifted slowly across the vast African sky, a sky which was endless; constantly changing in depth and colour. The biplane pilot had left Nairobi's Wilson airport in the heat of the early afternoon, climbing quickly to find the cooler air. She breathed deeply the smells of oil and petrol and doped fabric, marvelling at the blues and pinks and reds caught in a unique, unfamiliar light. Away to the right, in nearby Tanzania, rose the legendary Kilimanjaro, its three peaks standing as Hemingway had said: "As wide as the world ... great, high and unbelievably white in the sun."

The pilot smiled behind her goggles. The smile seemed to rearrange her age lines, softening the weariness that growing old can bring. The smile remained a moment longer, showing joy. On a day like this you could live forever. From a sky like this you could wish never to return. Her gaze went back to the cockpit, checking temperatures and pressures and fuel. All were as they should be. And somewhere beyond the curve of glistening cowling—Mombasa. Then, easing the nose above the horizon, she executed an aileron roll. The joyful rolls continued from time to time as the yellow biplane continued its journey east, its form and size diminishing with distance and the hazy heat of afternoon.

In that westernmost of the Channel Islands, Guernsey, it had been raining most of the day. One of those steady mizzles that accompanies a drifting fog from the sea. George Hinchcliffe did not mind. In a way he was enjoying it. For the first time in years he was totally relaxed. He had even dragged up a long forgotten line of Swift: "May you live all the days of your life." Not before time, perhaps. In the past it had been his wife's ambitions which drove him relentlessly on. Now things were different.

He activated the windscreen wipers of his parked car and peered through the glass at the grey shapes of small fishing boats bobbing in and out of the fog. The fisherman had told him the fog would come, at the hotel bar the previous evening.

"Fog?" Hinchcliffe had said. "How d'you know?"

The Guernseyman with the tanned leathery skin and cropped iron-grey hair had considered the Englishman for a moment or two before parting with his weather lore. "Many reasons. Seagulls flying round the lighthouse in the dark,

308

and the hair on my dog's back has felt damp all day. Also you can hear the church bells from a long way off."

"And that's it?"

The old fisherman frowned, as if to imply that that would be more than enough for most men. "The sunset tonight was bad . . . mark my words, there'll be a heavy fog tomorrow."

And he had been right. Hinchcliffe had woken that morning to find a grey blanket over the entire island. His eyes returned to the fishing boats. A car sped down the coast road, going too fast for the weather conditions, its tyres whispering urgently along the wet tarmac. The silence drifted back. That was the nice thing about this place. The tranquillity. Nothing like London.

The final pieces of the Blackhawk jigsaw puzzle had arrived on his desk last November. That terrible week when the crazy gung-ho American had downed a Russian reconnaissance plane and for a few hours NATO and the Russians had stood on the brink of war. But the Russians had held back. Outraged protests, sabre-rattling, but no more, thank God. And then, as the days went by, it had leaked out that the downed Tupolev had been an unofficial flight, piloted by some madman. Both air forces had them it seemed . . .

A year ago. God, was it as long ago as that? Quite amazing how time accelerated as one grew older. In the same way towns and streets and buildings seemed to shrink: he remembered that all right. Remembered the streets in Sheffield, the route he had walked as a small boy from his home to that of his grandparents. But when he went back he found everything smaller than it was in his mind. Even the distance from one house to another seemed to have diminished. Just like his days. He shrugged at the thought and returned to the Blackhawk.

It was November and David Courtney had produced the flight recorder as promised; although there did seem a number of curious aspects to the way he had got it. Not that Hinchcliffe was too concerned. He had the damned thing back; that was all that mattered. The transcript was a breath of fresh air. Some sort of metal fatigue problem: something that had caused an electrical malfunction which had resulted in the VIC system being locked on to the last verbal command from the pilot. The odd little character Blakeley had been right all along. He had said it wasn't the computer. British Aerospace went to work immediately to rectify the problem.

It was a few weeks later, after the election had returned Labour to power, when David Courtney knocked down his house of cards. One of MI5's agents had apparently sent in reports concerning suspected hardened laser sites being constructed in and around the Kola Peninsula—a Soviet step towards Star Wars. Futher intelligence gathering during the period of the NATO exercise Rolling Thunder had confirmed the initial report. Following that the government had had little option but to wind down the Blackhawk programme and divert funds into the Space Strike scheme. Now it was a race against the Soviets.

Even the American Senate had done an about-face and increased defence spending.

Hinchcliffe's anger had persisted over Christmas. Southgate-Sayers had won after all. In one way at least. In another, sadder way he had lost. The recurring numbness in his right hand had spead to his feet, then his left hand, and had finally struck him down on New Year's day. The overwhelming tiredness turned to lack of coordination and slurred speech. He was rushed to an air force hospital in Buckinghamshire. The diagnosis was multiple sclerosis.

When Hinchcliffe found out he went straight to the hospital. He would not have wished such a fate on his worst enemy. He met the air vice-marshal's wife at the hospital and had a long chat with her. A charming, if homely woman, she seemed to be taking it very well. Appeared quite chirpy. She would have her husband home in the summer. They had a big lawn, a huge garden. She would take him out in a wheelchair, and push him along the garden paths and show him the flowers.

Hinchcliffe's bombshell dropped in the middle of January. January 15. His wife Elizabeth died. It was nothing dramatic. She wasn't that kind of person. She simply went to bed one night and died in her sleep. He would always remember waking up that particular morning and speaking to her, and when she didn't answer reaching out instinctively and touching her. She was as cold as marble, and stiff. He had sat on the edge of the bed, head in his hands, for a long time full of emptiness and disbelief. It was late morning

311

when he reached down and kissed her gently on the cheek. Then he left the room and phoned the family doctor. He never saw her again.

It was following the funeral that he decided to retire from public life. Somehow there seemed little point in going on. The ambition, after all, had for a long time been hers. Now he would go away, find that country cottage he had always dreamt about. He was uncertain as to where the cottage would be until his weekend in the Channel Islands. David Courtney had suggested it; said he needed sea air, a restful atmosphere. Guernsey, he had added, was the ideal place.

The fog was still rolling inland from Cobo Bay as Hinchcliffe started the car and set out slowly for Grandes Rocques. One weekend in spring had made up his mind. Now he was waiting for the house purchase in St. Peter Port to be completed; then he could settle down to a life of pottering around the garden, and reading. Perhaps he would even take up fishing; something he hadn't done since he was a boy. In the meantime he was staying in a self-catering apartment in Grandes Rocques Court, experimenting with the cooker and a few local recipes the barmaid at the local pub had given him.

There was, it seemed as always, a touch of irony. Aeroplanes and pilots had somehow been instrumental in ending his career. The Blackhawk fiasco, Major Kitrell, young Maudsley. The threat of Soviet sabotage. Endless all-night sessions at the ministry. The strain had been too much. He liked to think that even if Elizabeth had lived he

312

would have still retired.

Now, coming to the peaceful island of Guernsey, he had imagined fishermen and flower growers . . . country folk. Instead he found the estate agent he was dealing with at the top of St. Julian's Avenue was an ex-air force flyer. And if that wasn't enough the owner of the apartment he was renting at Grandes Rocques was also a pilot.

It seemed they were shaping his life; working out all the future moves; planning his days. He smiled. What the hell, they could plan these sort of days forever, fog and all. After London this was paradise.

At that exact moment in London David Courtney was raising a glass of Dom Perignon. Not that he usually drank during the day—and even if he did his choice would not have been champagne. Today however was a special occasion. His daughter had given birth to a baby boy. Her first. And now David Courtney was a grandfather. He had taken the day off from the office and now sat with his wife Joanna at their Cavendish Square flat. A log fire blazed cheerfully in the Adam fireplace. He walked over to it and placed his glass on the mantelpiece. "So, how does it feel being a grandmother?" he said, turning to address his wife.

She looked up from the writing desk. "That must be the tenth time you've asked me today, David. And as I have already told you, I feel the same as I felt yesterday, and the day before, and the day before that . . . The fact that you seem to derive some pleasure from the prospect of growing old does not apply to me. Besides, I'm seven years younger than you; a mere slip of a girl." She smiled kindly and turned back to the desk, and the cards she was writing out for her daughter. "Do we have George Hinchcliffe's address, by the way?"

"In the address book."

"Eaton Square? I thought you told me he had moved to the Channel Islands!"

"Damn." Courtney went over to the bureau and rummaged through various drawers before eventually producing a compliment slip from a company called Gull Air. He handed it to his wife. "On the back."

"Who's the company?"

"Don't know . . . I think he's chartered one of their planes once in a while."

She laughed. "True to form . . . the original champagne socialist."

"I wouldn't say that . . ."

"I would. Anyway, how's he getting on down there? Must be rather lonely without Elizabeth."

Courtney strolled back towards the fire. "Lonely? George? No . . . no, I gather he's quite enjoying it. Best thing he could have done . . . retired, that is." He picked up the glass of champagne and took a sip. "You know," he continued, "this time last year he was on the way towards a nervous breakdown."

His wife looked round, surprise showing in her eyes. "I never knew that."

314

"I don't think he did," Courtney replied drily. "But I've seen the signs often enough in the department."

He picked up a log from the basket at the side of the hearth and dropped it onto the fire. A flurry of sparks rushed up the chimney. And George's breakdown would have happened if they had failed to retrieve that flight recorder. It had been close, though. Old George had never known just how close. The report from Karolyov saying he had obtained the "Scottish artifact"; followed by the cryptic message on the following day. The one that had read "The tenth commandment." That was when Courtney knew they had lost out to a more devious mind.

Nevertheless he had put the department wheels in motion. Since the Norwegian post office at Bodo had been the originator, and Bodo was inside the Arctic Circle, that seemed to indicate that Karolyov had to be making for Kirkenes and the border of the Soviet Union.

Knowing that the Russian would have planned the crossing to coincide with the sending of his second telegram did not deter him. He maintained the pressure; alerting his counterpart in Norwegian Intelligence; an old warhorse named Borthen. Their diligence paid off.

Alexei Karolyov, carelessly using the false passport name of Arild Hansen, had taken the mid-afternoon flight from Bodo to Tromso. Changing carriers from SAS to Wideroe he had then flown on to Hammerfest. Following a thirty-minute turn-round the plane—a de Havilland

315

Dash-7—had continued its journey towards Kirkenes. It was then that the intransigent Norwegian weather played its part. Fog. A thick grey shroud shutting down the airport at Kirkenes. So bad was it that the flight was forced to return the two hundred and seventy kilometres to Hammerfest.

Courtney now had half the Norwegian secret service sealing off every airport and road and port in the Finnmark area. Time was running out for Karolyov as the Wideroe airliner made its second flight to Kirkenes. It landed at 9 p.m. local time. By then the fog had cleared and it was snowing.

Karolyov, doubtless aware that his plans had come unstuck and that his arrogant second message to Courtney would now be working against him, tried to slip away from the aircraft. He nearly made it. The secret service men by the terminal missed him. Those waiting by the perimeter fence, cloaked in snow and darkness, didn't.

It was as Alexei Karolyov was climbing the wire that he was shot. He was a man fond of quoting the ten commandments of the spy trade, and the eighth, "Do what you like with traitors," had finally caught up with him.

Courtney took a packet of Rothmans from his pocket, tapped one out and lit it with his Dunhill lighter. Luck, he thought. Plain old-fashioned luck. As the old Arab proverb said: "Throw a lucky man in the sea and he will come up with a fish in his mouth." And the man they had flown back to Britain forty-eight hours after Karolyov's death had been lucky too. Up to that point he had been the prime suspect. What was his name now? Kitrell, that was it. Paul Kitrell. Yes, he'd been lucky in more ways than one. The two knife wounds had done surprisingly little damage. Then, after his hospitalisation and interrogation, he'd been spirited quickly and quietly away to some place in Africa. A lucky man. Courtney, like many another ruthless intelligence man, resented an independent spirit in civilians and would have liked to see charges, but none had been pressed. He wondered what had happened to Kitrell. Nothing good, he hoped. The man had been a pain in the neck, a rule-bending, insubordinate whistle-blower. At least he, Courtney, hadn't thought it necessary to play bloody cupid between him and that butch pilot girfriend of his. He smiled spitefully.

What the hell. It was all over. Passed. One more dusty file for the archives. He'd survived. He'd almost been sacked over the delayed Boris Gleb report, but he'd survived. The government needed him; he knew too many of their secrets.

He smiled ruefully as his sad, pale-blue eyes rested on his wife, on the still-blonde hair caught up in a bun at the nape of her neck. He'd never made love to a grandmother before, he thought. He threw his cigarette into the fire and went over to her, his hands falling lightly on her shoulders, expertly massaging the muscles through the thin silk of her blouse.

She smiled to herself and stopped writing.

"Why David," she said reprovingly. "Love in the afternoon . . . that's positively indecent."

In Mombasa it was hot and humid, the afternoon sun heliographing bright meaningless messages off the roofs of a nearby shanty town, whose rickety houses were built of flattened tin jerry cans.

Paul Kitrell made his way along the parapet walk of Fort Jesus for the last time. The book was finished. Gone. He had posted it thirty-six hours earlier to a New York agent. It had taken a year of his life, a year of sitting in one room for sometimes up to sixteen hours at a stretch, until backache, shoulder cramps and raging headaches had driven him outside. There, usually in the dead of night, he would walk off the pain, the cool air and the fragrance of frangipani serving as a herbalist's balm. And suddenly the book was with him no more. Suddenly the characters who had filled his days and nights with their chatter, who had sat with him, slept with him, argued with him, refused to be killed off when the plot dictated it—suddenly they had gone. He was more lonely now than he ever could have imagined. And that exposed the reason for his torturous work schedule. It had been to escape the emptiness he felt at losing Erica.

The memories drifted back one by one. He had been lying in the snow near the fence of the military base at Trondheim when the alsatian began sniffing at his face. Then a soldier had shouted something in Norwegian. It had seemed to take forever until he was being carried away on a stretcher; the jerky, jostling ride opening up the wounds he had so carefully packed with snow. The pain had returned long before they reached the small military hospital. He shouted for the soldiers to stop but they kept on walking, so that, by the time they lifted him onto a trolley and began wheeling him down a too-bright corridor, he was limp and exhausted. The last thing he remembered was the doctor in the white coat holding up the syringe with the long needle. Then nothing.

Some time later—two days as he was to find out—he was put on a "medevac" (medical evacuation) flight to Brize Norton in Oxfordshire. From there an ambulance took him to a private nursing home deep in the Cotswolds. Three days after that he had a visitor. The man, carrying about thirty pounds too much weight, was dressed in a dark grey suit, white shirt and a dark blue knitted tie. His pale-blue eyes, Paul observed, looked permanently sad.

"Glad you made it," the visitor said, pulling up a chair to the bedside. "How do you feel?"

Paul, still pumped full of drugs, half-smiled and said: "Fine. A few aches, but the doc says I'll be as good as new in a month or two."

"Good . . . do you feel up to answering a few questions?"

"Questions?"

The man smiled; the gesture failing to remove the sadness from his eyes. "Oh, nothing much.

Few details about the Blackhawk ... security, you understand."

Paul's mind sharpened instantly. The smooth quiet voice. No introductions. No name. Security. He'd run across FBI and CIA people before. They were just as secretive. This one had to be British Intelligence. Warning bells were clanging before the questions began.

"How did you first stumble across this Blackhawk story?" the man said.

"You know my brother was Major Kitrell, I take it?"

"Oh, yes. And that you contacted a man named Finlay in Scotland. After that our facts became a bit hazy."

Paul lying back on the pillow, slowly recounted the events from day one. He was careful to leave Erica out of the main part of the story, substituting Jamie Finlay as the person who had advised him on how to get the flight recorder transcribed.

The man with the sad eyes listened attentively until Paul had finished, then began to probe a little deeper. "One aspect that you haven't touched on, Mr. Kitrell, a minor one I'm sure, but we might as well clear up everything in one go as it were ... you mentioned, in the notarised statement found in your briefcase, that a Flight Lieutenant X had assisted you with the information on the Blackhawk. Perhaps we could ask you the name of that person?"

Like hell, Paul thought. Damn, he'd forgotten about that. He couldn't implicate Erica. Not now. "There's not much point," Paul said suddenly.

"He's dead."

The visitor looked slightly surprised. "Dead?"

"Jamie Finlay. Used to be a flight lieutenant in the RAF. I wanted to keep his name out of it as much as possible." The rank was a guess on Paul's part. If he was wrong it didn't matter. He had simply made a mistake.

"And how did Mr. Finlay find out so much about the aircraft?"

Paul managed a weak smile. "An old newspaper man with printer's ink for blood and you ask me that . . . bloodhounds rate a poor second when it comes to sniffing out news."

"And that's all you know?"

"That's all. Except I would like to know who the Russian guy was who almost cut my guts out in Norway."

The man took a packet of Rothmans from his pocket. "Do you mind if I smoke?"

"Not at all . . . do you mind if I have one?"

The man gave him a cigarette and lit it. "Now, you were saying something about a Russian in Norway . . . what gave you the idea he was Russian?"

"I spoke to him."

"I see . . . and he told you he was Russian."

Paul exhaled a thin trail of blue grey smoke. "I get the picture . . . there never was a Russian, and I never went to Norway. Is that it?"

"More or less."

"But we did get the flight recorder back?"

"I think we can safely say everything is in order, yes."

321

"And the problem ... the electrical problem with the computer ... I guess you know all about that by now?"

"As I said, Mr. Kitrell, everything is in order."

"End of story, uh?"

"An apt American expression, yes. Except you will be flown back to your country of origin—in your case Kenya—as soon as you're fit enough to travel. We would also like to suggest that no word of this is available for publication. I'm sure your years in the newspaper business have taught you sufficiently well ... repercussions, you understand?"

Paul nodded. "There is something I would like to ask. My brother Gene, Major Kitrell, was engaged to a Flight Lieutenant Macken ... I met her at Yeovilton. She told me she was going to Norway," his voice became a little shaky as he searched for the right words. "As she was on the same squadron as Gene, I assumed she was flying the Blackhawk ... I just wanted to know if she's safe ..."

The man looked around for an ashtray and, not finding one, used the saucer of a half-drunk cup of coffee on the bedside locker. Having extinguished the cigarette he stood up to go. "Off the record, Mr. Kitrell, Flight Lieutenant Macken's aircraft crashed in Norway six days ago. Search parties have since confirmed no survivor ..."

For Paul the nightmare had only just begun. Five days later—five days of more pain than his injuries had caused—he was returned to Nairobi for a period of convalescence. It was when he got back to Africa that he made up his mind. He would disappear, take what money he had left and vanish. One year should do it. He had told her he was going to write a book. That is what he would do. It would be dedicated to her.

Two days after arriving in Nairobi he had erased all trace of himself. He had now adopted his mother's maiden name—Houston. He would now go and sit in Mombasa and work. There would be no distractions because no one would be able to find him.

Now one year after Norway, one year of getting over Erica, he was going back. Back to Nairobi. Leaving Fort Jesus, leaving Mombasa. He had to earn some money, it was as simple as that. He had less than five hundred pounds and a fifteen-hundred-page manuscript. His only possessions. And if the book didn't sell? He smiled to himself. If it didn't sell, he'd simply rewrite it until it did.

He brushed the flies away from his face and set off again down the parapet walk. He looked at his watch. It was too early to go out to the airport. The flight to Nairobi wasn't leaving until five o'clock. He drifted aimlessly across to Treasury Square and ended up going into the government department's Ivory Room, more for somewhere out of the sun than anything else. The interior of the building was cathedral cool and had that musty smell which only a multitude of animal trophies can produce.

Half an hour later Paul re-emerged into the sticky heat of afternoon. The flat pounding of the afternoon sun on the white buildings was almost audible. The air was heavy, and in the distance he could see clouds piling up. The short rains were late, but they were nearly here. As if agreeing with his thoughts, he heard a rainbird's three-note call in the still heat. African afternoons, he thought, are only fit for sleeping. He made his way down the street then, searching for a taxi. It took him ten minutes, and a further ten minutes to wake the African driver and agree a price. Eventually, having collected the suitcases from the apartment he had rented, he set out in the taxi for the airport.

In many ways it had been a long time. Confined to one room for nearly a year. The journalist's discipline had helped him. When you have to produce copy on a daily basis year in, year out, it is not difficult to set yourself a schedule to write a book. Even so there had been the black days, the days he had thought of Erica, the days he had found a bar and tied one on, and bought the services of a hip-swinging Somali whore with kohl-smudged eyelids. The mornings after those nights had been the worst. Living in a world of strangers, where no one knew Paul Houston, with no conversation to eke out the lonely hours. Those were the mornings when he felt like ending it all. And she had always saved him. The book was for her, after all. Oddly enough, it had only been the first fifty pages which had been the stumbling block, and the further he progressed the more the characters had taken over. Until in the end they were writing the book for him, dictating it line by line. It was a river inside his head, flowing further each day. And when the river reached the sea the story was finished.

The taxi swung left into Kenyatta Avenue, the driver blasting his horn at a suicidal cyclist. Paul wound down the window as far as it would go, trying to catch the cooling breeze on his face. He checked his watch—four o'clock. Early enough to have a cold beer before checking in for the flight. And then Nairobi. What about Nairobi? Another newspaper job? Picking up the threads of something he had left off—it was the strangest feeling. He felt like a person misplaced in his own time, like a burnt-out soldier returning from a war. Except he had never been in a war to justify the burning. He closed his eyes and listened to the bump, bump, bump of the wheels as the taxi sped down Makupa Causeway towards the airport.

The yellow Stearman biplane was twenty miles from Mombasa. The sky was much darker now, the clouds sagging lower towards the coast. The sun shone eerily from time to time, peeping blood-red around the edges of blackening cumulus, casting a strange purple light on all it touched. Slightly ahead and left of the aircraft's track solid shafts of rain were moving south. The pilot was no longer smiling. She had been fighting the turbulent conditions for the last twenty minutes. She knew about the violence of thunderstorms. Erica Macken had been raised on a diet of little else. She reduced power and fought silently with the controls. Perhaps she should turn back. There

325

had been a bush strip about fifty miles away. She could land there and sit out the weather. She grimaced. She had come too far to be beaten by a thundery day. Damn it, she had come too far. A tremendous crack of thunder ripped the clouds and released a jagged streak of lightning. The Stearman reared like a frightened stallion, before Erica's hands could tighten the rein. The clouds were purple now, tumbling over each other, seething with anger. The sky blackened to almost twilight even though it was only just after four o'clock in the afternoon. The warm rain followed. In less than one minute Erica, sitting alone in the open cockpit, was soaked to the skin.

Ten miles to go now, she tried the radio again and was cleared to join the circuit for landing on runway zero nine. Only ten miles, she said to herself. A distant roll of thunder drowned out the engine note as she eased the aircraft down the sky. It was not unlike the distant passage of a jet aircraft. And those memories would always remain. Not that she remembered much of what had happened at the time of the crash. The air force experts had however come up with the only answer possible. She had been descending inverted when the Soviet missile had exploded in the tail area of her Blackhawk. The explosion had momentarily pitched the fighter forty-five degrees up and at that exact moment she had ejected. It was the tossing-the-bomb routine again. If a pilot dives at five hundred knots then pulls up to forty-five degrees and releases, he can toss a two-thousand-pound bomb four-and-a-half miles with an accuracy factor of three hundred feet—a method proven by the Israelis when they used their F-16s to blow away a nuclear facility at Baghdad in 1982.

Of course, in Erica's case the low-level trajectory her ejector seat had taken through the mountains, followed by the deployment of her parachute, had carried her even further, due to strong funnel winds. That the helicopter search parties hadn't found her was therefore understandable. She was presumed dead.

For two weeks after the accident Erica, who had badly sprained her leg on landing, used all of her skills to combat the arctic conditions. By the time the emergency rations she carried gave out, she was too weak to move. All that remained was a part of her orange silk parachute blowing noisily in the wind. And it was with that noise in her ears that she had crawled into her snow house to die.

Twenty-four hours after that, a platoon of Marines who were moving through the area during the period of the NATO exercise found her. They were certain she was dead. As was the winchman of the SAR helicopter which flew in forty minutes later. Her body was taken to the military hospital at Bodo.

The doctors were confounded. Clinically she should have been dead. Her stiff, frozen body was described as feeling like a piece of meat fresh from the deep freeze. So hard was her tissue that medical staff could not puncture it with hypodermic needles or intravenous tubes; and no thermometer had a scale low enough to record her temperature. And yet there was a heartbeat. Incredibly, after many hours wrapped in electric heating pads, she began to revive. As the medical profession do not list miracles in their list of cures, it was reasoned that Erica Macken had entered that eerie state of suspended animation similar to that of some hibernating animals. She became only the second known person to survive such a fate—the other being a young nineteen-year-old woman named Jean Hilliard who had crashed her car one winter's night in 1981 in Minnesota. Following the accident Jean Hilliard had attempted to walk through sub-zero conditions to find help. She was found the following morning fifteen feet from the door of a friend's house. Her condition and subsequent recovery were a carbon copy of Erica Macken's.

It was two months after the accident that Erica was transferred to Princess Mary's RAF hospital near Wendover, England. As a result of her ordeal doctors in Norway had had to amputate two toes on her left foot. Other than that frostbite had ravaged her once-beautiful features, leaving a web of lines which gave her the appearance of a middle-aged woman.

Now, descending through the stormy afernoon into Mombasa, she no longer cared. She had cheated death twice. Every extra day was therefore a bonus. The African controller's voice filtered weakly through her earphones asking if she had the airport in sight. She said she did. The African, whose voice was a mixture of boredom and indifference, cleared her to land. This was a new world to her, a slow moving world. Even the speech was unhurried. In a way she found it quite pleasant. It was a country for bush pilots. Big, untamed.

She sideslipped the Stearman onto final approach, fighting the gusting wind and the blinding rain. There was a moment of indecision. She had been away from flying for some time. She couldn't be sure she could manage the crosswind landing. Then her father was there beside her. There were no words, just a silent promise that everything would be all right.

The biplane rocked down through the turbulence, nearing the runway threshold. A group of pilots and mechanics were gathered in the open doorway of a large black hangar, quietly watching. Disbelieving the almost side-on approach of the biplane.

"Too much bloody crosswind," one shouted.

"Rather him than me . . . no one can land a crate like that in these conditions . . . and I mean no one."

They huddled closer together, as if preparing for the inevitable crash. The Stearman kept on coming, jinking with small rapid movements as the pilot anticipated the squally conditions. Then it was over the boundary and the engine note was sighing to a whisper. The biplane was a matter of inches from the tarmac when the pilot kicked off the drift and touched down with the grace of an eagle. Somewhere from the back of the group a voice let out a protracted, *"Beautiful."*

The Stearman, weaving from side to side,

taxied up to the hangar entrance. The low burble of its radial engine lasted a few moments longer as the pilot checked the magnetos, then shuddered to a stop. All that was left was the sound of rain beating on canvas.

Erica slipped down from the cockpit, gathering up her hold-all from the unoccupied rear seat as she did so. The men watched as her slight figure limped towards them through the rain. She was halfway when she tugged off her leather flying helmet. One of the older men was about to say something crude to the man standing next to him when he noticed the sag of weariness in her body, the hair already matted wetly to her head. This was a woman who had come a long way. Not just on this stormy African day; but through a lifetime of such days. It was in her eyes. Her home was in the battered old bag she carried, and when it was not there, it was in the sky.

The man moved out into the rain to greet the newcomer. For that moment she wasn't a woman, but a weather-worn reflection of them all.

It was half an hour later, five o'clock, when Erica left the hangar and walked towards the terminal. The rain had stopped now and the clouds had cleared. There was a smell of mimosa in the air. The engineers had dragged the aircraft safely into the hangar, and the pilots had found her a cup of coffee in their crew room. She had taken the opportunity to look in the telephone book—there were no Kitrells listed. There had been the usual small talk and advice on hotels, and how much one paid the taxi driver for a trip into town. Then they parted. The older pilot of the group had a routine passenger flight to make to Nairobi. The daily five o'clock run.

Erica looked up and saw a vulture wheeling silently in the now clear, late afternoon sky. It reminded her of a fragment of story, the story she had read on the page in Paul's typewriter. The story about MacKinnon, and the Indian woman, and Fort Jesus.

It had been during her period in the air force hospital in England that the MI5 man had visited her. No name. Sad, hungry eyes. Still convalescent and uncertain, she had told him everything. He in turn had admitted that Paul Kitrell was alive and well, and had returned to Africa. She started investigations from her hospital bed but they seemed blocked at every turn. She gave up. The man had said Paul knew where she was.

She waited for him to contact her. The court martial she had been expecting never came, but even so she was discharged from the service as medically unfit. It took three more months to get herself into shape, after which the civil aviation authorities issued her with a medical certificate of fitness. And still there was no word from Paul. She went back to Canada.

But she had to be certain. There'd been something about the MI5 man she hadn't trusted. His class, for one thing: *airmen and their women.* And his sad eyes hadn't fooled her. He was a man who wouldn't take kindly to being made to look foolish. And as the months passed, so her mistrust had deepened. Until finally, as November came round again, she had decided that, if she *was* to be certain, she had only one option.

Go to Mombasa. Find out for herself. And if Mombasa, then it had to be Fort Jesus. It was the place in Paul's story, the only place in Africa that had ever seemed important to him.

Her decision had been based on nothing else. Nothing but a hunch. But she had a gut feeling she was right. A feeling that if Paul was anywhere he would be here. She went into the terminal as a group of passengers were struggling through the departure gate and walking across the baked tarmac to the Otter aircraft about to leave for Nairobi. She looked hopelessly around, at people meeting people. Others saying goodbye. Where did she start?

A man in a khaki bush shirt passed close to her as he made his way towards the departure gate. He stopped, quickly stubbed out a small cigar in an ashtray, and just as quickly was gone. For Erica the aroma was a tripwire of memory. Distinctive. Paul had smoked cigars. The smell had been the same. She hurried to the departure gate, pausing in the doorway to watch the figure walking unhurriedly across the tarmac. The hair was the same, perhaps even blonder; and he was thinner. But it was Paul.

The right engine of the twin Otter was already whining into life as she ran out onto the tarmac, calling his name. The man kept walking. She stopped, unsure now. Then, almost in embarrassment at the thought of being wrong, she called again. This time his step faltered. The man slowed to a halt, turning his head.

Her voice was nothing more than a whisper when she said his name again. Then she was moving towards him, slowly at first; then, as their eyes met, she was running. A gentle breeze started up at that moment, carrying the heavy scent of mimosa and the tremor of far distant thunder.

ASHES
by William W. Johnstone

OUT OF THE ASHES (1137, $3.50)

Ben Raines hadn't looked forward to the War, but he knew it was coming. After the balloons went up, Ben was one of the survivors, fighting his way across the country, searching for his family, and leading a band of new pioneers attempting to bring American OUT OF THE ASHES.

FIRE IN THE ASHES (1310, $3.50)

It's 1999 and the world as we know it no longer exists. Ben Raines, leader of the Resistance, must regroup his rebels and prep them for bloody guerrilla war. But are they ready to face an even fiercer foe—the human mutants threatening to overpower the world!

ANARCHY IN THE ASHES (1387, $3.50)

Out of the smoldering nuclear wreckage of World War III, Ben Raines has emerged as the strong leader the Resistance needs. When Sam Hartline, the mercenary, joins forces with an invading army of Russians, Ben and his people raise a bloody banner of defiance to defend earth's last bastion of freedom.

BLOOD IN THE ASHES (1537, $3.50)

As Raines and his rugged band of followers search for land that has escaped radiation, the insidious group known as The Ninth Order rises up to destroy them. In a savage battle to the death, it is the fate of America itself that hangs in the balance!

ALONE IN THE ASHES (1721, $3.50)

In this hellish new world there are human animals and Ben Raines—famed soldier and survival expert—soon becomes their hunted prey. He desperately tries to stay one step ahead of death, but no one can survive ALONE IN THE ASHES.

Available wherever paperbacks are sold, or order direct from the Publisher. Send cover price plus 50¢ per copy for mailing and handling to Zebra Books, Dept. 2235, 475 Park Avenue South, New York, N.Y. 10016. Residents of New York, New Jersey and Pennsylvania must include sales tax. DO NOT SEND CASH.

THE SURVIVALIST SERIES
by Jerry Ahern